DANGEROUS SILENCE
A Dark Mafia Romance

The Adler Brothers

Audrey Rush

Dangerous Silence: A Dark Mafia Romance by Audrey Rush

Independently Published

Cover Photography from DepositPhotos.com
Cover Design by Kai

Paperback ISBN: 9798708532800

This is a work of fiction. Names, characters, places, and incidents either are the product of the author's imagination or are used fictitiously. Any persons appearing on the cover image of this book are models and do not have any connection to the contents of this book.

Dangerous Silence

PROLOGUE

Axe

Age 7

I wasn't supposed to be outside. The rule was to stay in the shop, but Shep gave me a popsicle and moved onto the customer in front of him. I might have been a kid, but I knew when an adult wasn't paying attention.

With my blue popsicle, I leaned against the walls of the butcher shop, looking down the street. Not many cars drove back here, but Shep could work in this neighborhood. As the last real butcher in the city, people drove from all over to see him. A drop of the blueberry juice went down my wrist. I licked it up.

Three men on the corner huddled together. I recognized a few of them, though I don't know why. A car stopped. The one wearing a black sweatshirt talked through the open window, and handed the driver a small object, like a fidget disc or something.

As the car disappeared around the corner, the man, the biggest one out of them, looked over at me. He was big, like he could squish my older brother with his thumb. Each stomp was louder than the last, until he was standing over me. I looked him in the eye like my father taught me. Veins like spiderwebs crisscrossed over his pupils.

"What are you staring at?" he asked. Spit flew from his mouth, landing on my nose. I flinched. "You too good to answer, pussy boy?"

"Hey," someone from his group said, "Ain't that Gerard's kid?"

"Shut up," the big man said. "I know who it is." I took a lick of the popsicle, still staring him in the face. "I know you're Gerard's kid." I took another lick. He knew my father? So what? A lot of people knew my father. "Gerard's got a pussy for a kid." He kneeled down in front of me, our eyes meeting at the same height. "Where's your daddy now?"

His face was round, his beard uneven. Why did he care so much about my father?

"Busy," I said.

"Too busy for his own son." The big man laughed, then stood up, blocking out the sun. He seemed taller than before. "You know, Gerard and I are good friends. He even took one of my fingers once."

I glanced at his hand. At first, all I saw was his thick metal ring, but then I saw it. His pointer was missing.

I raised a brow, then licked my popsicle again. Father always said the business could be demanding at times, and missing fingers were common. I had never thought anything of it. But why would he *take* a finger? What did he want with it? I didn't know what he did all day; only my big brother, Derek, was allowed in my father's office. Wil and I weren't allowed yet.

"Answer me, pussy boy," the big man said. I blinked up at him.

"My father probably threw it away," I said.

A punch seared across my cheek, banging my head back into the brick wall. A ringing started in one of my ears, vibrating through my head, then disappeared. I instantly regretted saying anything.

As soon as the world came into focus, another punch hit me.

"Come on, Baby Adler," the big man said, punching me again. "Stand up and fight me like a man."

"He's a kid, man."

"I didn't ask you." He glared at his friends on the corner. "He's still an Adler."

I glanced at the other two men, but neither of them did a thing.

"You're not going to snitch, are you? Your daddy doesn't like a snitch, does he?" the big man asked.

Another hit knocked my skull against the brick wall, hurting worse than the one before. He was laughing hard, crouching down, yet still bigger than me, but that didn't mean I couldn't fight. My big brother had taught me how. Holding my popsicle in one hand, I made a fist with the other, then hit the big man in the eye. Like he had done to me.

My knuckles pulsed. His head was harder than I thought.

The big man's mouth opened, then his eyes narrowed.

"You actually got me," he said.

I smiled, pleased with myself, but as soon as I saw his frown, I knew it was a mistake. He stood up.

"Your daddy isn't going to save you now," he said.

His fists railed into me, his ring catching my lip. Then again. The metal digging into it. My mouth hurt—hurt worse than a brain freeze. Worse than getting the flu. I dropped my popsicle and rammed my punches forward, but the big man laughed and hit me harder. My head turned towards the men on the corner. Maybe they could help; they seemed to care. But where were they? I could barely focus before another hit landed on my face. I spit; deep purple saliva landed on the floor, a mix of blood and blueberry juice. Had I bit my tongue somehow?

I couldn't catch my breath. The more the man railed into me, his ring catching on my bleeding lips and brows, the worse it got. My head hurt. Blood oozed out of me like a slushie. The world was fuzzy, and in the half-second between punches, I looked around. Where had the world gone? There was no one there. Not my father. Not my big brother, Derek. Not even my little brother, Wil.

The bell on the door jingled, and the big man stopped. Shep came out, blood on his apron, his hands on his hips. He looked at the big man. Shep wasn't tall like him, but he was built like a tire swing. The car sagged whenever he picked me up from tutoring. He was only about five feet tall, a lot shorter than my father, but sometimes I wondered if he was as strong. His gray eyes washed over the empty street. He pulled a cigarette from the pocket of his apron, resting it between his lips.

"You proud of yourself?" Shep asked the big man. He ran a hand over his shaved head. "Beating up a child?" He picked me up off of the ground and leaned me against the wall, propping me up like before. But I slumped down; my knees were weak; I could barely stand. I opened my mouth, but Shep lifted a hand, to stop me from talking.

"Why do you care?" the big man asked. "He ain't your kid."

Shep scowled, then turned to the corner. "And you two. You didn't help a child?"

The other men shook their heads.

"This ain't none of your business, old man," the big man said. He stood up, looking down at Shep. "I've got beef with his dad. This ain't got nothing to do with you."

A hint of a smile crossed Shep's face. Had the big man said something funny?

"Oh, his dad?" Shep asked. "I know his dad."

Shep immediately pulled out a cleaver from the pocket of his apron, bludgeoning it into the big man's side. It happened so fast I almost couldn't tell what was happening. With his other hand, he grabbed the man by his neck, pulling him down to the ground. Then the man didn't move. *Couldn't* move.

"Don't die on me yet," Shep said.

The other two men looked at each other. "Fuck!" one of them shouted.

Shep pulled a gun from his back pocket, shooting them both in the eyes. The sound echoed in the empty street. The men fell to the ground. He went to their bodies, pulling them up by the short hairs on the top of their heads, then used the cleaver across their throats. But the knife wasn't meant for that kind of motion, so he had to saw the blade back and forth until they bled like he wanted.

Each step he took rattled the earth. His shadow loomed behind him, stretching across the sidewalk. Shep looked down at the big man on the ground, whimpering beside me. He pulled him up by the head.

"Good boy," he said. "You didn't die on me yet."

Shep was always covered in shades of red; he owned a butcher shop, and I knew what that meant. But I had never seen him do anything like this. It was like being inside of a dream. Everything was blurry; my left eye was swollen shut and my face was tender and puffy. But Shep hadn't changed; the cigarette was still pressed between his lips. He motioned to me.

"Come here," he said. He offered me the handle of the cleaver. "Go on."

I took the handle, then stared down at the big man. He was more than twice my size, but I couldn't tell anymore. And with those cuts in his side, he was going to die, no matter what happened to him now. Still, I knew I shouldn't hurt him.

But something inside of me wanted to. To be powerful like Shep. To show the big man that even a kid like me, a so-called pussy boy, could cut him down to size. Make him smaller than me.

"Finish him off," Shep ordered.

The big man closed his eyes. Just like I had seen Shep do, I brought the knife down to the man's neck. The man choked, blood sputtering from his mouth and landing on my cheek. But the knife wasn't making a dent in his neck like it had done with Shep.

"Harder, Axe," Shep said.

I wanted to do what Shep told me, to be more like him. With all my strength, I brought it down again; this time it went through, the flesh splitting to the sides. I don't know why, but I was shaking. My whole body was numb. It looked like the man's skin would rip apart from the inside.

Shep laughed, a deep, hearty sound, like the warm bowls of soup he heated for me after tutoring. I furrowed my brows, looking up at him. What was so funny?

"It's time," he finally said. He patted me on the back, then grabbed the cleaver from me, finishing up by sawing with it until the man went limp, his blood pooling in front of us. Shep stepped out of the way, somehow keeping the blood off of his shoes. I looked down, horrified. Mine were covered in it. I wanted to take them off now.

"Pick up his feet," Shep said. "Let's get him inside."

The door to the shop jingled as we came in. The meat counter was full of the same cuts Shep had taught me: heels, rounds, shanks, rolled flanks, fillets, brisket, sirloins, rumps, and shoulders. Underneath the counter was a hidden freezer full of popsicles for me. I had dropped mine earlier. Thinking about that made me sad, but I didn't know why. It was just a popsicle.

And those were just men. Men I didn't know.

Why did I feel bad?

Shep nodded to the swing door. He rarely let me inside of there. We went through.

As I heaved the big man, helping Shep get him on the stainless steel table, I glanced around at the empty sink and the carcasses hanging from the metal hooks. Shep wiped his hands on his apron, adding another streak of red.

Did Shep butcher people too?

"It's time you learned," Shep said, locking eyes with me. "I'll teach you everything."

***

Age 10

I was good at it now. Not as good as Shep, but almost. Shep was the best. Even my father thought so.

"Shep can teach you better than I can," my father said. "He's the best enforcer we have."

I had known since I could remember that my father wanted me to be the lead enforcer one day, but until Shep started teaching me, I didn't know what that meant. For the following year after he saved me from those punks, Shep kept me in the backroom, showing me how to dismantle bodies for easier disposal. I still couldn't cut through the bones without help, but the stomachs were easier for me. We'd put them in these industrial-sized vats full of acid, checking on them every once in a while like a beef stew. By the third day, the corpses would be gone. Sometimes, we buried the bodies in the woods with pig and cow bones to throw off the scent.

Once I got the hang of that, Shep took me on my first run. I did as he told me, standing in the corner, not saying a word until Shep said it was time to leave. As he held a man by the back of his neck, the blood gurgling out of his throat, he turned to me.

"You saw how I did that?" he asked.

Use the gun to keep him still and compliant, then the knife as the final weapon. Yeah. I saw that.

I nodded.

"Good," Shep said. He finished the man off by bludgeoning the knife into the back of his head, and the man slumped to the floor. I went to pick up the corpse, but Shep held up a hand.

"We're going to leave him. It's a message," he said. I looked up at him, waiting for an explanation. "You don't mess with the Adlers."

Shep wasn't an Adler, but he had been working with my father since before he took over for my grandpa. He respected our family, and so we treated him like one of us. He always came to dinners at our house. My father would bring out the best whiskey, to celebrate in Shep's honor.

We had one more stop; I didn't catch much of the details. But as we walked up to the house, I recognized it. Our nanny's house, Fran. I hadn't been there in a long time. But when I was younger, if I wasn't with my tutors or with Shep, my brothers and I were with Fran.

What had Fran done to us?

Shep barged into her place. I stood in the corner. Fran's eyes flicked over to me. Shep spoke quietly to her, and when she raised her hands in defense, Shep put her into a chokehold. She gasped. Those wheezing breaths seemed louder than anything I had ever heard, begging for air. Her face turned purple, the veins in her eyes wide and red. Shep kept an elbow tight around her neck, but she pulled at his hand desperately. It was no use. Shep gestured for me to come forward.

I stayed still. It was Fran. Anyone else, maybe. But Fran?

With his free hand, Shep pulled a knife from his pocket.

"In the heart," he said, the handle pointed towards me.

I stared at Fran, her eyes so red they looked like apples. Why wasn't she fainting? She pulled at his arm. Shep gave her enough room for a lung-full of air, then pulled tight around her throat once again.

"Kill her Axe," he commanded. "She was a traitor to your family. Spilled secrets to our rival."

Her feet pushed on the floor, trying to maneuver herself out of Shep's grip, but she kept slipping, the screech of her feet against the hardwood floor piercing me. My vision blurred. Those gasps. It was all too loud. I needed it to end.

"Now, Axe," Shep said. "Like I taught you."

I couldn't think about it. I had to focus on what Shep told me. Fran was a traitor. She put us at risk. Gave our secrets to a rival.

We couldn't have that.

I brought the knife down on her heart with as much force as I could muster, breaking through her ribs to the heart. Her eyes widened and Shep gave her one last breath. Power surged through me, her body twitching against the blade with fight, then simmering down, dissipating. I brought the knife down again, and then again, the wet sound of the metal plunging into her chest overpowering the rest, until everything stopped.

A wave of heat washed over me. Fran was silent. Finally.

We were quiet on the way back to Shep's workroom behind the Adler House, where my family lived. Though it was filled with tools for torture and dismantling, it was considered the lead enforcer's office. One day, when Shep retired, I knew it would be my office. In the woods, we set the body in a hole Shep had dug the day before. It seemed strange; she had betrayed our family, and still, Shep knew how much she had meant to my brothers and me. It was almost as if he wanted to give her a proper burial.

She looked small in that hole, all bunched up. We shoveled enough to put a few inches of dirt over her, then added some pig bones from Shep's shop. Then we shoveled some more.

"Remember, Axe," Shep said, breaking the silence. "It doesn't matter if you care about someone. If they're not family, they're no one." He paused, leaning on his shovel stuck in the ground. Sometimes, I wondered if Shep meant blood relatives, or if he included himself with family. I was closer to him than I was to my own father; my father wasn't around much. Still, I took Shep's words seriously. Caring about someone, beyond your family, could be dangerous. Like it was with Fran. I continued on. Another shovel, then another. I wanted to get this over with. He grabbed his shovel again, resuming his part of the burial.

"The only time you spare a person's life is if they've saved yours," he said, adding more dirt to the hole. "Otherwise, it doesn't matter."

By the time we were finished, the fresh patch of dirt was flat, but noticeable. Shep grabbed some ivy vines from the sides of the trees and covered it. It wasn't visible anymore.

"You never know when you'll end up like this," he said, gestured at the plot. "Always make sure your loose ends are tied up. You don't want to leave someone in the middle of your life and end up like this."

He said it like his stomach hurt, and I wondered if he knew Fran, if that's why he made me kill her. What had she done, exactly? What secrets had she spilled? How many more people would die, because of what she had done?

He cleared his throat. "It's easier to make sure you never have someone to leave behind," he said. Dirt was smeared on his cheek. He wiped it away. "Trust me, Axe," he said. "It's easier this way."

***

Age 15

The wail pierced through the room, damn near capable of shattering a window. I covered my ears until it stopped. My father held the red ball of flesh with glee in his eyes. The tiny little thing looked like she had goo stuck all over her body, crusted over on her hands and feet, peeling away in the crevices. I was jealous of my brothers for getting out of this. While Shep had stayed hidden in the house with this flesh ball's mother for the last few weeks, he thought that we—my father and I—were worthy of her presence. Worthy. Of a *baby's* presence.

This was coming from a man who told me to always have my bag packed, to never have anything I would miss if I left it behind. Because life didn't wait for you to choose a time to die.

Here he was, with a fucking baby.

Shep beamed at her, a damn smile I had never thought was possible from a mafia enforcer. His cheeks were flushed, his chest pushed out. Flaunting himself. A daughter did that to him? I had a feeling he'd miss *her* if she was gone.

"She's beautiful, Shep," Gerard said, bouncing the baby in his arms. He made googly noises at the little pink ball. Her eyes wandered off, looking at the animals twirling in the mobile next to her crib. "You must be proud."

"You're damn right," Shep said. The baby's head was tucked into the crook of Gerard's arm, and gently, with more caution than I thought was possible coming from a mob boss, Gerard turned to me. "You want to hold her, Axe?"

I shook my head.

The two of them talked, marveling over a baby that couldn't even look straight yet. Crossed-eyed and grunting. Wow. How amazing. I pulled out my knife, flicking my thumb over the edge of the blade, wondering whether it was time to sharpen it yet. What was the point of bringing me here? I had no interest in a baby, even if it was Shep's child.

"Not in here, Axe," Gerard said. I held my thumb on the knife's edge. Did he think I was going to murder it? I knew it was a precious baby. I wasn't going to go anywhere near it with a knife. Gerard tilted his head. Shep glanced over at me, looking away from his baby for the first time since he had let us into the house.

I put the knife away.

Gerard gave the baby back to Shep, then came to my side, holding my shoulder, pulling me deeper into that nauseatingly pink room.

"Shep's retiring, son," he said. He turned toward Shep, and Shep gave that deep nod that I knew well.

"Why?" I asked. I grit my teeth. I knew exactly why, but I wanted to hear him say it. To admit the truth out loud.

"He thinks you're ready," Gerard said. That was bullshit. I tilted my head, narrowing my eyes at Shep. "He's ready to—"

"I don't want this life for her," Shep said. He moved his arms, rocking the baby, never letting his eyes off of her. I don't know what pissed me off more: the fact that he was a contradicting bastard, caring about something that could easily be taken away from him when he taught me to do the opposite, or the fact that he was giving up on a job that he had trained me in, as if he was too good for enforcing now. "But I need your help, Axe, for one more thing."

What could he possibly want? He came towards me, holding her. These days, I was a foot and a half taller than him, towering over him like a bridge.

"If Demi doesn't marry a good person by the time I die," he said slowly, batting his lashes at her until she cooed in amusement. *Demi.* He beamed. I held back a gag. "I want you to protect her. Marry her."

"Marry her?" I repeated, looking at Gerard.

Gerard nodded. "We already discussed this."

"Why can't Derek marry her?" I asked. "Or Wil? They're—"

"I would not trust them to protect her like I trust you," Shep said.

I hated this. Hated that I didn't have a choice. What was I supposed to say? No, take your baby and your perfect, *normal* life and go back to your dream suburbia, while I kill all of the traitors that you're too good to kill now?

"The decision has already been made," Gerard said. Because in our family, you didn't get a choice if the boss ordered it. I crossed my arms. I knew I couldn't fight it, but still, this was bullshit.

"If you say 'no,' I will find someone else," Shep said calmly. That made me straighten. That tone of voice, both a warning and a compromise. He was giving me a choice, but one that had consequences. I stared into his gray eyes, trying to read him.

"So you're saying to marry her. *If* you die," I said slowly. "That could be in a few decades."

"Or that could be tomorrow," Shep said, reminding me of his lessons. Always have your ends tied up. Don't be in the position where you leave anyone behind.

The hypocritical bastard.

"Do you need to retire?" I asked. "You're not that old. You could stay in the shop, taking care of disposal or something."

"Think of this as a lesson in letting go," Shep said. "You can't get too attached to anyone. Not even to your father or to me." He shook his head, his gaze gentle. "It weakens you. You never know when a person will be gone."

Gone. Not dead. He was already going soft around her.

"I'm not marrying a baby tomorrow," I said.

Shep gave a hearty laugh. Gerard chuckled too, and the baby grunted. "I'm not going anywhere anytime soon. Not if I can help it," Shep said. "Besides, she'll have plenty of time to marry someone she loves." He smiled at her, then turned to me. "But if the time comes, promise me you'll protect her. Keep her alive. Marry her."

Shep's words always did something to me. Gerard was hardly ever around. Derek wasn't even eighteen yet, but he was doing more for the mafia than I had seen our own father do. I respected Derek more than I cared about our father.

But when it came to Shep, I respected him. He had taught me everything, and he had saved my life. I knew that I would have died with blue-stained lips eight years ago if it weren't for him.

A life for a life. That was the only time you owed someone.

The room reeked of baby powder and piss, all radiating from her. I crossed my arms. I hoped she didn't smell like that forever.

"Fine," I said.

CHAPTER 1

present

Axe

"What is his name?" I asked, enunciated each word, making sure he understood me. The man before me was hefty, a few inches taller than me and twice as wide. It had taken help from Ron and Randy to get him strapped to the table, but now that he was completely restrained and spread out, he was helpless. Like the rest.

Sometimes, when it came to situations like this, I liked to inject a serum that would produce paralysis, so that they could feel everything but they couldn't move. But the serum left them speechless, too. If you wanted answers, you had to act accordingly.

But they were so loud like this.

Two gaping holes were in each cheek, whistling with his breath. His tongue flailed around in the pool of blood in his mouth. He'd probably drown in it if we didn't move quickly. Shep, though a pillar in his own right, had never been creative like this, which was one of the ways I improved our enforcement.

It was almost a shame not to send him back like this to the Midnight Miles Corporation. If Miles Muro's men kept disappearing, then he would catch on. But I knew that until then, it was best to keep him in the dark. See how much he was willing to do.

"I didn't—" he wheezed, his nostrils huffing out, the blood splattering to the side. "I said his name. Please."

"Cannon?" I asked. "I want a first and last name. Not a nickname."

"I told you," the man cried. A tear ran down his cheek, following the path of the last one. "Cannon. His name is Cannon. He goes by Cannon. Please. Don't kill me."

"I'm not going to ask again," I said. "Does your leader, Cannon, have a legal name?"

"I swear to God, man, I don't know. But I can—"

I brought the ice pick down on his forehead, piercing it through the skull. The pick squished through his tissues, blood gathering at the edges of the instrument. The silence that followed washed through the room. No more whistling noise. No more blubbering pawn. Sometimes, the pain was so intense that they gave up on screaming. Power always surged through me when that happened, making my dick hard. But I couldn't stand the whining and sniveling; it always seemed like it would never end. That's when I knew it was time.

I rolled my shoulders, then let my red-painted hands rest on the table.

This workroom, *my* workroom, had been in the family for generations. My great, great grandfather had built it for his brother to use as a space for enforcing. Made of solid concrete, soundproof, and over the years, decorated on the outside until it was camouflaged by the surrounding woods. There was no noise inside. Only the hum of the electric lights. The rustle of the cloth wiping my pick clean. The soft clicks as I laid my tools down on the table.

My brothers, though they had killed too, liked to brag about my capabilities, as a way to keep people in line. Axe, the killer. Axe, the Adler family's enforcer. But to me, enforcing, torturing, killing, disposing, were simply parts of my job description. A career in the mafia. The civilians out there, going about their daily lives, didn't think about what was going on beyond their bubbles. But seventy-five hundred people died in the United States each day. Why shouldn't a number of them be taken out by my hands?

It was a cycle. Life started, it went, then it came to an end. It would end for me too one day, and I would be ready for it.

My phone buzzed in my pocket. I let out a heavy sigh, then answered without a word.

"Any names yet?" Derek asked.

"Cannon," I said.

"Huh. Still Cannon." The microphone scratched, the murmur of the traffic in the background. He must have been on the road. "Keep working on it," he said.

We were at war with the Midnight Miles Corporation, with Miles Muro himself. I never dealt with the politics, but I knew the basics. Through the stupidity of my half-brother, Ethan, we had offended Muro by not delivering a captive we had promised. After that, he pretended to play nice, but insulted us with bad trades, then ended our alliance by sending in undercover soldiers to kill us.

My job, as the lead enforcer, was to figure out Muro's security situation. Part of that was finding out who Cannon was, and getting rid of him. Once Cannon was replaced, Muro's army would be at a disadvantage. And that's when we would strike.

"Turns out Muro's got major footing in our state, and some in Woodlands." That was the capital for the next state over. "Small agreements all over the United States, but mostly controls Brackston and Woodlands. Sounds like he wants to control Sage City before he deepens his hold elsewhere."

And we were standing in his way. "And the rest?" I asked.

"He's been causing shit everywhere else. Enough to piss people off, and big enough to scare the shit out of them. I sent Ethan to negotiate." Ethan had been on the run since stealing his woman from what should have been Muro's captivity. It was unlikely that Ethan would be able to secure assistance, but Derek and I both knew that he could help form better relationships. They stepped aside while we took down Muro, and in return, we would work out favorable arrangements.

Derek sighed. "It might take some digging to find people on our side."

Which was Derek's and Wil's job.

Once the war was over, I could go back to being creative. Killing Muro's men was never a drawn-out affair. I had to work quickly. Extract information. Dispose. And when Muro was gone, I could go back to being alone. The only time I was ever alone these days was in the workroom, right after a death. And still, there were several guards waiting around the perimeter of the workroom.

"Good luck," I said. My phone beeped, and I glanced at the screen. *Shep* blinked back at me. A strange sensation took hold of my stomach. I hadn't heard from him in years. Over a decade. The random call wasn't a good sign. "I have to go."

"Keep working on Cannon," Derek said. "Let us know what you need."

I clicked over to Shep's call.

"Axe," he said, his voice raspy. He hacked, backing away from the mic, barking up mucus. Once he finished, he continued: "You need to come here."

"On my way."

Shep lived on the other side of Sage City, a few miles away from the coast and far enough into the city that you only smelled the ocean on a warm breeze. His house was situated in a quiet neighborhood, one that he had moved to right before retiring from the mafia. A few cars were parked out front, some I recognized from family and friends. A yellow house with white trim, a blue chair on the front porch. On the side table, a tray of cigarette butts, the ash spilling out.

I knocked. An older man in his sixties answered, then motioned me inside.

In the living room, Uncle Ray acknowledged me, then stepped into the kitchen. The other men looked up, then followed him. A nurse was looking at the monitors at Shep's side. And lying on a hospital bed, was Shep. The man I had outgrown by the time I was fifteen, shriveled in bed, like a sun-dried peach. His spotty white hair growing in patches on his head. His sunken eyes, purple with exhaustion.

"Axe," Shep said, his voice hoarse. He barely lifted his eyes to mine. I took the folding chair by his side. He inched a finger toward me. "I'm dying."

That was clear. The strange part was that this one of the most notorious mafia men in Sage City, dying from a disease, rather than a hit. It didn't seem right. Where was the gash in his side? The bullet in his head? Then again, Shep hadn't been a hitman in many, many years. Still, it wasn't easy to watch his body wasting away.

"I want you to watch Demi," Shep said. "Marry her."

Marry? I knew that had been a promise made back when Demi was born, but that couldn't have been a true possibility now. How could we jump straight into being husband and wife?

And how do you tell that to a man on his deathbed?

"I can watch over her," I said. "But there's a war, Shep. The Midnight Miles Corporation is fighting against us. It's not safe to bring your daughter into our family right now."

"I understand, but you've got to—"

A fit of coughs broke through him, making his chest seize up. A dull ache spread across my body, making me numb. How was it that I could watch a man die, holes dug into his cheeks, an ice pick stabbed into his head, but watching a man barely on the edge of suffocation, his lungs giving out before him, somehow made me feel lost?

Eventually, the coughing stopped. His eyes were red and glossy.

"You've got to protect her," he said. He slid his hand onto my arm. "Watch over her. Take care of her for me."

I looked at his hand, holding me. As close as we might have been at one point in time, we weren't like that. Physical touch was out of place. But he needed it more than I wanted to refuse it.

I let my eyes wash over the room. On the wall, there was a gold-framed photograph of a toddler, dark brown hair like her mother, gray eyes like her father, holding a chicken, a cockatiel on her shoulder, and two dogs sitting on either side of her. And if I remembered correctly, the last time I had heard from Shep, when Demi was still a toddler, there was a cat too, just not in the picture. She was obsessed with animals, though I saw no evidence of any pets now.

That had been one of the last times Shep had spoken to me. After Demi's mother died, everything changed. It was solely up to Shep to take care of Demi, which meant that he cut off contact with me.

Not that I cared.

"I don't have room for animals," I said.

"I took care of that years ago," Shep said. A hint of a smile cracked his chapped lips. Took care of it? That meant there was a story there. One he likely had no energy to tell.

"She's barely eighteen," I argued. "She deserves a chance to find real love." Whatever the hell that was. For me, it was an excuse to get out of this mess.

Shep used all of his strength to move his chin back and forth, a dramatic movement that had the nurse straightening up and glaring at me.

"No," Shep said. "Love doesn't matter. Keeping her alive does."

By putting her in jeopardy so that she was living with me? When a war was going on and there were a slew of deaths ahead of us, and mine might be added to the list?

Keeping her alive.

Those words stood out to me. It wasn't a question of marriage or love, but life or death.

"I will keep her alive," I said.

"Good," he said.

A bright blue city car pulled up to the front, visible through the front window. Out of the passenger seat, popped a backpack and a duffel bag, then a person. Then the car drove away.

"Does Demi know about the business?" I asked.

"Of course not," Shep said with a hint of annoyance.

Another fit of coughs took hold of him. It was better for it to happen now before another visitor walked in.

The lock turned, and it seemed as though everyone in the room held their breath. We all turned to face the entrance. Through the screen, a person close to five feet tall was visible. She opened the screen door. The fluorescent lights flooded over her, illuminating her turquoise and violet hair.

Turquoise and violet hair. Bright. Like a damn mermaid.

"Dad?" she asked.

She ran to his side, glaring at me so that I backed away, giving them space. A sweatshirt was loose over her body, *PGU* written in athletic letters on the front. So Shep had let her go to college, then. I hadn't expected that.

The exposed skin of her neck flushed with red. She shook her hair, letting the waves of color fall in front of her face.

"Dad?" she asked again.

I leaned against the wall, taking her in. Here was Demi, all grown up. Swallowed up by a college sweatshirt far too big for her, with dreams of a life beyond Sage City. So far beyond it, that she would rather go to a small college town three hours away than live in a major city with her father. The kind of woman who needed to be free. Who needed choice. Adventure. Experimentation. Exploration.

And here I was, coming to rip that away from her.

"Come on, Dad," she said. "What's going on? Why didn't you call me sooner?"

Shep said nothing. He lifted his eyelids, and once he saw her, a full smile crossed his face. He wouldn't speak. The rest of us knew that he was trying to avoid having another flare-up, but Demi? She only knew that her dad wasn't speaking.

"Come on," she said. "What's going on?"

She flipped around. The group in the kitchen turned away, pretending to be busy cleaning and eating. The nurse buried her head in Shep's vitals. Then Demi's eyes landed on me.

"What the hell are you staring at?" she asked.

It took a lot of nerve to say something like that to me. I'm tall, with broad shoulders, thick arms, and one hell of a core. Anyone can tell I'm a man who likes to eat, but no one can deny that I'm built like steel. More than capable of taking a tiny mermaid girl, wadding her up into a ball, and throwing her back out to sea.

She was so sure of herself. So sure of me.

My scalp prickled. I cleared my throat, running a hand over my facial hair, then narrowed my eyes at her. The pungent smell of sour milk drifted from the bed. Demi shifted away, finally looking back to her father, the only thing that truly mattered to her.

CHAPTER 2

Demi

It was hot in that room, like we were all in a furnace, watching my dad roast to death. I pulled off my sweatshirt, leaving it on the floor, then grabbed his hand, tucking it inside both of mine. A loose strand of half-purple, half-blue-green hair, landed on our grip. I blew on it, not wanting to let go of him. The blue-green and purple color always reminded me of a sunset in a tropical paradise. Sage City had beaches, but I never thought of this place as paradise. It was just home. And my hair was a way to show Dad that I was on my own now. Hair he refused to let me color when I was in grade school. Said it was a waste of money. That I had beautiful, rich chocolate brown hair like my mother. Why would I ruin it with bleach and cheap dye?

But he hadn't said a single word about my hair. He even smiled at me. Like he was pretending not to notice what I had done, deliberately going against his wishes.

That's how bad his condition was. He didn't have the energy to fight.

"Why didn't you tell me sooner?" I whispered. I squeezed his hand and he grimaced. Heat washed over me again, a heaviness spreading across my chest. Was I that terrible of a daughter? I knew he was sick, but how had I been gone for three weeks and in that time, he had taken *that* far of a plunge? Did he think I wouldn't be able to handle it?

Why did I leave? Was going to college that important now?

I shouldn't have left. This was my fault. I could have done something. If I had stayed.

"You needed to be on your own," he said, his voice withered, half of what it used to be. A ball grew in the pit of my stomach, anger tightening my throat. I would have given anything to hear his voice full of rage, anger at me for bad grades, for bad behavior, for everything bad, bad, *bad*, just to know that he had that strength still inside of him.

But there was none of that left anymore.

I shook my head. "Bullshit," I said.

"Demi," he whispered.

My eyes flicked down. Yeah. Dad hated when I cursed. But I needed to get it out. I had thought we had at least a few more years left, but this? This sudden change? The nurse appeared on his other side, checking his IV.

"You have a nurse," I said, stating the obvious. She pretended not to hear me. "When did this happen?"

No one moved or said a word. Not even the ogre with the butt-shaped lips standing in the hallway. A tight black shirt covered his chest, matching his black pants, belt, and shoes. He sucked the color right out of the room. That ogre looked like he was itching to say something.

Then it hit me. Dad had held on, hadn't he? He had stayed strong until I was on my own.

"Damn it," I said. Tears welled in my eyes. "I should have come home sooner."

Dad smiled. "You're here now," he said. "That's what matters."

I swallowed a dry lump, then the ogre cleared his throat again. I snapped my head around, scowling at him.

"Give your father some dignity," he said.

I turned to the men in the kitchen, then glanced at the nurse. I didn't know any of these people. The nurse likely didn't know anyone, but the men? These extra people? Who were they? Why were they in my house?

It was an invasion.

"Give him some dignity?" I asked, my tone incredulous. "You want me to give him some dignity?"

"Leave him alone," he said. "Let him die the death he wants."

My heart ripped open at those words. The death. The death *he* wants. No—screw that. And screw that ogre for telling me what to do. For thinking he knows what my dad wants.

"Go screw yourself homeboy," I hissed.

"Demi," Dad said, slightly louder than before. And that single word broke my heart all over again. Dad couldn't tell me to behave. That's all he had: my name. My nose was filled with snot; I could barely breathe. But I wouldn't let myself cry. Not yet.

"I'm not leaving," I said.

"You are leaving with me," the ogre said.

"I don't even know you."

"Demi," Dad said again. He shifted his body, lifting his chin to the ogre. "Thank you."

The ogre nodded, then backed away, disappearing down the hall. How was that ogre walking through the house like he knew where everything was? Like he owned the place? It was my house. The house *I* grew up in.

It was easier to be mad at a stranger than it was to face what was actually going on. But I wasn't afraid of death. The ogre might have been afraid to watch a loved one die, but I wasn't going to leave my dad's side. I would have expected my dad to do the same for me. You couldn't be afraid to look at someone when they were at their worst; Dad had taught me that.

The people from the kitchen and living room said their goodbyes, and Dad lifted a finger to acknowledge them. I faced my dad, never turning to look at the strangers. In the end, it was Dad, the nurse, the ogre hidden in one of the bedrooms, and me.

"He'll provide for you," Dad said. He pointed toward the hallway.

"The ogre?"

"That ogre is named Axe."

The name sent a wave of shock through me. Axe? *That* Axe? The son he had never had? The one I grew up hearing stories about? Dad was always clunky on the details of teaching him to work in the butcher shop. But I knew that Axe went on to do the family business, instead of working in Dad's shop. That was him?

"Provide for me?" I repeated. "This isn't the seventeenth century, Dad. We don't do dowries anymore."

"You need to marry him."

"What? Why?"

"So that I know you're safe. I want to rest easy, Demi. Can you—" A coughing spell broke through his body, contorting him in painful twists. Suddenly, it felt like there were millions of people packed into that room, his choking sounds taking up all of that space, when in reality, it was empty. Once he could breathe again, he looked at me. "Can you do that for me?"

An acrid scent came to my nose, coming from Dad, like urine and rubbing alcohol and sour fruit. I shook my head. I wasn't going to marry a man I didn't know.

But what difference did it make if I lied? If I told Dad that I would? Maybe it was selfish of me to hold onto that right to choose my partner when this was my dad's one last request. But if Dad could slip to the other side, believing that lie, then maybe it would be easier for him.

I nodded, changing my response. "I will, Dad," I said.

His eyes closed. A minute passed. He was letting himself rest now. Each wheezing breath seemed to take so much energy from him.

"You were my brightest joy," he said.

I couldn't stop the tears from falling. They crashed onto our hands, wetting us both. How could he say those words now, when I had longed to hear them, or anything resembling them, for so long? When Mom died, we only had each other. You would think that her death would have made Dad kinder, but it was the opposite. He was strict, not letting anything slide. Not a single B on a test. Not a muttered curse word. Not a single bottle of temporary dye.

How could I be his brightest joy, when I could never live up to his standards? And how could I be angry, when he was dying?

I wiped my nose on my sleeve, leaving a trail of shiny snot. Dad's breathing shifted. The wheezing quieted, almost as if his body was giving him a break. But then it started up again, harder, deeper than before, gasping. He let out a wail, and the sound was desperate. It startled me. I flinched back, waiting for it to stop. Then I was angry at myself for my reaction. I had to be strong. Dad needed me to be strong. I grabbed his hand.

Every once in a while, this happened. His breathing quieted, then the gasping started, and he wailed so loud that I held my breath. The nurse took a seat on the couch, sitting to the side. Waiting for him. I knew it was time. I thought about my homework. About my college lectures. About Axe. Anything to keep my focus away from Dad's breathing. That rasping gasp, every molecule of air squeezing out of his chest in a drawn-out whoosh. It made my skin crawl, made my heart ache.

And then there was silence. Cold, dreadful silence.

I wasn't sure how I was supposed to feel, so I decided that I would pretend like everything was fine. Because the idea that Dad had waited until I was legally an adult to die, made me angry, and I knew that wasn't right. Why did he wait until his last words to tell me that he was proud of me? Why couldn't our last few years have been spent with joy instead of the lack of emotion, the strict discipline, his *need* for me to get As so that I could go to college 'and get a good life' for myself, like he loved to remind me?

Why couldn't I be a butcher, like he wanted so badly for Axe?

My muscles quivered. Dad's monitor buzzed in a long, dim sound. The nurse opened her mouth, and I knew the words she was going to say, but I couldn't bear to hear it right then.

I walked down the hall, finding Axe lying on my bed. *My* bed. The behemoth was sprawled out, reading a crime novel I had gotten from the free books section from my private grade school's library. *The Beginning of the End* was written on the weathered spine. What a gloriously ironic title.

"That's my book," I said.

Axe glanced up, those narrowed eyes pointed at me. But he didn't say a word.

"So I'm supposed to stay with you?" I asked. He didn't move. Kept those eyes trained on me. "Hey ogre, I asked you a quest—"

He leaped forward, pinning me against the wall, his hands on my shoulders. The movement was so sudden that I sucked in a breath, unsure of what to do. He smelled like rubbing alcohol, like Dad, but more metallic and musky. Maybe Axe did end butchering meat for a living, but not with Dad. Either way, he needed a shower.

His eyes bore into me, black and vacant. As if he could see what I was hiding.

But what was I hiding?

"'I'm supposed to stay with you,' isn't a question," he said. "It's a statement."

"But—"

"Don't call me 'ogre' unless you can handle the consequences." He sounded like Dad too: *handling the consequences*. I wanted to scream that Axe wasn't my dad, that he would *never* come close to being my dad, but I knew that would make me look like a bratty teenager. And I would just start crying.

And I wasn't going to cry in front of an ogre.

He let go of me. A tear dropped on my hand and I quickly rubbed it into my sweatshirt. I hadn't realized I was already crying. That sour scent wafted up to my nose, hidden in my clothes. Dad. But not in the way that felt like him.

"I'll call the funeral home," Axe said.

I nodded. I was grateful, but I didn't have the energy to say it.

Axe said something about an uncle coming to wait for the funeral home to pick up Dad. My backpack and duffel bag were already packed, so Axe grabbed them off of the floor, carrying them for me. I ran into Dad's room and grabbed the folded blanket off of the foot of the bed. I took a deep breath in: lavender detergent and a hint of ash. Dad's real scent.

I found another duffel bag in my closet and stuffed the blanket inside, afraid that if I took it unprotected through the front room, the sour smell would get on the blanket somehow. Axe opened the door for me, and we walked to a white cargo van, an older one with no windows in the back.

If it had been any other time, I would have commented that he was driving a kidnapper's van, but I didn't have it in me to fight right then. I guess I expected him to have a nicer car. The whole 'provide for you' thing made me expect luxury, I guess. But I was sort of glad his car was more lowkey than that. I don't know that I would have been able to put up with the class-differences-anxiety like I had attending a private school growing up.

Again, Axe opened the car door for me, which hinted at *why* Dad liked him. Even if he did push me against the wall and threaten me, it was as if he had only done it because I had earned the discipline. Otherwise, he was a perfect gentleman. His dark brown hair was short on the sides, but shaggy on top like he cared enough to cut it, but not enough to style it. Trimmed facial hair spread over his jaw and neck. His dark black, soulless eyes peered at the road as he started the car. The engine rumbled, but the radio stayed silent. What kind of person didn't listen to the radio?

Once we were on the freeway, I turned toward him.

"This is temporary," I said. Axe didn't say a word. Did I need to ask a deliberate question for him to make a single sound? "I'm a first-year at Pebble Garden University. I don't have time to stay here and pretend to get married."

I waited for him to flinch at the word, to show his commitment-phobe streak, but he didn't even blink. He kept his eyes on the road.

"Did he give you the marriage talk too?" I asked.

Finally, Axe gave a curt nod, showing that he *was* listening. How nice for me. A police car drove by the side, the sirens blaring. Axe changed lanes, getting out of the way.

"You know, I'm going to be a detective one day," I said. "Homicide." A half-smile crooked over his lips and I wanted to punch it right off of him. "You don't think I can?" The half-smile dropped, replaced by that dry stoicism on those butt-shaped lips. It looked like a chunk had been cut out of his bottom lip. Was it a scar, or had he been born that way?

"Oh, that's right. It needs to be a question-*question*," I muttered. "All right, Mr. Axe. How's this? Do you think I don't stand a chance at becoming a homicide detective? Because I can tell you right now, I have better grades than all of the students in my program."

He merged onto the off-ramp. Right before I was going to open my mouth to start ranting again, he said, "Why would I doubt your abilities?"

He said it in a low voice, like he wanted me to pay attention. I shut up then, deflated. I looked out the window. We were in an average part of the city inside of an apartment complex's parking lot. He didn't have a house. Maybe he owned the place?

Axe carried all three of my bags through a dim corridor with two units facing each other. He turned to one, then opened it with his keys. He gestured inside.

A mattress lay directly on the floor in the front room. Axe put my bags on the floor. To the side of the kitchen, in what should have been a dining area, was a set of filing cabinets and four locked toolboxes. A short hallway led to a bathroom and a bedroom.

Why did he have a mattress on the floor in his living room? Why did he have so many toolboxes?

And why did Dad think he could take care of me?

But I couldn't think about that or it would make me angry all over again. If Axe wasn't going to talk, to help me get my mind off of Dad, then I would find something else to numb the edge. I went to his kitchen, opening the fridge. Milk. A few different takeout boxes. A dozen eggs. Seeded bread. Mustard. A half-eaten container of deli turkey.

The man, at the bare minimum, was in his thirties. And he had no alcohol?

"You've got to be kidding me," I muttered.

Axe crossed his arms over his chest. I did the same. The next-door neighbor banged on the wall, screaming about her pudding. Or maybe she was screwing someone? It was hard to tell. I turned to look at the noise, but Axe didn't move.

Did he actually live here?

"I want to go back to Pebble Garden," I said.

"No."

My jaw dropped. "What do you mean, 'no'? You're not my boss."

"I promised your father I would—"

"My *father* said he wanted us to get married, and we both know that that's not going to happen." I pointed a finger between the two of us. Granted, he wasn't ugly… Okay, maybe he was kind of hot, but not in the traditional way. It was his size. Like he could smush me with his thumb. How he pushed me against the wall. Unafraid to do what he needed to do.

Which, in a sense, was also kind of creepy. But I didn't hate it.

"Why would my Dad want me to stay with you?" I asked. "You have nothing here. You don't even have a box spring. Do you have a job?"

"I come from a good family."

I found that hard to believe. But then I smacked my forehead.

"Don't tell me you opened up your own butcher shop," I said.

He shook his head. "Do you have any pets?"

Pets? "Why would I?"

"Shep told me you loved animals."

My chest tightened. I didn't want to think about that either. First, it was Mom. Then I got my first and only D on a report card. Next, my babies were gone too.

"Loved. As in, I *did* have pets. A long time ago."

But not anymore. Dad made sure of that.

"You'll be staying in town until the funeral," Axe said. "I can help with the arrangements. Make sure everything goes smoothly."

I wanted to hate him for barging in and telling me what to do, but I was grateful in a way. Because I had never had to plan a funeral before, and I wasn't sure where to start.

I froze, realizing something. He knew about my pets. That meant Dad had told him about me. That was years ago now.

And Axe remembered?

I had grown up hearing all about how amazing Axe was, how he could be better than any professional, how he knew animal anatomy even better than Dad did. But whenever I tried to lift a cleaver, Dad pushed me away. *It's not a business for women,* he would say. *You need to do something better with your life.*

But Dad, I—

You need a better life, Demi. Not cutting up meat like your old man.

"Give me your phone," he said.

"What?" I asked. "No. I—"

"I'm not going to ask again, Demi," he said, venom in his tone.

I don't know why, but a gut instinct took hold of me. As soon as my eyes landed on the knife block on his counter, I went towards it. I grabbed a steak knife, but right as I did, Axe ripped it from my hand, the blade scratching my palm, leaving a faint white line in its wake. The movement surprised me, made me forget to breathe. Axe held my wrist.

"Make no mistake, Demi. I made a promise to your father that I will watch after you. Keep you alive." He put the knife down on the counter, still holding my wrist. "But for the next few days, we're doing this my way. That means you don't leave this apartment unless you're with me. And there will be no alcohol or drugs. No phone calls. No text messages. Nothing. Got it?"

"What the hell? I'm not a—"

"You are under my rule." He tightened his grip around my wrist so hard I thought it might bruise. He slipped a hand into my sweatshirt pocket, removing my phone and putting it into his own pocket. "I expect you to listen," he said. "In return, I will help you."

He let go. My wrist throbbed. I stared up at him. He narrowed his eyes.

"Don't underestimate me, Demi, and I won't underestimate you."

CHAPTER 3

Axe

By the time the funeral came, I was itching to be back into my normal routine. Sharing a space with an eighteen-year-old who, most of the time, refused to talk to me, was easy. But watching over her, while a war raged outside of the apartment, was difficult. I was almost relieved when the funeral came, except for the fact that I hated large gatherings.

Because Shep was mafia, we had a plot at the cemetery lined up for him—we knew the owner personally—but when it came to the service, we had it at the Adler House. It was a large, but older home that had been in the family for generations. I gave Demi a quick tour, showing her the bathrooms, kitchen, and dining room, as well as pointing to where Shep's casket waited in the study. I asked if she wanted to see him then; she shook her head. I grit my teeth. Today was not the day to be resistant.

"Don't be afraid of death," I said.

She scowled. "I'm not," she said. My jaw twitched, and she turned toward the kitchen. I let out a deep sigh. For such a sheltered young woman, she certainly had Shep's bold attitude.

I stood at the edge of the yard, a beer in my hand that I didn't plan on drinking. I scanned the area, looking at the different arrivals. Plenty of older men and women. Some were probably from Shep's stint in the military before he was dishonorably discharged. And many were from our own team, the enforcing staff, all in one place, honoring one of our greatest men.

Which made the event an easy target.

The woods surrounding the Adler House were miles deep. Luckily, we owned most of the property, which gave us space to do what we needed. But because of the war, we had a large unit of men guarding the woods. The trees stretched up, the scent of pine mixed with a hint of savory dishes. Comfort food.

Wil, my younger brother, hit me on the back. A classic suit was fitted to his muscular body.

"Looking sharp," Wil said. My hair was styled for once, and I wore a dark blue suit with a red tie, like Shep would have worn. "How are you doing?"

He expected me to be upset, as most people would be if their mentor died. But in the beginning, Shep had taught me to let go of all connections, even with him; you never knew when someone would leave you, so you couldn't let anything hold you back. It was better that way; it gave me a chance to watch while everyone mourned.

I ignored his question. "How are the wedding plans?"

A smile lit up Wil's face. "I swear, Ellie is the best," he said. "There isn't a lot to plan. Makes it easy on us. I can't believe it's already here."

That was good for them, but I didn't care to hear the details.

"Did Derek tell you about Cannon?" I asked, changing the subject. Wil lifted a brow. I figured Derek hadn't. There had been too much going on, and Wil was a busy man. He took care of the gambling hall, Jimmy's, as well as oversaw the dealers that sold our product. "Muro's army is led by a man named Cannon."

"Is that his real name or a nickname?"

I shrugged. "I can't get anything else out of them."

At the word 'them,' Wil's eyes scanned the woods. "You haven't found many, have you?"

"Only two so far."

Wil nodded to himself. We had been upping our security in the woods, ever since Muro tried to ambush us with undercover soldiers. Luckily, we had destroyed his training camp and hired some of his ex-soldiers to our side.

But that didn't mean everything was perfect. It was far from it.

"Sorry to hear about Shep," Wil said, patting me on the back. Then he waved to another person, heading to their side. I scanned the place, finding that purple-blue-green hair instantly. Someone was speaking to her, an older couple, and Demi bobbed her head, clutching a soda can in her palms.

A heavy hand landed on my shoulder. Gerard, my father, with his salted-black hair slicked back, kept his chin lowered in remembrance.

"Shep was a good man," he said. I kept my eyes trained on the woods. "I'm glad you got to know him."

Did my father realize that I knew Shep better than I knew him? That Shep treated me like a son, a true son, more than Gerard, himself, ever had? But none of that mattered. Gerard was too busy playing games and getting high to notice what was going on around him. Almost as if he got Clara pregnant just to have his children take care of the family business.

I let out a sigh. Gerard squeezed my shoulder.

"You hear anything about Midnight Miles yet?" he asked.

He likely knew everything from Derek, my older brother, who was next in line to take over officially as the boss. Which meant that his question was prodding at something specific. I wished he would spit it out. But I refused to give in and ask him what he wanted.

"You hear anything?" he asked again.

When I was younger, eight or nine years old, my mother had thought I needed therapy. I didn't talk to anyone anymore, not unless I had to, and she thought that by sending me to a therapist, I would be fixed. That I would speak again. Gerard agreed with her, supported her whole-heartedly, found me the best psycho-therapist the mafia could afford. A woman who no longer had her license. Because working for criminals was better than working for civilians. It paid more. Made for more interesting cases. Even when the patient scared you.

But how do you fix a kid who watched people die almost every day of his life? Who has been told that he was meant to become the next lead enforcer, the next feared monster? A kid who every day, his mentor told him to never trust anyone, to keep his distance. Burned it into his mind that everyone, even the people you loved, could die tomorrow. That you could be next.

Gerard's fingers twitched on my shoulder. My therapist had stressed that I didn't have to speak to anyone, but that it would be kind to give them the courtesy of an acknowledgment. That always stuck with me. Courtesy. Acknowledgment. That's all anyone wanted.

Finally, I shook my head.

"Look, Axel," Gerard shuffled his feet. "I know you boys are concerned with Muro, but if he wants to negotiate, you should give him the chance." I didn't get the idea Muro wanted to negotiate. I said nothing. "I know that you boys are going to handle it your own way, but let's not get carried away with bloodshed."

Since the war began, several of our men had been killed. We had plenty to replace them, but that didn't make up for the fact that Muro was trying to take over Sage City, attempting to eradicate us from a place where our family had established a foundation for many generations. So I didn't understand why Gerard wanted to keep the peace.

Which was why enforcing was left to me, and not him.

"The funeral will begin in five minutes," Clara announced on the speaker system. Everyone turned to her. She stood on the back patio with a wireless microphone in her hand. "Please meet us in the garden."

The garden had strawberries, lettuce, the squash blossoms blooming, and a few trellises on the edge with jasmines clinging to the side. Plenty of folding chairs were lined up, as well as some cushioned seats for the elderly. The group shuffled forward, and Gerard found another person to talk to. I stayed on the edges, scanning constantly for danger.

The funeral celebrant went through the usual rituals, and when it came time for close friends and family to pay respects, everyone shifted in their seats. One of my men, Ron, went to the front, taking out the piece of paper I had given him earlier that day. He ran a hand through his wavy brown hair.

"Hi," Ron started. He glanced at the paper. "I used to work with Shep a long time ago. In fact, he trained me. Made me the man I am today." A few people nodded. Some of the people must have known that Ron was reading for me. Ron had been around for the last ten years, but Shep had been gone for almost twice as long. But I didn't need to claim my words.

"And while I never completely agreed with his methods, he taught me one thing."

Ron paused, looking around. He nodded at me, and I did the same. Our fellow enforcers kept their arms crossed. If there was a time to be sentimental, it would have been this, but it wasn't like us to show emotion. My eyes washed over the group of people, wondering how many of them knew everything about Shep, and how many didn't have a clue.

Demi's hair caught my eye, a splash of vibrancy that rivaled the bright yellow blossoms behind her.

"Death is inevitable," Ron continued.

At the apartment, Demi had chosen to stay in the bedroom, resting in a sleeping bag, only coming out when we had to make arrangements for the funeral. Most of the time, she deferred to me. What kind of chairs did she want to rent? Where did she want to hold it? Did he prefer a casket or cremation? In her mind, whatever I wanted was fine. The only preference she had was that she would not be speaking at her father's funeral. I didn't ask for a reason; I respected her wish.

And then this morning, when the time finally came, she took a steaming-hot shower. Left the door open. I looked in the foggy mirror, watching her. She had her hair wrapped in a towel, swirls of dye staining the fabric. Her skin was pink from the heat, her legs bare.

"There is nothing separating us from the animals we slaughter," Ron said. "And that means that you have to make sure that you are always ready to die."

What would it be like to marry her? There was no doubt in my mind that I wanted to fuck a young woman like Demi. And with the situation we were in, I could take exactly what I wanted from her. I could make her mine. I owed it to her father, and she would owe it to me.

Ron shuffled the paper in his hands, then continued: "Shep was ready to die, until he had something to live for."

That *something* was Demi. I had to do what Shep wanted; I had to keep my promise and keep her *alive*. And then I had to make sure that she stayed as far away from me as possible. Until the war was over. Until she found real love. Because Demi put me on edge, like a clock that couldn't catch up to the exact time. She was so damn sure of everything and she had barely even lived. How could anyone be confident in anything, even our next breath?

"Everything changed after he started a family. I admit I didn't care for the transformation at first, but eventually, it made me respect him more," Ron said. He took a breath, then looked out at the crowd, concentrating on the final words. "Because Shep showed me that there were just as many reasons to die as there were to live."

And that lesson stuck with me now. A reason to live. I had never had to protect anyone before. Watching over Demi was new to me.

"And I know that I will never forget that lesson," Ron said, then left the podium.

A murmur sounded through the crowd. A few people politely clapped too. Ron put his hand on my shoulder, then stood beside me. He was one of my top enforcers, and I trusted him as much as I trusted anyone.

"Thanks," I whispered. He nodded in response.

Once the ceremony was over, a few people swarmed Demi, some of which I recognized, which meant they worked for my family. I broke through the group. Demi's eyes peered up at me, gray and glassy, like her father's. I put an arm around her shoulder, guiding her small body through the house.

"What were they saying to you?" I asked.

"They were asking about his butcher shop," she said. "Whether I was going to take it over or not. They didn't know he had shut it down years ago."

Those were the small details that would reveal Shep's link to the Adler mafia. I pulled her through the backyard until we went inside the kitchen.

"You need to eat," I said.

She gazed at the food, then shook her head.

"I'm not hungry."

"You *are* hungry," I said. She had eaten half of a sandwich the day before, but that was it. "You need to eat, Demi."

A few people crossed in front of the window, and my eyes flashed to the view of the woods. I needed to keep her away from the people who knew about Shep's background in the mafia, but I also needed to watch the woods for intruders.

"Stay in here," I said.

I slipped outside, watching the scene, but nothing had changed. If it weren't for the black clothing, the event would have looked like a wedding or college graduation. Derek came by, saying he was sorry about Shep, and Wil came by again too, this time with his fiancée, Ellie. I shook hands with both of them, though I had nothing to say.

A hand grabbed my arm. I turned; Demi looked up at me. Her hair was tucked into a low ponytail, the waves of color washing down her back. Her skin was pale under the moonlight, her gray eyes bloodshot and tired.

"We've got to figure this out," she said. "I know you promised my dad that you'd marry and provide for me, but I can't do this." She sighed deeply. "I know my dad wants what's best for me, but all I've craved for the last eighteen years is freedom. And I'm not going to get that through being your wife." She crossed her arms. "We need to solve this. Like a practical matter. Not like some silly promise we both made to a ghost."

"A practical matter," I repeated. As in, an incident that could be dismissed.

"I want to go back to college. I want to study criminal justice. I want to help people," she sighed, "And I want to live my life. I can't keep letting him control me from beyond the grave."

I nodded again. I understood that.

"Do you think we can figure out a way for both of us to keep that promise, without getting hitched?" Demi asked.

Her cold eyes stared at me, begging for an answer. It would break Demi to know who her father was, and ruin her entire world view to learn those truths from me. I had to keep her alive, but I knew that didn't have to be through marriage. In the end, Shep would understand. It was the best option for Demi.

"We'll figure it out," I said.

"Really?" she asked, her eyes lighting up, full of misty clouds. "You're not going to tell me that I'm wrong?"

It was as if she expected to be denied every single time, as if she could never stop fighting for what she wanted. How hard had Shep been on her?

"Shep's house too," I said. "I'll help you sell it."

Out of the corner of my eye, I saw something shift in the woods. If it were an animal, it would move again and reveal itself. But if nothing moved, it could have been someone. A person trying to stay undetected. A soldier sent by Muro.

Another shift in the woods, several yards away from the first.

Then nothing.

"Axe?" Demi asked.

I looked down, meeting her eyes for a moment. They were full of truth, waiting for my answer. If she knew who I was—what her father had taught me—all of that respect would be gone.

But right now, I had to go take care of business.

"We'll discuss it later," I said. "Stay here."

I walked into the woods, leaving her behind.

CHAPTER 4

Demi

Axe walked into the woods like he was searching for a lost jewel without a treasure map. His eyes were penetrating, his attention focused. Part of me wanted to follow him to see what drew him into the forest. The other side of me didn't care. Not a single bit.

"Demi Walcott, is that you?" a fragile woman's voice asked.

A hand landed on my shoulder. I hated, *hated* when people put their hand on my shoulder. As if they wanted to show me how small I was. When I looked up, I realized it was because the woman needed a steady hand. The anger lifted from my chest. I didn't mind that.

"I haven't seen you since you were a baby," she said.

Another line I loved to hear. I thought of a million lines to spout off in response, but instead, I simply said, "And I don't think I've seen you—*ever*."

The woman laughed, her shoulders shaking. She fixed her brooch. "You know, your father was one of my good friends before you were born. He took good care of me."

"And me," another woman said. They both looked about my dad's age, maybe younger, though it was hard to tell with their hair dye. "I didn't know Shep raised such a—" the second woman paused, eyeing my hair, "—such an adventurous young woman."

I smiled, giving the widest, toothiest grin I could muster. "You know, that's what finally put him over the edge," I said. I leaned in, bringing my voice to a whisper, "He saw my hair and croaked. Couldn't take it anymore. Not with a little hellion like me."

The women laughed, though the one who had made the 'adventurous' comment gave me side-eyes.

"You've certainly got his spirit."

I glanced at the woods, expecting to see that ogre of a man looming through the trees like a storm spreading across the sky, but I didn't see Axe anywhere. I balled my fist, holding onto the funeral service pamphlet. I wanted to go home, but I had no idea where that was anymore. My parents had paid off the house a long time ago, so I knew I could go there, at least until we sold it. But I also knew that the dorm rooms back at PGU might feel better. Either way, home wasn't Axe's empty bedroom with the sleeping bag on the floor.

I pictured Dad's blanket over the top of that maroon sleeping bag. That's what I wanted. *Home.*

Maybe I needed to be by myself.

The two women kept talking, sharing stories about old times with Shep. Without announcing my departure, I went to the kitchen, leaving the two of them behind. I followed the stream of people to a side room, where a dining table was covered with every casserole imaginable, plus cheesy bread, chocolate chip muffins, a cherry pie, pizza, and pasta. I swiped a chocolate chip muffin off of the table, wishing I still had my sweatshirt to hide it in the pocket. The black dress I was wearing was nice—I guess Axe had sent someone to buy it for me—but it wasn't practical for hiding baked goods.

Tossing the muffin between my hands, I wandered back into the kitchen. A couple of people glanced at my hair, whispering to each other, and I pretended not to notice. That's the thing they don't tell you about brightly colored hair; people gawked at you all of the time. But I had only dyed it because I liked the colors and I wanted to do something for myself for once. To not care about what Dad thought.

It was funny how I ended up at his funeral like that.

Bottles of hard alcohol lined the countertop, with a cooler on the floor full of ice and red-labeled beers, one of Dad's favorites. I eyed the bottles, searching for tequila. I hadn't tried it, or any alcohol for that matter, but my roommate loved to brag about the pungent taste and the punishing aftermath; tequila was *her* drink. I wanted to see if it was true. Anything to distract myself until the end of the night.

I reached for a bottle of amber-colored liquid, but then hesitated. I wasn't supposed to drink alcohol. A pang of regret trickled in. Would someone tell on me?

Why did I care? Dad couldn't punish me.

But that nagging grew, scraping at my stomach. I couldn't break a rule at his funeral. Dad had always said that every rule had a reason behind it, which meant you had to *trust* that the rules were just. Still, would one drink hurt? I held the stem of the bottle, debating what to do, that gnawing sensation digging deeper inside of me.

"Whoa there, cowgirl," a woman said. She set down another cooler full of beers, then adjusted a few of the cans so their labels were facing up. Reddish-brown hair rested on her shoulders, too fire-engine red to be natural. She blinked her emerald eyes at me. "There are plenty of sodas and non-alcoholic beers in the fridge. Gerard's stuff, since he went sober. Or tried to, anyway."

Who was Gerard? And why was she talking to me?

"And you are?" I asked, raising a brow.

"Maddie," she said, holding out a hand. Then she smirked and wiped the cool condensation off on her black shirt, and held it out again. "You must be Demi."

"Did Axe send you?" I asked.

"He might have said something."

There was a playfulness to her smile, but I balled my hands into fists, annoyed at the situation. Why hadn't I grabbed the bottle like a normal rebellious college student? Why couldn't I break a damn rule?

"If I want a beer, I should be able to get a beer," I said. "It's *my* dad's funeral."

"I believe you were reaching for tequila," she said, "and I also believe your host has a strict policy about that."

I rolled my eyes and crossed my arms. "I'm sure there are worse things going on here, than an eighteen-year-old drinking a little."

"Huh. Well," she laughed. "You're probably right." She grabbed my arm. "Come with me."

She took me through the house to an empty room at the front with a large window pointed toward the street. An elegant wood-carved couch was situated near the view, with white and floral cushions, reminding me of teacups. Maddie sat down on it, her hips hanging off of the couch. I hesitated, but then sat down next to her. It didn't seem like the kind of couch you were allowed to sit on.

But why did I care? I didn't even know who lived in this house.

"So," I said, unsure of what to say. "Did you know my dad?"

"Hah, no." She smiled, grabbing an unlabeled bottle full of blue-green liquid. "But I know the Adlers. I work for them."

The lines on her forehead made her seem older. Maybe she was in her thirties? Part of me was irritated that Axe *and* Maddie thought it was necessary to safeguard me, but the other part was relieved. I had seen what happened when my roommate got drunk; that probably wasn't the best state for me to be in at my dad's funeral reception.

But again, why did I care?

She handed me the bottle. It must have been alcohol. That was probably why we were in this room, away from everyone, including Axe. *Screw it*, I thought. I took a swig.

"This tastes like juice," I said.

"I know," she said.

Was it juice, then? I guess that didn't matter either. "So what do you do?" I asked.

"Cleaning. Concierge. Shopping. Picking out dresses," she eyed my black dress with fluttering eyelashes. "Whatever the brothers need. And I see the dress fits perfectly."

I looked down at the dress. Black material covered all the way up to my neck and down over the tops of my thighs, with a sheer material covering my arms. How had she known my size? She was right; it was perfect.

"Thanks," I said.

She smiled, then gestured at the bottle. I handed it back to her and she took a drink.

"You want to talk about your dad?" she asked.

"Not really," I said. I looked at the muffin in my hand, slightly squished from carrying it. I hadn't had an appetite at all lately, and somehow, even the chocolate chip muffin didn't seem that great. I should have eaten it right when I picked it up. Maybe then, I could've stomached it.

"You want to talk about what's going on with Axe?" She watched me carefully, her eyes pinned on mine. I shrank down. "He can be hard to deal with."

"Don't want to talk about that either," I said. "But thanks anyway."

"There you are!" a woman said. Short hair surrounded her round face, and a man followed behind her. "I've been looking for you everywhere."

"Do you know them?" Maddie whispered.

"No," I said.

"Why didn't you speak at the service?" the woman asked.

I shrugged. "Not really in the mood."

"But you know that you'll always live with the fact that you didn't speak at the event that was supposed to honor your father's life. You understand that, don't you, dear?" The woman tossed her head. "I'm sure if you simply said that you loved your father, that would have been perfect. In fact, I think Clara could arrange something now if you'd like. Trust me, dear. I speak from experience. You need to honor his life."

And that was the point, wasn't it? *Life*. He was gone now. And I was living life. And I didn't want to share his last words with a bunch of strangers. Maddie gave me a look, and I hung my head, staring down at my lap. I wanted to scream. I wanted to punch something. I wanted to rip that woman's ugly earrings off and shove them down her throat. But it seemed like so much effort right then. None of it would've helped.

I needed to leave. But I couldn't, not until I found Axe.

"Anyway, I was telling Hubert how amazing of a man your father was," she said.

"But he did, you know, butcher those—"

"Wow, you must be Mr. and Mrs. Johnson," Maddie said, grabbing their hands and shaking them enthusiastically. "My name is Maddie Vela." She stood in front of me, covering me from their view. "So do you personally know Ms. Walcott?"

"Well, we met when she was little."

"Still in the womb?"

"Well, not exactly—"

Maddie tilted her head to the side, then put a hand behind her back so that only I could see. She pointed to the kitchen as if to say, *Save yourself while you still can!*

"But I'm telling you," the man said, "The things he did, didn't make him an amazing man. He was a terrible person. Butchering so many of them. To pretend he was any less is a disservice to—"

"Go on, Demi," Maddie whispered. "I'll meet up with you later."

I inched through the kitchen, avoiding eye contact, but every hot gaze beamed down on me. The more people realized that I was her, *Shep's daughter*, the miscreant who hadn't given a speech, the more anxious I was to get out of there. But what had that man, Mr. Johnson, said? Was he a vegetarian? Against butchers? I put my muffin on the counter. A lot of people were vegetarian these days, so those kinds of comments had been coming up more lately. I passed the bottles and beers, not bothering to look this time, and wandered out into the backyard. Darkness was settling over the sky, making everything seem quiet. But not quiet enough.

I walked into the forest. The ground was covered in heavy vines of ivy, the leaves pointed and washed with creamy streaks. Cool air lifted up from the ground, greeting my bare calves. Axe was out here, somewhere, looming around in the darkness. Or maybe he had left. It would have been a cruel joke to leave me there with the wolves, but he had no reason to look out for me. We had both agreed that our manufactured relationship wasn't the best option for either of us.

I kept going until the buzzing insects were louder than the noise from the reception. I started thinking about Dad, whether he would have been mad if I drank at his reception or the fact that I hadn't said a word at his ceremony.

Dad had always been hard on me, never letting me make a mistake. Was Dad like that with Axe? Strict to the point of making him feel inferior? After Mom died, when I got my first D, I came home and all of my pets were gone. No tweeting cockatiel. No clucking. No barking at my feet. No purr against my chest.

I thought about what the guy had said during the ceremony: *You have to make sure that you are always ready to die.*

Dad never seemed attached to anything. When it came to my pets, he didn't have any sympathy when I cried. He had taken them to the shelter or given them away. *Why do you think you deserve them?* he had asked.

I didn't know how I was supposed to feel now. And that pissed me off more.

A low gasp, like air being squeezed out of a bag, caught my ears. I turned, peering through the trees. It was hard to see. I went forward.

"Axe?" I asked. A figure straightened, growing in height, a long arm gripping an object in its fist. As I got closer, I realized it was round, like a skull. The figure was holding another person by the head. The tall figure took a gun out of his pocket and held the barrel against the person's skull. The bullet shuddered through the barrel, going through the bone and flesh. The explosion was soft though, dulled.

Someone had committed murder.

Adrenaline instantly rocked through me. *Come on*, I thought. *Think.* I reached for my pockets, trying to find my phone, but my hands were clammy and energy pulsed through my veins hard. Shit. I had forgotten Axe had taken it. I peered out from behind the tree and saw the figure again, coming closer. Those dark eyes reached mine, the dull light from the reception reflected in them. Haunting me. Coming closer.

Axe.

I ran towards the house as fast as I could. Someone would be able to help. Axe leaped toward me.

"Someone help!" I shouted. Then someone from the side pushed me over, my body crashing into the ground, the roots and rocks biting my skin. The person, another man—not Axe—lifted a gun, aiming it toward my head. Death at my father's funeral. A final end to the Walcotts.

A bullet pierced through the trees. The man fell forward, falling on top of me.

Axe stowed his gun. My pulse raced. He had shot two men. And I had almost died. Had he saved me, or was I about to die too? He pulled me into his thick arms, putting me into a headlock, his other hand pushing on the back of my skull until my vision darkened.

I pushed against his arm. "Let me go!" I shouted.

He dragged me through the woods. I kept fighting, so he maneuvered me against a tree trunk and punched me in the chest, knocking the wind from my lungs. I gasped for air, unable to find it, falling forward, and he caught me, throwing me back into that headlock, dragging me once again.

"You can't get away with this," I said.

But what had he gotten away with? I had almost died. He had saved me from one of the men, hadn't he?

But he had still killed another man before that. What the hell was he doing?

He opened a door in front of us. A click of a switch. Then light flooded around us, and he pulled me inside. Concrete covered every inch of the room, like a warehouse or a parking garage, and the lights above flickered, a gentle hum filling the room. Metal cabinets with locks. A toilet and a sink. A chain saw hung from the wall. Knives stuck to a magnetic rack. And restraints. Two cages. And so many metal objects that I had no idea what they were for.

Every vein in my body throbbed.

"Who are you?" I asked. Axe let go of me and I dropped to my hands and knees. He bent down to open up a wooden box, about the size of a large dog crate. He fumbled with the lock, then the wooden slats on the sides fell open, revealing a cage with thick bars. There was no way I was going in that. I had to do something. I grabbed the first thing I saw on the table—a baseball bat—and swung it into his back in a loud *thwack!*

He stood up slowly. Then he turned and looked down at me.

"Get in the box," he said.

Hitting him with the bat hadn't fazed him. My fingers quivered, but I stilled them.

"No," I said.

"Get in the box," he repeated, his tone firm.

"I'm not getting in your box."

"Don't tempt me, Demi," he said.

Those words held in my chest, knocking back and forth until I felt them all over my body. *Don't tempt me.* Because fighting back would only tempt him to kill me. Just like he killed those other men.

But there had to be a way out of this.

"You don't have to do this," I said.

He grabbed me by the hair and swung me around like a doll until I was on all fours. I held the sides of the cage, resisting as hard as I could, but he pushed me inside easily.

"This isn't you," I said.

I turned around, hunched in the cage, practically in the fetal position, and faced him. I tried to think of anything I knew about Axe. He didn't owe me anything, and yet he had helped me plan my father's funeral, and had agreed to marry me because it put Dad at peace. He could have let me die just now, but he hadn't. He had saved me.

"There's good inside of you," I said, almost like a threat. "You're not the monster you think you are."

He crouched on his knees, tilting his head. A hint of amusement flickered in his eyes, then vanished.

"You don't know anything," he said.

He folded the wooden slats, covering the bars of the cage, locking them into place. Darkness swallowed me, leaving behind a small hole of light.

CHAPTER 5

Axe

A wave of heat crawled over my skin. Demi was in a cage now, but that didn't make me feel any better. A third Midnight Miles soldier was out there, and I needed to take care of him before I did anything else.

"You're a man of your word," Demi said, her voice muffled. "You made a promise."

And what good was a promise to a dead man? A dead man who had lied to his daughter for her entire life.

"You're a good man, Axe."

I wanted to laugh. I had been born into this life, trained to be a murderer. There was nothing good about me; I was numb to my core. Everyone had their task, and mine, right then, had to do with getting rid of Muro's slime.

"You made a promise," Demi repeated, her voice quivering.

It was finally getting to her. That strength was falling, knowing that she was trapped. I kneeled down again, looking into the peephole. It was about the size of a round coaster, enough to give her air and some light, but not enough to stick her hand through to try and escape.

Her gray eyes found mine; fight pulsed in her pupils.

"You don't have to do this," she said, her tone menacing. "If you let me go, I won't tell a soul. But you need to let me go, Axe. Before you make a very big mistake."

I smiled. The grin washed over me. Oh, the mistakes I had made didn't begin with Demi Walcott. They began long before she was born. That very first time I took the knife from her father's hands.

That was if you believed in right and wrong.

She kept speaking, making up nonsense to convince me to let her go, but common sense was working its way into her brain too. Her eyes shifted beyond me, then stilled with the truth; if this was my torture lab, then killing those men wasn't a mistake. Nor was putting her in a cage 'an accident.' It was a passion.

"If you make any noise," I said quietly, "I will cut your tongue."

She stared at me, her eyes racing back and forth.

"You wouldn't," she said.

"I would."

"But you promised my dad you would—"

"I promised your father I would keep you *alive*," I said sharply. "We never agreed to what that meant."

My boots thudded on the concrete. The door swung and closed quietly. I stood outside of the workroom for a moment, checking my weapons and rope, acknowledging the guards at the sides, then let my eyes adjust. There was one more soldier out there. I had to work quickly.

I traveled through the woods. A tree lay on its side. A few yards down, another tree was too close to its neighbor, the roots growing up out of the earth. If you didn't know it, you would miss it and trip over the roots hidden by the ivy. But I knew these woods better than the apartment I slept in.

A dark figure was crouched, peering at the reception, a sniper rifle on the ground, aimed through the trees. I came closer, step by step, waiting as he looked for the right target. I swooped in behind him, pulling his neck into a tight noose, then dragged him through the trees as he tried desperately to get some air. I pulled it up, letting his weight hang on the rope. I could have killed him there, but I wanted to play. And I wanted Demi to see how much of a mistake this was. Because mistakes didn't happen on purpose, and I was going to use every last second of this man's life to prove that to her.

I opened the door to the workroom, wrung zip ties around his ankles and wrists, and right before I knew he would expire, I opened the rope, giving his lungs freedom. He gasped.

"It's you," he said. "*You.*"

I hoisted him up, letting him drop onto the metal table. The baseball bat was underneath him, but causing him discomfort.

"You!" he said again, sneering at me. His breathing hoarse.

"Tell me about Cannon," I said. "What's his name? His real name?"

"Cannon will never bow down to you."

I huffed. I never expected Cannon to obey me. I expected him to die.

"What's his name?" I repeated.

"I'm not telling you shit, mother fucker!"

I let out a sigh, letting the sound float between us. How much could Demi hear?

"You're wasting my time," I said.

I went to the wall, finding my favorite bone saw and cleaver. The table creaked and clanged as he wiggled his way off, falling to the floor and knocking into Demi's crate. I kept waiting for her to speak, to ask this man for help, but she never did. Putting the knives down on the top of Demi's crate, I pulled the man up by his bruised neck and slammed him on the table once again, power surging through my bones.

"Fuck, fuck, fuck," the man cried. Saliva spit from the sides of his mouth, sputtering like a foaming pot on the stove. "Don't kill me, man. It's not about you. It's about your dad. It's about your dad—"

"What about Gerard?" I asked.

"I need to kill him. The rest of you are bonus. Just him. Kill Gerard. And then—"

None of this was new information. I already knew Muro had a distaste for my father. I grabbed the bone saw off the top of Demi's crate and brought it against his leg, bringing it back and forth, more pressure on the bone, slicing through the marrow, then down again to that easy flesh.

He wailed, his screams growing, sweat dripping from his face, his panting breaths harsh. But those screams, those damn screams. They only made me want his silence more. I went for his arms next. Once I was done, blood oozed from the open wounds. His body stopped shaking, dulling into silence. I put the knife down. Moved his hand until it was on the table next to him. The leg, heavy with his boot, dropped to the floor.

The tension released from my body, a lightness filling my head. My mouth was dry. I had water in one of the cabinets. I knew I should drink some.

Still, even in the silence, Demi was quiet. I hadn't felt this relaxed since she had first come into my life.

I grabbed a bottle from the back in one of the cabinets, chugged it until it was empty, then considered giving one to her. As I neared the box, I stopped, waiting for a noise. If I listened carefully enough, I could hear her breathing. Steadied. Then stopped. Then steady again, as if practicing, trying to stabilize.

I wet my lips. The image of her wrapped in a towel crossed my mind, the wet strands of hair on her back, the dye on the towels, her bare legs. I could push that fucker off of that metal table, slam her onto it, and claim her as mine, once and for all.

My cock twitched thinking about it. The fear in her wide eyes. The glassy look on her face as she came to understand the fucked up man her father had promised her to.

It would be easy to kill her. Shep had no other family. The mafia men who knew about Demi would assume she had gone back to college. And by the time someone cared to look, it wouldn't matter what had happened.

I leaned on the box, admiring the smooth wood, remembering the day I had made it. Afterward, I had treated myself to time with a sex worker. I had tried a girlfriend once because my mother insisted on it. But when my girlfriend saw how I acted in private, she went running. I wasn't going to chase after someone I was vaguely interested in, so instead, I chose sex workers. They were easy; they knew what was expected. The day I made the box, the woman had been a sweet talker, telling me how handsome I was, how sexy my scarred lips were. Anything to make another buck.

But Demi was nothing like that. She knew what she wanted, and what the world owed her.

And yet she knew nothing about the real world. Nothing about her family's history. Nothing about me.

My cock pressed against my pants, heavy and rapt for her. I unbuckled my belt, the leather sliding from the loops, then set it down on a clean spot on the table. Undid the top button, unzipped the fly. Pulled out my cock. Gripping it hard until the blood visibly throbbed in the head. I thought of Demi.

Knowing how strict Shep was, and that she had gone to that private girls' school, I knew there was a good chance she was still a virgin. Tight as hell. Untouched. I could ruin her with one hearty thrust.

She gave a sharp intake of air. My cock pulsated at the sound. I swallowed the saliva gathering in my mouth, then licked my lips, thinking of her crouched inside of there, waiting for me. Demi had never tried to flatter me with false compliments like the sex worker had. Demi was pure, she knew what the world was made of, and she knew that she deserved more than what I could give her.

Wasn't she right?

A flash of that night with the sex worker came into my mind. Nothing had worked. No matter how tight she squeezed my dick, no matter how hard she clamped her lips down on me, nothing would make me come. Every few seconds, she'd pull off my dick and moan, her doe eyes and fake lashes blinking up at me. *You taste so good, baby*, she said. *You're such a treat.*

Still, I felt nothing.

It wasn't until I pulled out a gun and held it to her head that I got anything real out of her. *What are you doing?* she had asked, her hands shaking. But I didn't move. Kept the gun aimed at her head. *Are you insane? A gun?* But I had told her I was armed. I had told her what I liked. She must have thought I was joking.

Do you think it's loaded? I asked.

Her lips quivered. I put a hand on the back of her head and shoved my dick down her throat. She whimpered, a tear rolling down her face, and I knew then, that those emotions were the only real thing that I would ever have from her. From any woman. Every single woman feared me. I would never have a moment where someone trusted me.

And so I came then, down her throat, filling her mouth with my jizz. She coughed it out, couldn't stop crying. Once I was done, I showed her that the barrel was empty. Then I pulled out our negotiation form, pointed to the gunplay box. I dropped it and left her sobbing on the floor.

I leaned down, unlocking the padlock on Demi's crate. Once I removed the bar, the wooden slats would fall to the sides, and Demi would give me those same eyes, the pure adrenaline-soaked fear that I craved. The scent of it was musky and full of heat, and I relished in that scent, knowing the power it gave me.

The sides of the crate clanged down onto the concrete. Demi's eyes washed over the man's leg on the ground, then to the corpse on the table in front of her. She turned her neck, looking at me. Those wide eyes caught me, held me in their stare. She grew still, then her lips parted. Wet. Her eyes took in my cock. Her pupils dilated.

Everything about her was soft, yielding to me. I kept stroking my cock, each pump harder than the last, watching as her tongue flicked over her lips. She was sitting with her ass on the floor of the cage, her legs bunched in front of her, but the slightest movement of her ankles showed that she was spreading herself. She probably didn't know she was doing it, but she was opening herself for me.

Curiosity was laced between us. Was it hers, or mine?

Where was the fear? Was she following my instructions? Or was she that enraptured? What was she trying to hide?

But Demi didn't hide anything.

And her eyes never left me.

CHAPTER 6

Demi

The head of Axe's cock was a deep red, sometimes a dark purple when he gripped it, the angry veins twisting around his shaft like they were struggling to get free. My eyes were glued to him, and his eyes were stuck on me too, feeding off of me, bulging out of their sockets like he would die if he couldn't have me. As if he was about to unleash a demon on the world. And on me.

I should have been afraid. I should have been wondering what was wrong with him. But I wasn't. A man's amputated leg lay on the ground, just out of my reach, and yet I was staring back at Axe, never letting my eyes leave him. Was I scared that if I moved or broke our eye contact, that he would kill me? Death was hovering over us, seeping into our souls. And yet Axe wanted to fuck himself while looking at me.

I didn't feel like myself. Power swelled inside of me, knowing how much he wanted me. I was in a cage, a damned cage, and yet Axe was so enraptured by me that I couldn't move. Couldn't look away. How could a man put you in a cage, then look at you with such lust in his eyes that you felt drawn to him, as if lust were a tangible, physical web being spread out between the two of you? Wrapping the silky threads around us until we both spiraled into nothingness.

He came closer. Put his hand down, leaning on the cage. Thrust his fist over his cock, the shaft a dark red. He had the key to the lock in his other hand, but he didn't reach down to open it. And he didn't hurt me.

When the pleasure bubbled up, Axe groaned, a satisfyingly primal noise, and the come shot out of him, dripping over the cage, getting on his hand, landing on me. His eyes closed, and his body shook with each pulse, like it was taking the life out of him.

I had no idea that an orgasm could be that powerful.

I reached up, stroking my finger across his palm leaning against the cage. He glanced down, a shudder rolling through him, our eyes meeting for a moment in that aftermath.

He stood, zipped up, and buttoned his pants. I opened my mouth, putting my hands on the bars, trying to figure out how much I was willing to risk when it came to my tongue. But he bent down and closed the wooden sides shut over the cage again, the padlock clicking into place. The key turning in the lock echoed in the crate as if it were directly connected to my eardrums.

I angled myself, looking through that peephole. Axe ran a hand over his face, then went to a corner I couldn't see. A faucet turned on. Water splashed in the sink. When he returned to view, he rubbed a clean cloth across his face. It was fascinating to see someone take a person's life, then do something normal, like clean his face. Axe had always seemed aggressive—the way he randomly turned on me always caught me off guard—but I hadn't expected this. He wasn't simply a murderer; he had a full-on torture room.

He checked his gun, then put it in his holster and went toward the door. He clicked off the lights, and the quiet buzz dimmed to silence. I pressed my hand against the bars and the wood, watching as he left. The door closed behind him. Darkness swallowed the room.

What had just happened?

***

I dreamed of Dad. Before he closed the butcher shop, his white apron had been his classic staple, strapped across his chest, splattered with blood like a badge of honor. But in my dream, it hung over his sickened body, thin and frail, like a doll wearing an adult's clothes. *Run, Demi,* he said. My heart quickened. *Run while you still can. Before he takes your legs too. Before he takes your will to fight.*

My head bumped into the top of the cage, waking me up. I wasn't sure how much time had passed. There were no windows in that room, at least none that I could see, so it was hard to tell what time of the day it was, or if another night had passed.

First, Axe removed the body of the man, then wiped the table clean. Then, a few different times, he brought me food. Removed the wooden slats, then set the food right against the metal bars so that I could grab it. A chunk of cheese. A molasses roll. A peanut butter and jelly sandwich. Survival should have kicked in, making me eat those things, and while my stomach grumbled, I didn't feel hungry. Not in the way that I normally did. And I knew that if I accepted his food, the more likely I would be to see him as something other than my captor. A sick game messing with my head, trying to convince me that Axe was providing for me. He brought me food. Killed for me. Kept me alive.

So I refused to eat. Refused to see him as anything other than a deranged killer.

My legs ached from being in the fetal position, but there was enough room that I stretched my legs into a tight butterfly. The door swung open, hitting the wall in a loud thud. I angled myself to the peephole. He was carrying another man. This one was smaller than the others, but Axe rammed him onto that table, and his body tumbled like it weighed a million pounds.

This is a case study, I told myself. It was easier to live with the situation that way, pretending like I was still in school, getting ready to take down criminals like Axe. Did Axe work for someone, or did he work alone? Was he simply twisted, or did he have a heart? Why hadn't he killed me yet? Why had he saved me? Was there anything left inside of him?

Axe began moving the man's legs into buckles at the end of the table.

"Fuck you," the man screamed. He pushed himself up onto his hands. "You killed Mike. And I'll kill you!"

Axe stared at the man for a moment, then he punched him, sending his face straight down. It stunned the man, but only long enough for Axe to find the other buckles to bind his arms. Next, he strapped his forehead and neck.

Axe braced himself, leaning over the man.

"Who is Cannon?" Axe asked.

"Cannon? Cannon?"

Axe went to the wall, picked a long, thin instrument with a sharp end on one side and a blunt edge of the other, and brought it to the man. He pressed it into his cheek.

"Where is Cannon?" Axe repeated.

"The hell are you doing that for?"

"Where," Axe paused, leaning closer, pressing the pointed end into the man's cheek, "is Cannon?"

"I ain't telling you shit!"

Axe removed the instrument and pressed it into his throat, letting the first half-inch linger in his neck.

"Where is Cannon?"

Who the hell was Cannon?

"He lives in Brackston," the man gasped. "A few miles away from the headquarters."

"And how secure is his place?"

"High tech. But he lives by himself. Too proud to have help."

Axe pressed the instrument into the man's throat, inch, by inch, until the instrument stopped at the hard table. The man swallowed, blood gurgling in his mouth. That wheezing sound filled the air, each breath with the whistle of air being let out of a balloon. My heart raced in my chest, and every muscle in my body tightened. That noise. I was back with Dad, watching as life left his body. Those wails that came out of nowhere. His last gasps. I covered my ears.

Axe said something in a low voice to the man, and I moved my hands. I needed to hear this.

"Your choice," Axe said.

"Please," the man begged, his voice trembling. "Make it quick."

Axe did the same thing, piercing the man's neck an inch lower this time. And the man's breathing was louder, more erratic, like his body couldn't decide whether to rebel or give up. Axe moved, piercing him again, and again, methodically, until finally, the man shuddered, and the rasping breath stopped.

How did anyone deserve this?

Axe got another instrument from the side of the room, tools I actually recognized. A bone knife, cleaver, and scissors. He cut off the man's clothes, his body limp, then started butchering him, using deliberate force against the flesh. Like Dad.

Had Dad known about this?

He couldn't have. That was impossible. Dad had to be as clueless as I was, otherwise he wouldn't have let Axe get anywhere near me. And if I thought about the man like a cow being cut for steak, I could remove myself. It was normal. Axe was butchering beef.

But I knew he wasn't.

He turned the body, lifting it up. The air pushed out of the man's lungs in one final wheeze, so loud that it startled me, surging me back to that living room with Dad. I yelped a short squeal, then immediately covered my mouth. My own breathing hitched, too panicked to do me any good. I pressed myself against the box, pushing toward the back, as if those few inches could save me.

The thump of his boots came closer. I held my breath.

He removed the padlock, letting the wooden slats crash to the floor. I raised my eyes to meet his.

Narrowed. Black. Seething.

He unlocked the cage. I stayed pressed against the edges. Then he pulled me out by the hair.

"Fuck!" I screamed.

I immediately jabbed him in the face with my fist, then used my other arm to cross from the back.

Axe stared at me. My hands seemed to hurt more than he did.

He pulled me into a bear hug, and that chemical smell, laced with the metallic scent of blood swallowed me. I tried shifting my arms, but he grew tighter, fighting me without much effort.

Taking my wrists behind me, he pulled them into a zip tie. I kicked as hard as I could, but he still zip-tied each ankle to a metal chair. I sneered at him, huffing through my teeth. In the back of the room, Axe washed his hands slowly, then he grabbed an instrument from one of the locked cupboards, meeting me by the table.

I had to think. I had to do something fast.

But *what?*

He twisted a knob at the bottom of the instrument until the bolts loosened, then he screwed it to the table. The top had a long arm with two pincers and another knob to tighten them. What the hell was it?

After taking another chair in front of me, Axe gestured with his hand to move forward.

"No," I said.

"Lean forward," he demanded, his voice monotone. As if this *was* normal to him.

"No," I repeated.

I truly thought that if he wanted to kill me, he would have done so already, but when he grabbed the hair at the back of my head and pulled me forward, holding me in place while he moved the contraption closer, I started to think of how stupid I was. If Dad didn't know this side of Axe, then what else was Axe hiding? What else would he be willing to do?

He opened my mouth, but I clamped my teeth down, grunting, not letting him get through. Then he grabbed my chin and pinched it tight, the pain shocking me until I opened my jaw, letting him grab my tongue and bring it out. He put it between the two pincers, then twisted the knobs until I was stuck.

Each twitch of my tongue irritated me. Drool instantly pooled in my mouth. I couldn't move from where I was seated, but I could still feel those involuntary spasms from my tongue. Any time I moved, the pincers squeezed tighter. My eyes watered. The pain spread from those tiny points like little fingers of death latching on to my nervous system.

He flicked a pocket knife open, letting the blade gleam in the light. He leaned forward, his knee bumping into mine, and he took the knife, skimming it over my bare legs, streaked with dirt and muck. Taking the point of the knife, he pressed it into my thighs, drawing a white line, until I moved, trying to get away from the knife. He was making me spread my legs, the dress bunching at my hips. He dragged the knife closer to my pussy, so slowly that I thought I might die.

He raised a brow, his eyes meeting mine. His mouth opened.

"Sensitive," he said. Drool spilled out of my mouth. I panted like a dog. "Are you a virgin, Demi?"

A wave of heat washed over my face, decreasing the pain for a millisecond, then it crashed back into me. He was asking that question *right now?* I knew I had to answer. I gave a small nod.

"I asked you a question, Demi."

I nodded vigorously, wincing at the pain. He lifted the knife from my skin. Still staring at me, his eyes always unblinking.

He spread his fingers, letting the tips rub against my inner thighs. They were thick, like the blunt end of a brush, but the softness of the touch made me quiver. He inched closer to my pussy, and as I wiggled my hips, I impulsively moved closer. What was my body doing? He was a murderer!

He took his thumb, rubbing it through my underwear against my clit. I sucked in a breath, but he kept his thumb there, moving it back and forth, watching me. Seeing exactly what I would do. Heat waved through me, and he pulled my underwear to the side, his eyes hungry, drinking me in. His fingers brushed in midair, almost touching my slit, but he never pushed inside. I closed my eyes.

He sat up straight, the chair creaking underneath him. I opened my eyes, letting them fall to his groin, where his monster of a cock was hard and heavy against his leg. I brought my lips together and it lessened the pain, but as soon as I opened them again, the pincer clamped down tight.

He looked me in the eyes, reading me. Was he deciding my fate? To fuck me, or kill me? He could have killed me and I knew he wouldn't have thought twice about it. And I knew, by the way that his cock twitched, that he wanted to fuck me.

But he held back. He kept looking at me.

I spread my legs further, grinding on the chair, my underwear still disheveled, exposing me to the metal. I told myself it was an act of survival—get him to want me more so that he desired me *more* than he wanted to kill me—but it wasn't that. It was this strange need, being helpless like this, with a man that took my punches and wanted me so bad his cock turned purple. And he still wouldn't fuck me.

Yet.

He brandished the knife again, holding it up to my eye. We both watched as he brought the blade to my tongue, the sudden searing pain jolting through me. Drops of blood landed on my thigh. I closed my eyes tight. Then he removed it, going to the other side. The hammer of pain shook through me again. He was actually doing it. Slice by slice.

Suddenly, he undid the knob, the pressure releasing, and as soon as I could, I closed my mouth. The metallic liquid rolled over my teeth, two flaps on either side of my tongue catching on my molars, like the burnt skin on the roof of a mouth. How deep had he actually cut? Would I feel any difference?

He stood, going again to the wall, finding a large ring attached to two straps, a buckle between them. The ring was wide, big enough to fit my fist through. He put it in my mouth. I pulled at the restraints, but I didn't make a noise this time. I knew I couldn't go anywhere.

With my jaw wide open, my tongue flailed, the dull pain aching at the sides, and again, he went to another cabinet. But this time, he pulled out a black dildo. The rubber smell made me gag, the sound wet in my throat.

He held my chin, shoving the synthetic cock down my throat, and I choked so hard that it shot out of me. Then he did it again, and again, until finally, I took it, going past the curve of my throat. Tears washed down my face, the intensity building, but his eyes were on me, watching me intently. Haunting me. Holding me. Never letting me go.

A wet spot of pre-cum wet his pants. The impulse to lick my lips made me moan. There was no way that I could bite him with this gag, so why wasn't he fucking me himself? And why did I want him to do that? He leaned in, our faces almost touching, and he pushed the dildo inside, pumping it down my throat.

I started choking, coughing on saliva, and he pulled back, his eyes growing dim. He cut the ties around my ankles, then the one around my wrists. Then he pointed to the toilet and the sink in the corner, his hand on his holster. I relieved myself, washed my face, used the saltwater rinse as he instructed, his eyes on me the entire time.

Once I turned back to him, his arms were crossed over his chest. He handed me a bottle of water, and I hesitated. I still wasn't going to take anything from him, but I knew I needed water. I drank the entire thing, the sudden fullness giving me sharp pains in my stomach, making me forget about my cut tongue. He sighed deeply, then pointed to the cage.

"You can't," I started, but then I stopped. My tongue was heavy, but I tried again. "You can't keep me in there forever."

"I'm not," he said. Then he grabbed my hair, shoving me into the cage. Pulled up the wooden slats.

Then he locked it tight.

His boots pounded around the room like a slow heartbeat. Then, after a while, he switched off the light, but the door never opened and closed. Had he left? Once my eyes adjusted, I peeked through the hole.

His back was against the ground, right beside the cage. His eyes closed. His hands resting on his stomach.

He was trying to sleep.

He was trying to sleep?

I sucked in a breath, trying to figure out what was going on. In an attempt to get comfortable, I squirmed in the cage. The wooden slats creaked. Axe shifted. What was the point of sleeping beside me? There were so many locks on the cage. He knew, better than anyone, that I wasn't going anywhere.

Then his breathing calmed, steadying to a slow rhythm. He was asleep. He was comfortable then, not worried about me escaping and killing him in his sleep. His apartment was close. I knew that. He could have easily been sleeping on his mattress or in that sleeping bag at that moment. So why was he still here?

I closed my eyes, listening to his breath, finding comfort in it. The pain in my tongue throbbed, but I let his breath wash over me. Let him lull me to sleep.

CHAPTER 7

Axe

I rubbed the back of my head. My shoulders ached. My entire back was tight. I took a deep breath, stretching as I stood. Demi stirred in her crate. She needed something to eat.

Outside, a woodpecker was knocking into a tree, and the overcast sky let thin beams of light leak through the trees. I headed back toward the Adler House, stomping through the woods. A spider web, glistening with dew, sparkled in the light. The spider waited on the edge, a wrapped and bundled meal waiting on the opposite side.

I let myself in through the back door quietly. I preferred this time of the day when no one was out yet. After taking a piss and washing my face, I scouted the kitchen. In the refrigerator, there was a container full of my mother's tomato and basil soup, a cold bottle of water, some diced fruit, and a store-bought slice of cheesecake. I took an apple from the counter for myself, the hard crunch breaking through the quiet of the house. I didn't know anything about Demi, nor did I care to know. But I knew she had to eat.

The best item for her tongue was the soup, so I grabbed it, heated it up in the microwave, then went back to the workroom. The wood slats creaked; she must have been stretching—as much as she could, anyway.

I unlocked the wooden slats, then moved the soup next to the cage. Her skin was clammy, her cheeks pale. Still, she turned her chin.

"Not hungry."

I took a deep breath. "You haven't eaten since before the funeral."

"So?"

"You need to eat."

I opened the door, shoving the plastic container inside, but she put up her hands, pushing it back out.

"I said, I'm not hungry."

She smacked it away, some of it spilling to the side. I jerked it around, trying to make sure that more of it wouldn't fall. My heartrate spiked. Why was this tiny woman refusing to eat, when I could have killed her right then? When I *should have* killed her right then.

Maybe that's what it took. A gun to her head. Maybe then she would eat a damn bite.

I sat down on the chair to the side, putting my head in my hands. The only reason I wanted to keep that promise to Shep, was because he had saved my life. That was the only time you owed a man. All I had to do was keep her alive, but that meant she had to eat.

She put up the back of her hand to her forehead, her eyelids fluttering. "I don't feel good."

You don't say.

I stared at the half-eaten apple, wondering if she'd eat that instead. But screw that; it was mine. If she wasn't going to eat, then fine, but that wasn't going to stop me. The crunch of the fruit's flesh interrupted the silence, and Demi perked up, looking over at it.

"Dad told me about you, you know," she said. I didn't look at her; I took another bite. "Axe, the young man who could *really* make a career out of a butcher's life, he'd say. Axe, the only man he thought was better than himself." She snickered, then looked down at her nails, her head bobbing back and forth in fatigue. "What a fantasy that was."

A few minutes passed as I worked on the apple. Demi kept moving back and forth, almost as if she couldn't stay still, or wouldn't let herself. She stared at her feet, then watched me eat the apple as if I was the one in the cage and she was visiting the zoo. She had a way of unnerving me.

"Before my mom died, Dad was strict with me, but she kept him in balance, you know?" she said. "He'd want to discipline me for getting a B. Would always threaten to take away my pets. But Mom would tell him that my babies were my passion. And all he had to do was look at me hugging those furry and feathered fluffballs close to my chest, and he'd melt too. He'd ask for that same kind of hug, and he'd remind me that I needed to study harder. Even if I was in the third grade and didn't know what studying was."

The idea of Shep hugging anyone sounded like bogus. In fact, when I had heard that he had gotten his wife pregnant, I had been surprised that they had sex. Everyone had needs, but Shep had always stressed that you couldn't hold onto anything. And nine months of making a child sounded like holding onto a hell of a lot.

It wasn't the Shep that I knew. Something had changed him.

Love had changed him.

Demi ran her fingers through her hair, catching knots. The tendrils were damp with oil and sweat, and she was ripe. Saliva dried up on her face. Cracked skin at the corners of her mouth.

"He didn't want me to go to PGU," she said, still talking to me, or to herself, I didn't know. "He thought the local community college was fine, that I could transfer wherever I wanted. But I *begged* to go to PGU. It was close enough that I could come home if he got sick, but far enough away that I didn't have to if I didn't want to."

Her voice started drifting at those words, as if she was ruminating over the situation, wondering if it was a mistake. Even though Shep had raised her, her whole view was backward. She was holding onto his death, blaming herself for something that was beyond her control. The disease took his body; there was nothing she could have done to prevent that. Staying home with him wouldn't have changed his fate.

"If your father didn't want you to go to PGU, he wouldn't have let you," I said.

She perked up, craning her neck to see me.

"I think that's the most words you've ever said to me," she said. I took another bite of the apple, turning so that my shoulders faced away from her. Just because I was in the room, didn't mean that I had to pay attention to her. All of that rambling. I should have cut out her damn tongue instead of leaving it there.

So why hadn't I?

Was it because I wanted to fuck her tongue? Was it because I wanted to feel it on me?

Was it because I *liked* hearing her talk about this side of Shep that I didn't know?

"I think you're right," she said. "Dad never let anything go unless he wanted it to happen." I let out a breath and she sucked in through her nostrils. "Is that tomato soup?"

"Tomato and basil." Her stomach grumbled, loud enough to fill the room. "You need to eat."

She stared at the container, then turned to me.

"What happened to you?"

I flinched.

"What do you mean?" I asked.

"There's always a reason, right? A reason why someone turns out bad. Abuse. Neglect. *Something.*" She shook her head. "In the criminal justice program, there's this whole unit on mental health. Behavioral Health. I think that's what it's called? Anyway, I haven't taken it yet, but I have a third-year friend who told me about it. Basically, the whole idea is that if we look more closely at the mental health of our *youth*, then maybe a lot of crimes could be prevented."

That was an incredibly simplified way of looking at it. No college program could account for being born into a crime family. What did her college say of toddlers who had been told, since they could remember, that one day, they would make people sleep forever, and make their family proud?

"Or, like, you know, putting criminals in behavioral therapy instead of prison."

And what did you do for the people who tried going to therapy? Whose family would never be arrested, because we had so much blackmail on the local jurisdiction, that any law enforcement ate out of our hands? What happened to them, when they were stuck like that?

Not everything could be solved through textbooks and schooling. But Demi would never understand that. In her world, school was law, and laws were just. A part of me admired that rationality in her. I had never met someone who thought that way; I wished that I had that world view myself.

But I knew that there was no truth. Everyone had their dark secrets.

"You know, like maybe you had some sort of trauma. And if your parents didn't leave you to kill rabbits, then maybe you wouldn't be killing people now."

I stared at her. Killing rabbits? How about helping to kill a grown man when I was seven years old? Sure, he tried to kill me, but giving me that power over a man's fate was something that shifted my entire world view. Nothing was forever. Life could be taken from you in an instant.

"It doesn't work like that," I finally said. "You don't put someone in therapy and expect that to be the answer." I stood up, looking down at her. "The person has to *want* to change things. They have to believe that by following the protocols, everything will be better. But sometimes, even if you do follow the rules, it's not better." I leaned down, meeting her almost at eye level. "No matter how much you try." I shook my head. "You have to want to change."

And I never wanted to give up the power that controlling someone's life gave me.

Demi tilted her head, her brows furrowed. "Are you saying you don't want to change, then?"

I wasn't saying anything. I grabbed the container, shoving it back into the cage. "Would you, please," I said, raising my voice, "eat the fucking soup so I can leave?"

She stared at me, her sleet eyes daring. She had seen me kill multiple people, knew that I wasn't afraid of harming her too. Still, she leaned into the cage, closer to me, her expression full of passion.

"I'm not eating. If you want to keep me 'alive,' like you promised my dad, then you need to let me go."

I sighed. Then I took the soup. Put it on the table. She held her breath, her eyelids fluttering as she realized that I didn't care. If she wanted to starve herself to death, then, by all means, be my guest. It wouldn't be the first time I had watched someone starve.

I lifted the wooden slats. Locked them into place. Went to the door.

But something stopped me. I turned back, looking at that wooden box. Rage filled me to the brim. I had this woman, a young, intriguing, aggravating-as-hell woman, who wouldn't eat a single bite of food to survive. A woman who thought she was better than the life she had.

I stomped back to the box, taking a spoonful of soup from the container and sliding it through the peephole. Most of it would fall, but some of it might catch her.

"Eat the soup," I said. "Lick it off the bars."

"I'm not eating—"

I grabbed the key and unlocked the cage again, yanking the bars open from the top, then grabbed the container of soup off of the floor and shoved it onto her face, streaking her skin with red.

"Are you too good to eat food from me?" I growled. I pulled her against me, wrapping her in my arms, swallowing her body with mine. "Too good to take food from someone who should be rotting in jail." I wrenched her arms together with one hand, then used my other hand to take the spoon and hold it on her cheek. "Understand this, Demi. You are the one rotting in a cell. The only reason you're alive is because I haven't killed you yet."

Finally, her mouth opened, perhaps to resist me, to fight back, but I shoved the soup in there. It was cold now, but I held her chin shut, waited until she swallowed. She glared at me, her eyes like a silver lake, waiting for the moment to strike.

If I tried to feed her, tried to keep her alive, did it matter if she chose to die? Was that still keeping my promise? But a promise to a dead man didn't matter. So why did I want her to eat?

Because she looked so damned faint that she was on the verge of collapse. I shoved another spoonful in her mouth, but she closed her teeth, so I smeared the red liquid on her face, and then slapped her.

"Open your fucking mouth."

Finally, she relented. I put in as much as I could, then made sure she swallowed. Another spoonful. Then another. Until all of it was gone and her stomach stopped growling. She stared at me the entire time, peering up at my dark eyes, trying to read my soul. But there was nothing there, and soon, she'd understand that. Something exchanged between us then, like a shift in electricity; we finally understood each other. As much as I hated it, *no,* I did not want to kill Demi. But I needed her to be under my control.

"If you learn anything from me, let it be this," I said into her ear as she took the last gulp. Her throat moved in a circular motion, swallowing steadily. "Your dad was as evil as me," I said. "Worse." He may not have been as creative as I was, but he had trained a seven-year-old to be a killer. There were few things that would ruin a life more than that.

Demi didn't budge. I could tell she didn't believe me. It was beautiful, in a way. She was confident in her world.

Perhaps it would take showing her what I meant. Giving her a chance to see it with her own eyes. I couldn't bring back Shep, but I could show Demi exactly what he had taught me. And maybe then, I would rest easy by sending her back to her father.

But first, there was a wedding to go to.

CHAPTER 8

Demi

I stared at myself in the mirror. Axe's mother had left her curling iron and blow dryer for me. The hair dye had bled on her rose embroidered towels, just like I had warned Axe, but he didn't care and claimed that his mother wouldn't either. Axe had brought my bags from his apartment, but I hadn't packed anything that would be appropriate for a small wedding. Of course, Axe had taken care of that. This time, the dress Maddie had bought for me was light and whimsical. Yellow with pink flowers near the hem. She must have thought I was a sunny gal. Makeup rimmed my eyes, courtesy of Maddie too, and though I felt better, I still didn't feel like myself.

A floral print covered the wall, a little old-fashioned and stuffy. Two porcelain dishes sat on the edge of the sink with rose-shaped soaps. A stack of hand towels, all embroidered with that same, delicate rose, were hung up and pressed, as if they had never been used. His mother must have really liked her flowers. There was a window in the corner with wooden blinds, but Axe had shown me the alarm there.

One movement, he had said, *That's all it takes.* Then he gently pushed the device, and a piercing noise interrupted us. He stopped it.

He was standing outside of the bathroom, waiting for me. My best bet was to try and escape while we were at the wedding itself—if that's where we were actually going.

I sighed, then headed to the door. When I opened it, Axe was leaning against the opposite wall. His hair was styled, a navy blue suit tailored to his body with a dark red tie. The same outfit he had worn to my father's funeral. He straightened the knot, then looked at me, taking me in from my toes to my head. His expression stayed drawn.

"You use the same suit for funerals and weddings?" I asked. He gestured to the side, and we walked out of the house. "Are you that hard for money? Why don't you just steal from the people you kill?"

"Not a priority," he said.

The money, or the suits? I lifted a brow, but then shrugged. I should have stopped trying to understand him after I saw him murder the first victim, but I couldn't help it. I was curious.

We walked to the work van, and I caught a glimpse of his gun, tucked away in the holster. That morning, when he brought me inside the house, putting a full plate of food in front of me, he had held his gun, to threaten me into eating. But he didn't need to do that at all. This time, I couldn't stop myself. I needed the calories. He had already won with the soup. What was the point in giving up food now?

In the car, I turned toward him. "You said this is a wedding?" He nodded once, keeping focused on the road. I thought about the funeral, how I hated being in a group of people I didn't know, especially when they all seemed to know me. Now it would be the opposite; I would be the only one who was an outsider. "I don't know anyone," I said.

"You know me."

"Do I, though?"

A few minutes passed. We merged onto the freeway, and I glanced at the ocean passing to the side. We had gone to the beach as a family a few times, but never again after Mom died.

"My old therapist will be there," Axe said. "You can ask her about my behavior and the law. All of the trauma that made me so screwed in the head."

My gut sank at those words. It hadn't hit me at the time, but I knew now that it was presumptuous of me to assume that I knew his life better than he did. I grit my teeth, the annoyance aimed at myself rather than him, then settled back into the chair. His therapist would be there. Someone he knew from before. A person who had tried to help Axe, to make him a better person. Who had done more for him than I had.

A woman.

Did I feel threatened by his therapist?

"Old?" I asked. "You said, *old* therapist?"

"I don't see her anymore."

I leaned on the door, sighing to myself. Either way, it shouldn't have bothered me.

Axe parked, then got out of the car, opening the door for me. He offered me his arm, but I stormed ahead. Maddie was waiting by the path ahead of us.

"Hey! You survived," she said, then she laughed. "Kidding, of course. How've you been?"

"You know he's a psycho killer, right?" I said. She turned over her shoulder to look at Axe. "Don't look! He'll know I'm talking about him."

She smirked. "I think he knows."

My stomach dropped. I don't know why that shocked me.

"You knew," I said. "You knew this whole time."

"Oh, come on," she said, pushing my shoulder playfully. "If you clean someone's house for a year, you can kind of figure out if they're a psycho killer."

"But Axe doesn't have anything in his apartment."

"Exactly! What's he hiding?"

"I'm not joking," I said.

"And I'm not either. But let's check the facts." She leaned into my ear, taking my arm and leading me down the dirt road. "Axe has been keeping you locked up in his workroom." My eyes widened; so she did know! "And when it comes to the family, you know *way* too many secrets for them to let you go now. So if I were you," she poked me in the arm, "I'd shut up, smile, and enjoy the wedding." My jaw dropped, and she saw another woman with light brown hair waiting in the trees. Maddie squealed. "You look gorgeous!" she shouted, running over to her. The two of them disappeared into the brush.

I wasn't sure how I was supposed to take that. He came from an *entire family* full of secrets? If they were anything like Axe, his family had dangerous secrets. And I was supposed to be okay with that like Maddie was?

How much did Dad know?

"All right, she's ready!"

We all sat at a picnic table, big enough to fit the six of us. Maddie joined Axe and me in the back. On the front side, with their backs to the table, sat two men and a woman.

Axe leaned down, whispering in my ear, "Brother, father, mother."

I rolled my eyes. Like I cared.

For the most part, the wedding was traditional. They said the vows you always hear in the movies, and the bride, of course, looked like a ray of sunshine, and the groom looked like Axe, though younger, and seemed actually capable of smiling. I glanced around, studying each of their faces. I knew, by looking at them, that they were all criminals. I was the only person there with an inkling of a moral conscience.

Axe adjusted, his leg rubbing against mine. The heat of his leg made me think of the way he handled me, his eyes boring into my soul, looking at my pussy as he dragged the knife along my inner thighs, shoved a rubber cock down my throat. Like it would never be enough. And for some reason, that made me giddy. Made me want to spread my legs for him, to show him that I could take it. That I could take him.

But I buried those thoughts. He was a bad man. A murderer. Someone who needed to be corrected.

But he had also saved me. Promised my dad he would keep me alive.

And I was alive. More alive than I had ever felt.

After the ceremony, Maddie immediately ripped off her sundress and jumped into the river with the oldest brother, while the rest of us sat at the picnic table. Axe's mother's whitish-blond hair was blinding under the sun as she served the food. The officiant went past us. Axe turned his head, watching her go. Then he left me there and went after her. The therapist.

I bit my tongue. I don't know why.

Axe's mother pushed a plate with a fresh baguette, arugula, mozzarella, turkey, and pesto aioli. She had made the soup that

Axe had literally shoved down my throat. I wouldn't turn down her food again.

"This is nice," the father said, his voice deep. His pupils were dilated, or maybe they were darkly colored? It was hard to tell in the sunlight. "No talk of war. No talk of enemies. Just family. Just love." War? What enemies?

"Gerard," the mother said. Axe's mother had almost said his name with an accusatory tone. Gerard. Had my father known him?

"It's always *just* family," the newly-wed husband said.

I turned back, looking at Axe. He was still talking to the therapist, his face stoic. What was he asking her?

I turned back to the table. I couldn't be curious or jealous. Those emotions were unreasonable.

But I couldn't stop myself. How could Maddie act so nonchalant about the whole thing? How much did his family know? Why was the therapist leaving so quickly? Was she scared of Axe?

"You know he's keeping me hostage," I said.

Gerard laughed. "He's keeping you *safe*," he said. "Like your father asked him to."

"My father would never have allowed this."

"Your father trusted my son," Gerard said.

Axe joined us, and a hard silence fell heavy on the group. It took a few minutes of eating before his father, Gerard, went onto the rambling the same escapade about how nice it was to enjoy a wedding day without talk of war, to focus on what mattered. Love. Family. It seemed forced, and no one seemed to buy it. Especially not me.

Gerard left to go on a walk with his wife, leaving the rest of us alone. Axe spoke to his brothers privately, then turned to me, nodding towards the trees.

"You want to walk the loop?" he asked.

What choice did I have? I shrugged.

The trees were bright, yellow sunspots speckling the tops of the leaves. I hit my neck; a mosquito was nibbling on my blood. Axe rubbed his hand over his gun absently, like it calmed him to know that it was there. Or maybe he was thinking about murder, the different ways to kill someone. I didn't know. I wasn't sure I wanted to.

And yet, I couldn't stop wondering about it.

"When I went to therapy," he said, breaking the silence, his words causing my chest to seize up. "I was eight and a half, maybe nine years old." He wasn't thinking about murdering at all; he was thinking about therapy? "I had stopped talking, almost entirely. Rarely said more than a word a day. I was working with Shep full-time. We had a tutor that could work with me, so I eventually got my GED, but why? When..." His voice trailed off. Then he shrugged. "Anyway, Mercia, my therapist, once I told her about what I had done, she had said that there was no saving me. That I could never change the past. That I could either learn to live with who I was, or I could compartmentalize it, save it for a time when I needed it most."

What kind of therapist said something like that? "So what did you do?" I asked.

"I stopped being ashamed of who I was. And I stopped going to therapy."

Courage swirled within me; I had to know. "What did you say to her?" I asked. "Just now?"

"That she tried," he said calmly, "And that I was always meant to be this way. Nothing, not even therapy, was ever going to change that."

A heavy weight settled in my stomach, thinking of that young boy who had been told that there was no saving him. Because that was wrong. He might not have had a soul or a drive to make humanity better, but there was something inside of Axe that cared about others. Why else would he actually style his hair for his brother's wedding? Why else would he promise to keep me alive? And why would he keep me alive, when we both knew it would be easier for his entire family if I was gone?

He could have left me in that cage. But he hadn't.

And yet he truly believed that he had no heart.

"I shouldn't have said that stuff the other day. About therapy. Your past," I said. I bit my bottom lip. "It was wrong of me to assume I know better than you."

His lips twitched. I swear it was a half-smile.

"I'm not going to apologize for who I am," he said, locking eyes with me. "Your father helped to make me this way."

I ignored the reference to my dad. I didn't want to know what that meant yet.

"Did you start talking again?" I asked.

"Communicated, somewhat, yes. But other than that, what's the point?" he shrugged. "You're the only person who has talked to me this much."

I sucked in a breath. How was I supposed to take that? Did anyone in his life *want* him around?

"I'm a killer," he said. "Nothing, not therapy, not prison, not love—" My lips pressed tight at that word; why had he included love? "*Nothing* is going to change that."

"That doesn't give you an excuse," I said, bunching my brows. "Just because you had a bad childhood, doesn't make up for what you've done."

Suddenly, he slammed my body into a tree, pressing me against it. The bark dug into my back, scraping against my bare shoulders. He breathed down on me, sneering. But we were close. So close I could feel every pulse of his body as if it was sewn into mine. His lips, that bottom curve jagged with a scar. For some reason, I wanted that scar on me. I wanted his mouth, his tongue, his teeth pressed into me. To see what happened when he stopped holding himself back from me.

Because there was something inside of him. It might not have been good, or pure, but it was enough. And that's what kept me alive.

I licked my lips, and his eyes flickered, looking away. He let me go. I stumbled back to the path.

"I'm not trying to argue that," he said. Then he looked at me, waiting for me to speak.

"Then what are you trying to say?"

He stared at me for a moment. "I don't know."

We stood between the tall trees. The faint ticks of insects. The splash of the water on the shore. It was hard to remember that we had both grown up in Sage City, nurtured by the same man, and yet between our fifteen years, we had different lives. We were opposites in so many ways.

But this time, there was no blood on his clothes. No person dying between us. There was no tension to tie him down. It was just Axe.

"Why are you telling me this?" I whispered.

He thought about it, seeming to choose his words carefully.

"You're sure of what you know," he said, "but you don't know the whole story. Your dad wasn't a butcher."

I furrowed my brows. Yes, he was. "What do you mean?" I asked.

He sucked in a breath. "I want to show you what I mean. If you'll let me."

I bit the inside of my lip. It was raw, chewed to a pulp out of nerves and boredom. Did I want to know who my dad really was?

What would the truth do to me? Could I live without knowing?

No. I couldn't. I had to know.

"Okay," I said quietly. "Show me."

He took my hand; the touch warmed me. The man had shoved a rubber cock down my throat, had tackled me, almost cut off my tongue, but holding his hand made my cheeks flush.

"We'll go tonight." He led us, tracing our path back through the loop toward the park bench. "You know," his lips twitched into a half-smile, then faded away, "They won't teach you this stuff in your college classes."

I smiled. I had a feeling he was right.

CHAPTER 9

Axe

Brackston was an hour or so from the wedding reception, and though our cars were scattered, we were all within a few miles of each other. My brothers, including the newlywed and his wife, and a few of my men, were ready to take down Cannon. With the information I had provided, Derek and Wil were able to find the exact location of Cannon's home, which was close to the Midnight Miles Headquarters.

One of my men had been tailing him. Cannon was consumed by work; he never went anywhere by himself, except home. If we got him out of the house by using a decoy, then cornered him, we could take him out by himself. Muro's army would be forced to find a new leader, and would therefore be at a disadvantage, and more vulnerable, once we attacked them.

When we arrived, it was dark. The hills were shadowed on either side of us, the buildings popping up like black clouds. Demi bit her nails, staring out the window.

"Are you nervous?" I asked.

"Why would I be nervous?"

I thought about pointing out her tick but decided against it. What was she thinking? Was it about her father? I suppose it didn't matter, but it was amusing to consider myself.

Cannon's neighborhood was spread out. A thick wall guarded his house. To the side of the neighborhood, there was a peach tree orchard and a large, square-shaped community center that was under construction. From there, we looked at his place. Scaling the wall and standing in the darkness of his oversized patio wasn't an option.

There were likely sensors once we crossed into his territory. We needed him out of there.

Demi stood beside me, wearing all black. We had changed at the reception before coming here. I gestured toward Ron.

"You've got the coke?" I asked.

Ron patted his pocket. "Ready."

I turned to the rest of the group. "As soon as Cannon steps onto the sidewalk, we shoot."

"Got it," Derek said.

The rest of us situated ourselves around Cannon's home. Not many of the houses seemed like full-time living arrangements, so we peered from the shadows of the neighboring houses. Demi stayed by me in the frame of the community center. She had instructions to get in the car and drive like hell, should anything happen.

But nothing would happen. I wouldn't let it.

Ron, in oversized clothes to make him seem smaller than he actually was, pressed the call button at the gate. He nodded at the security camera.

"A delivery from Muro," he said. "Gift from the boss man."

The gate unlocked, and Ron went inside. He had a microphone on him, so I listened in through my earpiece.

"Hey man."

"What do you want?"

"Muro sent you this." The rustling of a pocket. "To thank you for your hard work."

"Is that right?"

"Yeah. Says he should never take your skills for granted. But hey man, my car broke down." Their feet shuffled as if he was pointing back toward the gate. "Can you take a look? I know nothing about cars."

"You're on your own."

The door banged shut. A few seconds later, Ron walked out, hands in his pockets. He crossed the street and got into his car.

"All right," Ron said into his mic, "Plan B. What's the scoop, boss?"

All we needed was for him to get out of his house. If we went inside, Cannon would have the advantage, and it would be hard to attack him.

There were eight of us, plus Demi. As we regrouped in the shadows of the community center, I looked at each of them, trying to decipher the strengths we had. Wil and Derek were too recognizable to bring Cannon out, but I stopped over Ellie, Wil's newly-wed wife. Her light brown hair was still styled from the wedding, but like the rest of us, she had changed into a more practical outfit.

"Ellie," I nodded to her. "Pretend to be a whore. Lure him out."

"What?" Wil squinted his eyes at me. "You want my woman to do *what* now?"

"If we want to do this the most efficient way possible, that's our best option," I said. "Ellie can pretend to be a sex worker, ask him to take her out *before* they do anything, then we attack. If we try going against him as is, it will be deadly."

"It's eight against one," Wil said. "I'm sure we can handle it without letting that bastard touch my wife." He leaned in closer. "My *wife,* Axe."

I didn't understand his need to always remind me that she was his. No one was arguing about that.

"Besides, he'll know it's me," Ellie said. She had a fair point. She had been forced to work in one of Muro's side projects before meeting Wil.

"I doubt it," I said. "Every man who worked at the Skyline Shift is dead."

Derek turned to Wil. "It's not like he's actually going to get anywhere. She just needs to show a little cleavage."

I turned to Demi. "Your skirt is in the car?"

"It was a dress, but yeah."

"Go get it."

When Demi returned, I took my pocket knife to the dress's hem, making it short enough in the back to show off her ass. Wil fumed the whole time, his jaw clenched.

"It's not going to go anywhere," Ellie reassured him. "I'll stab him if he tries anything."

"And then I'll gouge his eyes out."

By the time Ellie changed, she looked the part. Demi shook her head.

"But that was such a nice dress," Demi said.

"I'll get you another," I said. Demi raised a brow at me, but I turned back to the group. "Your line is that you want him to take you to a restaurant. One where you need his help to get you a reservation."

"Will that actually work?" Ellie asked.

"Do things to draw attention to your tits, and he won't notice," Derek said.

"Why don't you send her?" Wil asked, pointing at Demi. "She's younger. Looks more the part."

"The hell is that supposed to mean?" Demi asked.

"Your hair."

"Demi is not going anywhere," I said in a low voice.

"Why not? All we need is a decoy. What do you care about her? She's—"

"She's *not* going anywhere," I repeated. Demi was not from this world, like Ellie was. Wil stared at me. Even in the dark, his face red. "Ellie has training. Demi doesn't."

"I used to take kickboxing lessons," Demi said.

That wasn't training like Ellie had. I turned back to Ellie.

"Do you want to go?" I asked.

"Yeah," she said. "It's to bring him out, right?"

Wil glared at me, his eyes narrowed. Then he sucked in a breath and turned to his wife. "You're armed?"

Ellie tapped her hips. "Got my knives."

I turned to Demi. "You can wait here," I said, gesturing to the community center and the orchard, "Or lie down in the car. That's one of the safest places."

"I'm good," she said.

"You're good?" I raised a brow. "There will be a lot of bullets in a few minutes here."

"My dad was always packing." She shrugged. "I was with him when the butcher shop got broken into once."

I stared at her for a moment, her eyes stormy. It was hard to read how she was feeling. I'm sure she thought that the burglars were after Shep's money and that he turned them into the police.

But her emotions weren't my responsibility.

We got into position, angled around the home. Ellie walked down, showed herself to the camera, then walked inside. Wil cracked his neck.

"Calm down," Derek said over the earpieces. "He'll be dead in a few."

"He better be."

On the mic, we heard Ellie and Cannon talking, and then their footsteps came closer to the gate. We all shifted into position.

Cannon came into view, his hair cut close to his leathery head. He stopped at the gate.

"Wait," he said.

"Come on," Ellie said, pulling his arm. "I'm starving." He shoved Ellie out of the way. She smiled, pretending as if it meant nothing. "Let's go. That steak is not going to eat itself."

Cannon stared in the distance, then turned to where Demi was waiting.

Had he spotted Demi?

He pulled out his gun.

Ellie swung her arms towards him in a quick movement, knocking the gun out of his hand. But he elbowed her in the face, her nose bleeding. Without missing a beat, Ellie grabbed her knives and the rest of us started firing. Cannon shrunk back into the shadows of his house.

I ran forward, Ron and Derek following me. Wil ran to Ellie. The rest were watching the perimeter, making sure Cannon didn't make a run for it. Demi stayed in the nook of a tree. At least she was staying out of it. Warmth fluttered in my chest. But why?

There wasn't any time to think about it. I kept moving forward, stepping through the gates, ready to search the house. There were no audible or visible alarms, but there were cameras in every available space. Cannon was likely watching the footage. The best we could hope was that one of us would distract him while the other killed him.

I turned the corner, going through an office, the filing cabinets lining the side of the room, an empty bottle of whiskey on the desk. A jack and jill bathroom attached. Then through another bedroom, empty except for a recliner facing the window. Out of that door, and into a kitchen. I kept the lights off, inching through the space, not making a sound, ready and armed for whatever came. Bullets echoed in another room, and I rushed toward the sound. Derek and Cannon were in a standoff, Derek's arm bleeding. Cannon turned toward me, bullets flying, but I shot him in quick succession, hammering him to the ground.

I lifted my brow at Derek to ask his status. He held his wound. "It hurts like a bitch," he said.

"Where's Ron?" I asked. Derek tilted his head back. Hearing us over the earpieces, Ron appeared behind Derek quickly. Luckily, he was unharmed. "Drive Derek to the doctor," I said. Ron nodded.

The two of them headed to the car, while I went outside. My eyes instantly went to the community center, finding Demi. A look of fascination was stretched across her face, her eyes wide, her gaze pinned on me.

Me.

She was okay. That was good.

I turned to notify my other men to search the house for info, but Wil stomped towards me. He swung a fist, but I blocked his punch. He sent another, and another, until we were rolling on the ground.

"You idiot!" he said. "You could have—"

"She chose to help!" I yelled.

"Wil," Ellie said. "Stop it!"

Finally, Wil punched me in the nose, the pain like a lump of burning coal dropped onto my face. Using my legs, I threw him off of me. Pressure swelled in the bridge of my nose, and I sat up, holding my face.

Good job, brother, I thought sarcastically. What a stupid fight. I turned to Ellie.

"You did good," I said to her. "Thanks." She tilted her head, and Wil stood in front of her.

"Cut the shit, Axe," Wil said, fuming. "You don't put my bride in the middle of danger when you've got other people who aren't family that you can use at your disposal."

I glanced at Demi. Sometimes, I had felt closer to her father than I had to my own. That wasn't family, but it was *something*.

"You both knew the possibilities," I said to Wil. "You don't want to spend your wedding night defeating the enemy, then fine. Go have your perfect honeymoon." I stood up. "The rest of us will work."

"You are a dick," Wil said. He turned to Ellie. "Let's go."

Growing up, fights like this between us brothers blew over. Wil would cool down eventually. My men approached, and I told them to scout the house, to report anything they found to both me and Derek. They dispersed.

My nose seemed fine, but the blow had given me an instant headache. Demi came to my side, offering me her hand to stand up. I took it. We walked back to the car.

"Where's that look?" she asked.

"What look?"

"The one you have after you," she paused, "you know."

It was hard for her to admit what I was capable of, but she was still interested in my thoughts. I tilted my head, then turned back towards the car.

"There's a difference between execution and murder," I said. "That was execution. Quick. Efficient."

"And murder?" she asked.

"You get to decide what happens. You can take a moment to think. Figure out new ways to experiment." Demi bowed her head. "Does that bother you?" I asked.

She shrugged. "I'm trying not to think about it too much."

In the car, Derek called, then sent me the address for Harris Markson, a politician in the area who had ties to Miles Muro. My job was to take him down a notch, see where that left his relationship with Muro. We headed toward the next destination.

"You know your dad," I said, "He worked for my family."

"How?"

I wondered if she assumed that he simply butchered the remains for us. After what she had seen with Cannon, did she still expect her father to be fairly innocent?

"He was the lead enforcer before me," I said.

"Enforcer?"

I nodded, letting that settle in. "I'll show you what enforcing means."

CHAPTER 10

Demi

As we drove through Brackston, a dull weight settled in my stomach, making me quake with anticipation. The town that was more industrial than the trees and coastline I had grown up with in Sage City, and noticing that made me bite my lip. I ran my tongue along my teeth, stroking the bumpy scarred edges mindlessly. I was trying to make sense of it all. An enforcer? Logically, I knew that enforcing meant that when it came time to put a law or a rule into action, you had to *take* action. I had seen what Axe had done in his torture room. Was that enforcing too? And if so, what did that mean about my dad?

We stopped in a quiet neighborhood with sprawling yellow and blue houses, matching white trim, bushes of flowers in the front. Axe took a street, parking next to a jungle gym. I raised a brow, but he put a hand on mine. Electricity surged through the point of contact.

"Wait here," he said.

My heart caught in my chest. What was he doing *now*? Especially now that he was making me wait in the car.

He went down the street, hopping a fence, disappearing into a backyard. And it was then that I knew as screwed up as it may have been, even if it was for my own safety, I didn't want Axe to die. I was worried about him. I closed and opened my fists repeatedly, trying to release the tension.

About ten minutes later, having almost bitten off my nails, he finally reemerged from a different part of the street. He slid into the driver's seat, closing the door behind him.

"So what'd you do?" I asked.

"Secured some persuasion."

I wasn't sure what that meant, but it seemed inappropriate to ask. After we left the neighborhood, Axe drove us to the other side of town. We pulled into a business park. A squat, three-story building with white walls and a pink rooftop was our destination. *Harris & Hall Law Practice* was written on a sign outside of the door. I swallowed the lump in my throat. He was going after a lawyer?

Axe called someone, whispered to them. Then he hung up.

"Cameras are out," he explained.

Well, that was good. I guess. "Am I staying here this time?" I asked.

He motioned toward the building. "Let's go."

Axe bent his neck to pick the locks, and I kept my eyes up at the moonless night, counting the few stars I could see. Breaking and entering was the smallest crime that I had witnessed that night, but still, I didn't want to look. It felt like an admission.

The building was dark, but the windows along the entrance lit the empty lobby. We took the stairs to the third floor, following it down the corridor and through the main shaft of the building to where a single office was lit, glowing like the last coals of a fire. A couple laughed, then the woman moaned. These people weren't working late.

Axe motioned for me to stay by the wall. He removed his gun, pulled back the hammer, then turned the corner.

"Harris," he said.

A man with black hair and a woman with an unbuttoned shirt startled. The woman screamed. The man flung her off of his lap.

"What the hell?" She pulled her shirt shut over her chest.

"Whoa, buddy," the man, I'm assuming Harris, said. "No need to bring a gun here."

He seemed so casual, like he was convinced it was a joke.

Axe shot the woman in the face, her body falling to the floor, then he went toward the man. Sweat beaded on the man's brow as he hid his face behind his hands.

"Holy shit. You fucking killed her, man. Do you know who I am? I can have you killed. You know I—"

Axe shoved the back of his pistol into the man's forehead, knocking the words out of him. The man fell silent, his eyes blinking rapidly. Then Axe pulled a lock of curly brown hair from his pocket. The man's eyes widened.

"You know what this is," Axe said. The man froze in fear. "You know who it belongs to." The man's eyes shifted back and forth, and Axe lowered his voice even more: "You're going to put your hands on the chair. You're not going to move. And unless you want me to kill your mother, wife and child, you're not going to make a single sound unless I ask you a question. Do you understand, Harris?"

Harris nodded, then put his hands on the chair, shaking the whole time. Axe moved methodically, each movement calculated, strapping him to the chair with zip ties, going over it with duct tape. There was a window in the back of Harris's large office, all of the blinds drawn, casting the two of them in a dull silhouette. A set of shelves was to the side full of law books. A bright spin caught my eye: *Crime and Evidence: A Modern Approach to Law*. It seemed vaguely familiar, like a book from one of my college reading lists.

Once Harris was restrained, Axe stood in front of him, his shoulders straight, his chin tilted down.

A tear slipped down Harris's cheek. I wondered who the curly hair belonged to. Was it his wife's? His daughter's? A son's? Harris had seemed confident until Axe brought out the lock of hair. There was an infinite amount of intimacy in it, and invasion, showing that Axe had crossed over from the world of business into the personal, making someone close to Harris vulnerable. Did Axe hold anyone that close?

Axe's hair was ruffled now, the styling cream from the wedding no longer holding up to the chaos. His skin had a light sheen of sweat. A hint of that metallic scent came off of him too, almost as if his body was cleaned with the metal of a gun. I couldn't imagine Axe loving his family like Harris did. Instead, I pictured Axe being willing to die *in place of* his family.

But was that enough of a reason to justify him torturing Harris? Did it justify killing that woman who clearly wasn't associated in any way?

No. It didn't. So why was I still trying to understand? What did this mean to Axe?

What did Dad mean to Axe?

"You know Miles Muro," Axe said. The man nodded. "You help him launder for his arms business. Got some lawmakers to look the other way when it came to certain business regulations, yes?"

The lawyer shook his head. "No. It's not that. It's—"

"Cut the bullshit," Axe said. "You're not going to help Muro anymore." Axe paused, waiting for Harris to argue. Axe circled the man, each step heavy with power. "You're going to drop Muro as a client, and put him on the blacklist for all of your other associates. And on top of that," Axe stopped behind the man, "you're going to report him to the Feds."

"The Feds man? I can't do that. He'll kill—"

"And there goes your mother," Axe said. "Don't worry about what Miles will do." He held up a knife to the man's throat, letting him feel the hard edge of the blade. "Because your wife? Your son?" He slid the knife against the man's cheek, a single line of blood beading at the cut. "I'll make you watch as I make them beg for death. And once I give it to them, I'll kill you too."

Axe stabbed the man's leg above the knee. The man opened his mouth, holding back a wail, not wanting to make a noise again, learning his lesson. But his breathing quickened; he couldn't get enough air.

"Whether they live or die doesn't matter to me," Axe said, ignoring the man's obnoxious breathing. "I only care that you do exactly as I say. Then we won't have to worry about your wife or son, just your mother."

A chill ran through me. I wanted to believe it wasn't true, that no one could be that cruel, but Axe had already killed that other woman. And I had seen what he could do to make someone ask for death.

"For good measure," Axe said. Then he stabbed the man again, lifting the knife and bringing it back down, making a pin cushion out of Harris. Harris whistled through his teeth.

"Remember, Harris," Axe said, leaning down. "I will enjoy killing you and your family a lot more than I will like letting you live. It's in your best interest to not give me any reason to return."

Harris nodded, his eyes closed, tears running down his cheeks. Axe cut through the tape and the zip ties, leaving Harris still shuddering in his seat. Next, he carefully wiped his hands on a small cloth, then pocketed the fabric. Then Axe nodded to me, motioning toward the door. I ran to the bookshelf and grabbed *Crime and Evidence*, lifting it to Harris, who still had his eyes closed.

"Hey," I said. Harris didn't move. "Uh, can I have this? I need it for school."

Harris's eyes opened wide, shocked, seeing me for the first time. He glanced between me, then to Axe, who nodded. Harris turned back to me.

"Yes. Take it. Take whatever you want."

I tucked it under my arm. "Thanks," I said. The man grunted. I followed Axe back to the car. Outside, he gave a sideways glance, eyeing the book. I plopped into the passenger seat of his car, then looked at the cover. Blue with gray and purple prisms covered the front, making it look like so many other college textbooks. I opened it, scanning the pages.

We made a stop back at that neighborhood, then headed back to Sage City. I let out a sigh. Though the radio wasn't on, it didn't bother me anymore. I had gotten used to it. There was so much noise, that just listening to the rumble of the engine, the tires rolling against the road, the air pressure of the wind as we passed—all of that was enough.

I tried so hard not to think about it. But my hands twitched with my thoughts, desperate to figure it out. Why had he killed them so easily? It didn't make sense.

After a few minutes, I turned to Axe. "Did you have to kill them?" I asked. "His mother. That other woman. Both of them had nothing to do with whoever this man, Muro, is. You know that."

"His mother was collateral. And the other was a witness," Axe said, his eyes never straying from the road. "Your dad taught me that."

"My dad?" My jaw dropped. "My dad wouldn't kill someone like that. I find that very hard to believe."

"Shep told me that you couldn't think about it. Collateral damage is necessary to make a point. And the bottom line is that if a person is a witness, you have to kill them. She had seen me; she knew that we weren't supposed to be there. And I couldn't keep her in line like Harris." He shrugged. "You can't think about it. Her life is over. That's it."

I stared at him. "My dad would have never killed a woman like that."

"He did," Axe said. "Many, many times."

A tremor ran through me. But how could he?

"Bystanders?" I asked.

"Witnesses," Axe corrected. It was as if bystanders suggested innocence in his eyes, and he needed me to know that they weren't innocent. Their crime was being in the wrong place at the wrong time.

I stared at my hands, hands that I had gotten from my mother and father. If Axe was telling me the truth, then what did that mean about me? Was I a killer too, like Dad? Or were Mom's genes more dominant inside of me?

Had my dad ever really been a butcher? Or was he someone else? Did he live a separate life?

This had to be a bad dream.

"When you were four," Axe said, "You asked Shep if you could open up a farm for dogs and birds." The image of a red shack popped into my mind, the one we had kept in the backyard for Dad's tools. A shack that always stayed locked. I had never questioned it. But now, I had a sick feeling in my stomach. "You wanted as many pets as possible. And for your birthday that year, Shep got you another dog. You cried of happiness. Cried because you couldn't believe how happy you were."

My heart sank. It was only a couple of years later when he took them all away from me.

"I know it seems like I'm not telling the truth," he said, "But think back. If you look at the clues, you knew it was there."

I closed my eyes, shaking my head. He must have been telling me these stories to prove that he knew Dad. That he knew me. When I thought about the night when the burglars came to the butcher shop, I realized something. After Dad made me hide in the freezer, he took me through the back door of the shop. He always had blood on his apron, but this time, it smelled different, more rancid, an animal I didn't recognize. *I've gotta deal with this*, he had said, kissing me on the forehead. *Do your homework in the car. Don't leave. If you need anything*, he handed me his cell phone, *Call.*

Did you call the police?

Dad didn't answer, but smiled and walked back into the butcher shop. And that, I realized, was one of my clues. He hadn't answered. And I had never seen the burglars. I assumed he had them tied up.

Tied them up, then killed them. Like he had taught Axe.

I covered my face with my hands, my whole body shaking.

"He was a monster," I whispered. "My dad was a monster."

My chest tightened like I couldn't breathe, but I squeezed my cheeks, trying to figure out what I was supposed to do. This was a mess. A horrible mess. If Dad was a criminal, then what did that make me, especially with everything I knew now? Was I another accomplice? A bystander? A witness?

Or was it in my blood too?

"The way I see it," Axe said, tilting his head toward me, "There are always two sides to everything. There's a side of us we present to the world. The kind we craft, tailor to expectations. And then there's the side we hide, the part of us that rarely sees the daylight. That's what Shep taught me." I cringed at my dad's name on his tongue, but Axe continued on, "It's why I don't feel guilty. Everyone, you and me included, has a time to die. I took over Shep's job when he had you." Axe shrugged. "In your eyes, your father was a hero. Your guardian. Your protector." I sniffled. Hero seemed kind of strong now, but I respected him, and I knew he never let anyone harm me. "But you never saw the whole picture of who he was."

I held onto those words, thinking about them. *So I took over Shep's job when he had you.* That meant that once I was born, Dad had changed. Maybe he *was* the good man that I always thought he was.

But that didn't mean that this side of himself stopped existing.

Now, more than ever, I had no idea of how I was supposed to feel when it came to Dad. Who was he? And what did that mean for me?

I looked up at Axe. What was he hiding?

"Which side do you present?" I asked.

"I'm an enforcer," he said. "I'm not hiding anything."

I wanted to call him out, saying that was bullshit. That according to him, *everyone* hid a side of themselves, but I sank back into the seat. The vastness of the night made it seem as though we were stuck inside of a time loop, never able to find the sunrise.

"Then why don't you talk to anyone?" I asked.

He was silent then, but I didn't push it. We had covered so much that night. Understanding that everyone had a good and bad side was one thing, but to ask Axe to answer that same question was too much for both of us. I could barely handle learning this about my dad. I'm sure, though he would never admit it, it was hard for him to face these truths too.

"You could leave," Axe said. He nodded toward the door. "The next time we stop. Open the car door. Never look back."

That knowledge made my stomach turn. I looked at the handle, long and slender. I imagined my hand grasping it, breathing air that belonged to me for the first time.

But I knew I couldn't go out there.

What horrors would be waiting for me, when my past was marked with blood?

"You would kill me if I tried," I muttered. "Wouldn't you?"

The only answer he gave was a short glance in my direction. Both of us knew that what I chose to do didn't matter. I wasn't going anywhere.

Maybe Axe was right. Maybe there was a side of me that I was hiding from myself.

By the time we made it back to his workroom, he let me get comfortable but then waited for me to get into a larger cage, lying on the ground, long enough for me to stretch out. I bit my lip, thinking about it. There were no wooden slats this time. Would he watch me? Would he sleep there again tonight? Would he sleep in there with me?

Why did I want him to be there beside me when I fell asleep?

I slowly bent down, hoping that he was watching me. Then once I was inside, I turned around, looking up at him. As he locked the cage, he stared at me. His cock was bulging, slightly hard, from looking at me like that. Defenseless in a cage.

And it turned me on too.

I spread my legs, waiting to see what he would do. His eyes fell to my pussy, covered by my pants. His cock twitched.

Instead of being ashamed, I let myself feel what I wanted. I grabbed my breasts, imagining they were Axe's hands. His dark eyes held mine, and he unbuttoned his pants, unzipped them, pulled out his veiny dark-red cock. He played with the tip, rubbing his finger across the hole, then pumped it hard. I lifted my shirt, keeping my eyes locked on him.

"Touch yourself," he said. His words sent a chill down my spine. I inched the pants and underwear off of my hips, spreading my legs once again, dipping my fingers inside of my slit. The tenderness of my fingers made me shudder, and I used the moisture to play with my nipples. I might have been a virgin, but I knew what I liked.

"No," Axe said, his voice low and husky. "Fuck yourself."

A surge of energy clenched in my chest. He wanted me to do *that*. I penetrated myself, matching his rhythm as we fucked ourselves, staring at each other. Axe wanted me, and I couldn't decide how I felt. Was I grateful that he was giving me distance by keeping me inside of a cage? That he wasn't giving in to his desire to take me? Was I ashamed that being confined like a prisoner turned me on? Or was it frustrating? That I wanted him to fuck me *now*, to get this stupid v-card over with? That I wanted him to take me like I knew he wanted?

Or would he kill me if he did?

That thought alone made me soak with desire, knowing that Axe had that much power over me. Life and death, none of it mattered to him, but when he looked at me, he knew what he wanted, and all I wanted was to hold onto that power over him. My dad was a monster. Maybe I was a monster too. Maybe wanting Axe like this proved that. Everything in my life was a lie, and maybe that made what I wanted okay. And I wanted Axe. And if that's what I wanted, why couldn't I have it?

CHAPTER 11

Axe

It became our habit. I made Demi fuck herself until she was exhausted each night, and while I wanted to uncage her—to let her spread herself out comfortably, at least during orgasm—I kept her locked inside. She had the power, and the conscience, to go to the police. No one would listen to her in Sage City, but she could seek help outside of our jurisdiction.

But did the knowledge of her father's past change her opinion on what 'justice' was?

The sun never shined in the workroom, but my internal clock kicked me awake. I headed to Brackston in an SUV with a group of my men in tow. With Cannon out of the way, we had to act quickly. Eliminate as many of Muro's men as we could before they changed tactics. And Derek wanted us to get rid of the computer servers.

A tall, skinny building with mirrored windows like aviator sunglasses, contained the Midnight Miles Headquarters. I had never seen Muro before. All I knew was that he wanted to kill our family, and had been willing to send armies into the woods to murder us.

Ron called me on the secure channel on our com-sets. "Ready, sir."

While a decoy pretended to be a routine maintenance service at the checkpoint, we would have a few of our men break into the back of the building. Then, once they were done destroying the servers, the rest of us would attack.

It was simple. Figure out his capabilities. Get rid of them.

"All right," I said. I scanned the building, looking up at the top floor, wondering if Muro was watching right then. My finger twitched, itching for Demi. What would her reaction be to an operation of this size? But my instincts had kept her locked inside. It was safer for her there.

The wall in front of me was big, but nothing I couldn't scale. Once I heard our maintenance decoys pull up to the checkpoint on the earpiece, I motioned for my two men to head into the headquarters. They let themselves down over the wall, then headed to the back entrance of the building. I listened on the earpiece to our decoys; they were stuck at the front entrance, arguing with the guards.

"Air conditioning? We just had that serviced."

"I have it here. See? Midnight Miles Corporation. Routine maintenance. Every second week—"

"Maybe your boss likes it cold."

"I'd hate to see him get upset."

"Status for the main hub?" I asked over the earpiece, referencing the servers. No response. I glanced around, looking for Ron, who gave me a thumbs up. But nothing happened. No one came out of the building, despite the two men breaking into the bottom floor. Derek had told me that they always had one guard on duty in that lobby. Why hadn't I heard a bullet yet?

"Might take a minute, sir," Ron said. But I could already tell from the tone of his voice that he knew something was up too. "Shall we start the second phase?"

Time ticked forward. My hand twitched against the trigger.

Then an explosion sounded, dull against the surrounding walls. My pulse quickened. Then a crash of bullets sounded and a swarm of men came out of the building.

"Shit!" one of my men shouted on the earpiece.

They lurched out, coming toward the wall, bullets flying in angry bursts. Three times the number of men we had. We blasted back, some of us scattering, using distance to split them up. They scaled the wall, coming after us.

"Come out you fuckin' Adlers," one of them said. I came out from cover and shot him in the head. Just then, a bullet grazed the side of my ear.

"Damn it!" Ron yelled.

The bullets came out in a stream of fire. Ignoring the pain, we took them out, one by one, some of our men falling too. I realized then that they knew we were coming. That's why it had been too easy. We had a rat in our ranks.

But I kept firing and dodging the bullets.

Then Muro's men dispersed, shouting at each other. Muro's men were down, but not nearly enough of them. We gathered quickly, heading back to Sage City. Ron sat in the passenger seat next to me.

"Vic and Alan?" I asked, referencing the two that had gone into the building.

"Gone, sir," Ron said.

I clenched the steering wheel. Like anyone, Vic and Alan had their deaths written in the stars, coming one day or another. I didn't have any attachments to them, but I trusted them to get the job done.

And now they were dead.

"The servers?" I asked.

"Gone too," Ron said.

At least there was that. But still, I hated losing good men for stupid reasons. We had underestimated Muro. And while we had more men back in Sage City, I knew we needed backup. The next time we fought Muro, we couldn't make the same mistake.

In Vegas, there was a security team we sometimes used at our resort and casino. Veil Security Services had been sold to a new owner and later disbanded, but I knew the original owner. He did mostly charity cases now, but if he knew anything about Muro, he'd join forces.

"What's the plan now, sir?" Ron asked.

"We head back," I said. "Regroup. Figure out *why* they knew we were coming."

"You think there's a rat, sir?"

It seemed like it. I crossed my fingers that the rat wasn't stupid enough to be one of my men. Or I would strangle him myself.

It was then that my burning ear registered. I touched it; the blood had caked over. It wasn't bad, but had taken enough flesh with it that blood painted my neck. A few inches in one direction and I would have been dead too.

Opening the door to the workroom, my eyes fell on Demi and I let out a deep sigh. A pleasant warmth filled me. She was lying on her back, her legs crossed at the knee, reading the book she had taken from Harris's office. Her hair fell over that gray floor in a wash of color, bringing it to life. She perked up, her eyes flicking to mine, lighting up.

Why did I feel so hot?

"What the hell, Axe?" Her eyes dropped, her lip pouting. "You're hurt. What happened?"

I blinked slowly, taking in those words. Demi, as much as she hated everything I stood for, wanted to know what had happened to me. Rather than bring it up right then, I held onto that thought, not wanting to ruin the moment.

I changed the subject. "Good material?" I asked, gesturing at the book.

"Fascinating, actually. It has this whole section about crime rings," her voice was light. "I guess I should have seen the signs sooner. The whole 'mafia' thing."

I smiled, then, a real genuine smile, something I hadn't done in a long time. Despite everything she knew, she was still intrigued by crime and law, and still saw the order in the world. But beyond that, she had feelings for me. Cared about whether or not I was hurt.

No one had ever truly cared before.

"You know you stole that from a victim," I said, letting the side-smile stay on my face, teasing her. "How does that settle into your world of the just?"

"I didn't *steal* it," she claimed, exaggerating her words. "He *gave* it to me."

That was like saying I 'gave' duct tape to Harris. "Under duress," I said. She shrugged. "Do you plan on giving it back?"

"Maybe," she said. Then she shook her head. "No."

And there was her answer. She smiled too, but her eyes fell to her lap. She fidgeted, folding and unfolding one of the pages, crossing the crease with her thumb. I don't know why I said it, but the words came out of my mouth before I could stop them—

"You didn't do anything wrong," I said. "You're my captive. You were only doing what I said to do."

She shook her head, forcing a smile. "You said it yourself," she said. "I'm not much of a captive if I don't try to escape."

"You know I'd kill you."

"But would you?" She tilted her head. "I guess that's the question. You promised my dad you would keep me alive. Killing me would break that, nulling that promise." She gave a small smile, then shook it away.

She stared at me then, her hands holding that book tight. The pages were already worn, as if she had held them so tight her sweat had damaged it.

"What happened?" she asked again, her voice soft. "Who hurt you?"

For once, I thought she deserved to know the truth.

"We tried to take down Muro's army," I said. "Someone told them that we were coming."

She sighed to herself. "Those mother fuckers."

I laughed, and she startled, looking up at me, her eyes wide. My laugh wasn't anything that sounded natural; I didn't have much use for it. But it was amusing to hear her be upset at someone she had absolutely no control over. To hear her pretend to be on my side.

Or maybe she was.

"You're defending a criminal," I pointed out to her.

She put up a hand. "Okay, good or bad, evil, all of that aside, someone hurt you. That's what I know. You didn't do that yourself." She glared at my ear. "And someone hurting you isn't right."

"What if that person was trying to defend themselves?"

"I don't know," she said. "Maybe you're defending something too."

There wasn't much in my life that I did to protect others. I worked for my family, bled for my family, but did I feel anything for them? Loyalty. Trust. Would I do anything for them? Yes. But was that love?

Perhaps it was a certain type of love.

Demi's gray eyes stared into mine, and I swear she was searching for something, but I didn't know what. I told myself that whatever I was feeling, was because of that promise to Shep. I kneeled down, brushing my fingers along the open spaces of the cage. She put her hand against mine. Her skin was colder than the metal bars.

"What are you defending?" she asked.

Family was the easy answer, the answer that I knew and held onto, but how did that explain my relationship with Demi? I wanted more of her, and at the same time, I wanted her away from me. If I felt *anything* toward her, that put me in a weaker position. Made it so that I was vulnerable. Demi could die too, at any moment, like I could.

But that didn't mean I needed to accept that fate.

I leaned against the side of the cage, my back to her, looking at the door. She turned her back to mine too, leaning against me. Her book crinkled; she was back to reading it. Life was simple to her back in Pebble Garden. College gave her options. She had to go back.

But we had other problems to deal with first.

Once Muro was out of the picture, I could figure out what to do with Demi. Could focus on protecting her and finding an alternative situation in which she could live the normal life she dreamed of.

Which meant seeing if Zaid, from Veil Security Services, was still around. If he was willing to band together one last time. It meant a trip to Vegas.

I could leave Demi in the cage for the next couple of days. Or I could bring her with me.

One of those options seemed more entertaining than the other.

CHAPTER 12

Demi

As I gazed up at the giant resort, it was crazy to think that this morning, we had been in Sage City, and now, we were in Las Vegas. After waking up from another dream about my dad, Axe had told me we were going to Las Vegas. He had driven through the day and into the night, and because I had been having fitful sleep in the cage, I slept through most of it. But at ten o'clock at night, the Sin City was still bustling.

The sign for the Opulence Hotel and Casino was in gold cursive, glowing like a mirage. I couldn't decide if the building looked futuristic or tropical—it was a three-sided structure that stretched into the sky, but the front looked as if it had been swallowed up by a tropical forest and regurgitated palm trees. The water from the massive fountain in the front sprinkled my skin with dew. A few people eyed me—was it the hair, or my baby face, advertising that I was only eighteen in a place for twenty-one-and-up-year-olds?

Axe kept me close to his side and didn't let anyone come near me. Dressed in a short olive cocktail dress, Axe in his blue suit and red tie, we blended in with the crowd. But when we went through the casino, going down a forest green and mud brown carpet, I skirted too much to the side, nearing a blackjack table, and he yanked me back in.

"Stay on the path," he said.

"Why?"

"You're eighteen." He eyed the room, looking at the different security dressed in vests, wearing headsets. He glanced at me, then added, "We can't mess with that here."

A warm buzz crawled over my skin; Axe had actually answered my question. That was one of the ways I knew Axe was nice to me. I felt privileged that he wanted to tell me the answers. So I listened, treating him like we were friends. He might have been an objectively bad person, but if I looked at it his way, that there were two sides to everyone, then maybe *this* was the good side of him.

After we got clearance from the concierge, we were escorted behind a red rope to a private elevator, which took us up several floors. It opened into a dim lobby with deep blue walls and purple lights in the corners. A woman in a necklace that connected to her gold dress offered us flutes of pink-colored champagne from her tray. Axe lifted a hand, declining her offer. She walked away.

At first, I was disappointed that he hadn't let me try it, but then I was flush with insecurity. Why couldn't we mess with security here? What made it so bad for me to be eighteen?

"I'm not supposed to be here," I whispered in a harsh tone. "They'll find out I'm not old enough and kick us out."

He gave one shake of his head and walked to the bar at the center. I followed closely behind. He approached a man with gray hair and light eyes.

"Marshall," Axe said, shaking the man's hand. The man's face lit up. "How've you been?"

"Is that *you*, Axel?" He pulled Axe in for a bear hug. Axe let it happen but didn't hug back. "How's your family? Your brothers? I heard little Wilhelm got married."

Wilhelm? *Wil* was too old to be called little. Wasn't he? "Yes, recently," Axe said.

"And I see you finally found someone too," the man, Marshall, said, winking at me. Axe put an arm around me, bringing me closer to him. A deep blush covered my face, making me hot.

"Is Zaid around?" Axe asked.

"Can't say that I've seen him," he said, clearing his throat. He glanced around, as if waiting for someone to sneak up on him. Then he turned back to Axe. "But you know, he sold his company. Last I heard, he doesn't come around anymore."

"He still owns a penthouse here," Axe said.

"Right. But he must rent it out." The man shrugged. "He might still be a local. Not sure."

"Where does or did he live?"

"Now, I know I was his client for years," the man smiled, "But he kept that a secret too. If you go to Sour Times, you might find someone who knows."

"Jones's place?"

"I think Zaid used to have a client who worked there part-time." His eyes lingered over me, hanging onto my breasts, then dripping down to my sex. "Unless you'd like to stay for some fun. I can see how much more I can figure out for you."

My face went hot, and Axe's grip tightened on me. "We'll be on our way," Axe said, sternly. "Thanks."

"Gone so soon?"

Axe guided me away, then he whispered, "If he says one more word—" But then he stopped, biting his tongue. What was he leaving out?

We drove back through the city. The flashing lights never stopped, but instead of being proud in the sky, they were shorter, near the ground, as if people couldn't be bothered to look up that far. A flat building with orangish-pink paint had a sign that said *Sour Times Casino*. Unlike the Opulence that reeked of decadence, this place made me shiver. It seemed scummy, like the bottom of a shoe.

Axe led me to a corner of the room to a slot machine that had a giant, furry animated cat on top wearing a thick gold chain and slippers. The machine buzzed with a disco tune as soon as I sat down.

"I've got to find someone," he said. "Stay here. Don't talk to anyone."

I raised a brow. "You think I want to make friends here?"

"If someone tries to talk to you, tell them you're with the Adlers."

"You like holding onto that name, don't you?" I asked. "We're not in Sage City anymore."

"We own a resort and casino back on the Strip," he said. Of course they did. His family was part of the mob. I should've stopped asking questions by now.

He disappeared through the maze of machines, and I leaned back in the seat. Curiosity made me want to figure out what Axe was doing, but I also knew that if Axe was telling me to do something, that I should listen. I had learned quickly that he rarely spoke, but if he did, he did so with purpose.

Though the indoor smoke was thick, the slot machines themselves were empty, as if ghosts were smoking around me, not actual people. About ten minutes passed when I finally got the nerve to touch the buttons on the machine. There was a chance that I could gamble and no one would notice that an underage adult was using the machines. But I also knew there was a reason for those rules—perhaps a stupid one, but a rule nonetheless. Still— if I pushed a button but there wasn't any game playing, was that breaking the rules?

And why did it matter if I pushed a button? Was I really *that* worried? After all I had been through, I shouldn't have cared.

Taking a deep breath, I jabbed a button. Nothing happened. So I went for my wallet.

"Screw it," I said.

I added a five-dollar bill. The machine lit up, making the cat's eyes turn bright pink, and I pressed the red button. The wheels spun, and then a picture of a lemon, a seven, and a Siamese cat lined up. I pressed the button again, watching as I wasted away pennies. Fifteen cents per button press.

Right as I was about to use my third to last draw, the machine boomed with an orchestra of meows, and I lurched back in the seat. The screen started an animation of cats lining up for battle, using slingshots with bell toys.

"You here with someone?" a man asked.

I glanced over. The man was in his forties, black shaggy hair at the sides of his head, gold-rimmed sunglasses, his skin pale. I turned back to the machine.

"I said, you here with someone?" the man asked again.

"Piss off," I muttered. "Leave me alone."

"What's that?" the man said, putting his hand on my arm.

I cringed. Why was he touching me? He knew I had heard him.

"I said, leave me alone," I said in a stern voice.

"But honey, you're here all alone, aren't you?" He grinned, his teeth stained yellow, the shade of his sunglasses. "I can see you're too young to be here. You know what happens when you break the law in Jones's territory?"

I blinked. What was his problem?

"But I can help you," he grinned. "All I need is a little gratitude. You know." He brushed the back of his fingertips down my arm. My skin crawled.

"I'm with the Adlers," I said. "I'm not alone."

"Funny you say that *now*," he laughed. "I don't give a fuck who you're with. The Adlers haven't been here in ages. Too good for us. But not you," he winked, leaning into the machine. "Not you, little pet."

Where was Axe? He squeezed my arm and I revolted.

"Don't you fucking dare," I whispered in a harsh tone.

"That sounds like a threat."

He grabbed my arm and jerked me out of the chair and I swung my purse, hitting him in the face, which stunned him enough that when I jabbed him in the face, he blinked, rubbing his eye. He glanced to the side, and two other men came out from behind the machines.

"You want to help me with this?" the man asked.

They took steps toward me. One of them grabbed my hands, forcing them behind my back, while the other held my chin, pinching my face.

"This little bitch was breaking the law," the first man said. "Jonesy wouldn't like that."

"Hmm," one said, then tightened his grip on my chin.

Shit. Where was I supposed to go?

"Police!" I shouted. "Please! Security! Help!"

"Little pet, we *are* the security," the first man said, leaning into my face. The other two chuckled.

My face was on fire, sweat dripping from my arms.

"You're making a mistake," I said.

"We'll see about that," the first man said, lifting his spider hands to touch the bodice of my dress.

An elbow came flying, hitting the man in the nose. Before he could process, another one knocked into the third man holding my chin. Then Axe spun around, breaking the neck of the second one, but the man was still holding onto me and almost pulled me down with him. Axe grabbed me by the chest and pushed me against the wall, and the shock of it stunned me as I watched him tear the men apart. I slid to the floor, my eyes widening. One by one, he killed them all. Three men by himself.

As much as I hated it, I was relieved he was there. That he was helping me.

But where did it stop? No matter how much blood flew out of the corners of the men's mouth, he kept punching until their faces were dented inward. A few people from the sides of the room had gathered, giving us space, and no one seemed to care. Hell, I didn't even move. I didn't know what to do. He was defending me, but by now, the men got the picture. He didn't need to destroy the corpses too.

Finally, someone coughed, and that broke him out of his trance. He sat on his haunches, then glanced at his bloody, swollen hands, wiping them off on his pants.

Then he looked at me. "Let's go," he said.

Without a word, the two of us left the casino. Axe nodded at the bouncer, and he nodded back. What he had done was accepted here; no one hid behind the curtains of what was morally right or wrong. So what did that mean for Axe? For me?

In the car, Axe turned back onto the freeway, and we headed back toward the Strip.

"Where are we going now?" I asked. It had to be well into the a.m. I couldn't imagine the night getting any worse, but I knew we had so much ahead of us.

"To rest," he said. "But early tomorrow, we've got an appointment to make."

CHAPTER 13

Axe

Similar to me, Zaid liked mornings, and even earlier appointments. Though I had known him for many years, I had never been to his home. There was no need, and I respected a man's privacy, which I knew, like me, Zaid valued more than most. To find that he lived in the terrain at the foot of Mount Charleston wasn't a surprise. In the soft light of dawn, I parked the van along the driveway, gravel crunching under the wheels. Stepping out of the van, Demi flicked the hair out of her face, then zipped up her pink hoodie.

We went around a small plot of succulents to the entrance.

"How do you know this guy again?" Demi asked.

"We worked together a few times when I was doing a job down here."

"Oh."

Curiosity and disturbance always danced together in Demi's face. She wanted to know everything, and yet she knew that the more she understood, the harder it would be to hold onto herself, that purity that still lurked within her. Luckily, when it came to Zaid, there wouldn't be anything to worry about. No fights. No death. It was simply a discussion with an associate, then an eighteen-hour drive back to Sage City.

I knocked and Demi shoved her hands in her pockets. The door opened, revealing a brunette with curled hair and bright eyes. A rose gold infinity collar was tight around her neck.

"Hi," she said hesitantly, looking up at me. "Who are you?"

"Axe," I said. "An old associate of Zaid's." I tilted my head. "You must be Heather."

"I am," she nodded and turned to Demi. "And you are?"

"Demi," she said. The two women shook hands.

"Come on," she said, motioning for us to come inside. "I'll show you to the study."

Zaid had creases near his eyes from age, and matching scars on both sides of his face, striking through his eyes. One of them was a shade lighter than his skin tone, while the other was tinted pink, which meant it had to be new.

"Axel Adler," he said. "It's been a long time."

"Quite a while," I said.

This time, when I shook his hand, I gripped it firmly, hitting him on the shoulder, glad to see him. He had been a decent contact when I needed help down here, and it was hard to find good work. Zaid nodded to Heather, exchanging a silent communication.

"Come with me," Heather said to Demi, pulling on her arm. "I'll show you our garden out back."

Demi looked at me, and I gave a subtle nod. The two of them disappeared, and I turned back to Zaid.

"What brings you to this side of the country?" Zaid asked. We took seats in the middle of the room, along two chaise lounges facing each other. The room was large, with bookshelves along the walls and a fireplace roasting to the side. It wasn't surprising that Zaid had a modern, well-decorated home. He had always liked his spaces neat.

"Know anything about the Midnight Miles Corporation?" I asked.

Zaid closed his eyes, then opened them, spliced with a look of death.

"I am acquainted with Muro." His eyes trailed to the giant window at the back of the room, giving a full view of the shrubbery beneath the mountain. "He was one of Eric's friends."

I didn't know Eric personally, but I remembered the name from when Zaid and I worked together. Zaid had a grudge against Eric, and though that had long since settled, it was clear that the relationship was still not a happy one.

"Muro attacked my family," I explained. "Sent in soldiers to kill us. Disrespected us. Killed our men." I straightened my shoulders, staring at him. "And it won't stop until his corporation, or my family, is gone."

And I wasn't going to let Muro kill us.

From the window view, the two women walked out into the yard, carrying mugs of steaming liquid. Slivers of shadows illuminated them in the morning light.

"I know you sold Veil Security Services," I said. "But I wouldn't have come here unless it was important."

His glazed eyes lingered on the window. Demi and Heather were sitting on the edge of a planter box, talking to one another.

"I have some old contacts that would be happy to help," Zaid said. "And I'll be there myself. I know you'll return the favor," Zaid said. There was no doubt in my mind about that. "You have a plan?" Zaid asked.

Not yet, but with Zaid's help, I felt stronger about the outcome.

"I'll contact you with the details once it's finalized," I said.

In silence, we watched the two women. Heather was talking, while Demi's mouth was hanging open, as if stunned by every word that came out of her mouth. And yet she leaned forward, as if she needed more details, anything she could get her hands on. I loved that innocence about her. She never seemed to let anything discourage her curiosity.

"Who is she?" Zaid asked.

I paused, trying to find the words. Though I trusted Zaid, I wanted to keep Demi safe, to let her hold onto that innocence. Talking about her and claiming her as mine, even privately to Zaid, would put me in the position to claim her again, and potentially put her in future jeopardy.

I could have said she was my captive, but those words seemed off. You didn't take your hostage on a trip without bringing the cage with you, though I had honestly considered that idea for other purposes.

"She's my mentor's daughter," I said. Zaid nodded. But a knack grew inside of me, burning the longer I thought about it. She was more than that. How had I let that happen?

We said our goodbyes and left the house. In the car, I could smell Demi next to me, that soft scent, like cherries picked from the vine, rubbed with sweet sweat.

The plan was to go straight back to Sage City, but an hour and a half through the desert, Demi turned to me.

"What's the plan?" she asked. "You need me to drive?"

"Do you need a break?"

"My legs are killing me."

The next off-ramp led us to a dusty town with a motel and a burger joint. I don't know what possessed me, but the thought of staying with her in a nothing-town seemed almost nice. A break from reality.

"You want to stay here?" I asked. "Overnight?"

She smirked at me. "What? You don't like the indent of the window on my face?"

The sides of my lips twitched, and she grinned, knocking her shoulder into my side. I paid for the room in cash, then we took some fast food from next door back to the motel. Onion rings, fries, burgers, and milkshakes.

She crumpled the cheeseburger wrapper, then tossed it into the can.

"Did you see Heather's necklace?" she asked. I had, though I wouldn't consider it a necklace. I nodded. "Do you want to talk about it?"

What was there to talk about? I waited for Demi to say what she wanted.

"It was a collar, wasn't it? Like a master-slave kind of thing," she said.

A hint of a smile crossed my lips. Though I had never desired a 'slave,' I saw the appeal. To have a woman who saw you and respected you, as her owner, made me stir. Seeing Demi in that cage when she looked up at me had alighted a similar fire inside of me. A darker one.

Master and slave thing? "Yes," I said.

"What do you think about that kind of stuff?" She shuffled, bringing her knees up, holding her arms around them. "Do you have an opinion?"

Her gray eyes were darker in the dim-lighting, her face pale, a faint glob of melted cheese by her bottom lip. I leaned forward, wiping my thumb across the yellow smudge, brushing it away, then licking it off of my finger. She sucked in a tiny breath, her chest held tight.

I leaned back. "It takes a surprising amount of trust to have a true master-slave relationship like Zaid and Heather have," I said.

Demi nodded to herself, then mouthed the word 'trust.' "But do you like it?" she asked.

"Like it?"

"Do you think it's hot?"

I smiled then, a full one, my teeth bared. "Why?" I asked. "That's a curious question from someone who believes in clear cut definitions of right and wrong."

"Hey," she shook her head, "That's not fair."

"Isn't 'that kind of stuff,'" I said, emphasizing her words, "*bad*?"

"People should have the right to explore their sexuality," she said. "You know, when I went to PGU, I was on a mission to try everything that Dad had kept me from. There are a bunch of dances between my private school with the boys' school, but he *never* let me go." She shook her head. "The only time I saw boys my age was if Dad happened to take me to the grocery store and they were there with their parents too. Anyway," she shrugged, "I got my hands on beer, and tequila, though I never actually drank it. And I *almost* went to a frat party."

"You seem proud of this," I said.

She lifted her shoulders. "That's when Dad called. Anyway," she rolled her eyes, giving a deep sigh, "Back in the dorms, my stupid roommate had told everyone I was a virgin with a capital V. No one wanted to fuck me, scared that I'd be clingy or something. It was like she had given me a plague," Demi said, pretending to shudder, "But I knew I'd find someone to take it at that frat party."

I pressed my teeth together, glad that I didn't have to kill any dumb frat boys on top of Muro's men.

"What did you do instead?" I asked.

"I watched porn," she said, then she blushed. "Well, my *roommate* watched porn with her boyfriend, and I was in the room. The assholes."

We stared at each other for a moment. Was she lying? Trying to hide that she had sought it out herself?

No... Demi didn't lie. But she would be shy about unchartered territory.

"What did you watch?" I asked.

"Lots of stuff," she said, her voice quiet. "You know. They tied the women up. Played with them. Beat them."

"And?"

"Sometimes they cried. And sometimes, they came," her cheeks were bright red now, as if her head was a red sun going down behind her cool-colored hair.

"Did you like it?" I asked.

She closed her eyes for a moment, and when she opened them, they were trained on me.

"Yes."

My cock twitched. She was certain about this too. "What did you like about it?"

I sat beside her. The bed dipped between us, both of our hands leaning into it. I wanted to throw her on the bed and make her answer, but I wanted to hear it from her mouth, when we were like this.

Equals.

"They seemed so helpless," she whispered. "I wonder what that would feel like." She looked down at the bed. "But I've never even been kissed."

My teeth clenched. She had done so much since meeting me, and yet she hadn't done *that*? What idiots had passed on that opportunity? But kissing wasn't something I was willing to do. Kissing meant love, meant affection, and while I knew I felt *something* for Demi, I wasn't willing to open up to those emotions.

But making her feel helpless? That, I would indulge.

"Do you miss it?" I asked.

"Miss what?"

"College."

"Oh," she said, then she laughed to herself. "Not as much as you would think."

A few moments passed, where the air was laced with heat. I turned on the air conditioning as high as it would go, and let my eyes linger over Demi as she tucked her legs underneath her. In gym shorts, almost all of her legs were naked, though that big college sweatshirt hung over her body, covering her pussy. The looseness of the material made me want to explore every inch of her: the soft curve of her waist, the flesh of her hips, the bells of her breasts.

"You know I've never done anything," she said. "Not kissing. Nothing."

I sucked in a breath, then turned toward her. "No head?"

"No."

My cock twitched, thinking about the dildo I had shoved down her throat, shaking my own jizz on her face through the holes of the cage. I would need to change that soon.

"Have you ever been eaten out?" I asked.

A flush covered her face. "No."

The funny thing was that I had never done it either. My interest, sexually, was most of the time, perfunctory. The sooner it was over, the better.

But I thought about Demi's pink pussy lips, dripping wet with arousal, lapping it up and feeling her legs shake underneath me.

"We could try," I said. "If you want."

"We could."

Without speaking a word, Demi edged herself to the top of the bed, lying back on a pillow. I took off my shirt, and she stared at the hair on my chest, my muscular arms, a tattoo of a hatchet on my bicep. With her thumbs in her waistband, she inched down the shorts and underwear, and once they were past her knees, I pulled them off the rest of the way. A sweet smell came from between her legs, and I lay on my stomach, laying closer, the soft dark hair grown out on her pussy, matching her dark brows. Some hairs were short, evidence of stubble growing out, but most of the hair was long and curly. Demi had taken to shaving while she was in college, but with me? She didn't have that option. I wanted to bury myself inside of that hair. I loved it.

I stuck out my tongue, swirling it around the bead of her clit, glancing up at her as I did. Her eyes glossed over, completely focused on watching what I was doing. I sucked gently at first, and she tipped her hips closer to me, wanting more. Invigorated, I grunted, pressing my cock into the bed as I licked her pussy lips, tasting her, relishing in those tender folds. She moaned and I pulled her hips closer, bringing her to me. Then I stuck my tongue inside of her, tongue-fucking her until she whimpered in heat. She grabbed my head, burying my face in her thighs, but I grabbed her wrists, putting them firmly down on the bed.

I lifted my head, looking down at her, her juices covering my scruffy face. I tried to communicate without words. I loved that she wanted me so badly she was willing to wrap her legs around me, but her pussy was mine. It was mine to devour and worship, all fucking mine.

I put a hand on her pussy, letting my thumb flick over her entrance. That flush spread across her chest, up her neck, the hair on her head a puddle of blues and purples on the white sheets. She opened her lips, unsure of what to say. *You're mine*, I said, narrowing my eyes. *No one has ever touched you, because if they did, I would chop off their arms. Their legs. Their dicks. They're lucky you're still mine. And I'm going to take every inch of you.*

"You're mine," I said, with an edge to my voice. *Don't you dare tell me otherwise.*

She gave a subtle with her chin. I bent down again, bringing my tongue to her beaded clit, sucking on it until she bucked her hips forward again and moaned. Damn it. I wanted to fuck her right then. I wanted her to melt into pleasure until she was out of her mind, when she couldn't stand it any longer, when I couldn't take it either. But she didn't need me in her life. Not like this. But *fuck*, I wanted her so damn badly, and it was hard to resist her when she thrust again, her hands itching on the bed, her inner thighs shaking. I pressed down on her knees until they were flat on the bed, and lapped up her arousal.

Sitting up, I put a finger at the entrance of her pussy. She bucked her hips forward, wanting to feel my finger, wanting to feel me. I watched her, my cock hard against my thigh, bulging and aching to be deep inside of her. I rubbed the head through my pants, and she bit her lip.

"What do you want?" I asked.

Her eyes widened as if she couldn't believe that I was asking her a question right then. She smacked her hands down on the bed.

"Axe."

A smile lingered across my lips and her jaw dropped. She wiped a hand across her forehead, bucking her hips so close that I had to back away.

"What do you want?" I asked again.

She bit her lip. "Damn it, Axe. I want *you.*"

With those words, I pulled myself on top of her body, rubbing the tip of my finger along her pussy lips, wetting it, about to come in my pants just from feeling how aroused she was. It was hot as hell.

"I'm going to finger you, now, Demi," I said.

I wasn't afraid of a virgin. But I had to protect her, and that meant keeping myself away.

But that didn't mean I couldn't take this.

She stared into my eyes, glazed and full of desire. I stuck my finger inside of her, her velvet walls parting, her eyes rolling to the back of her head. She whimpered, moving her hips towards me, and I massaged her inside, staring into her eyes, shuddering with her. Sweat dripped from her brow, her bottom lip quivering in desire, her eyes glossy and mine, all fucking mine. She was so damn beautiful. She was completely at the mercy of this pleasure, of knowing that I would take everything she had to give me. I had never been with someone like this before, sharing this kind of intimacy. And neither had she.

I never let go of her stare. Demi was one of the first women who could actually look at me and see the real me. The violence.

The brutality. The ugliness. And she was still here. She wasn't afraid. Whatever we were doing, she might have had her idea of what was right in the world, but it didn't stop her from wanting me. I could be with her, show her every facet of me, and she stayed, saw past it all, even dwelled inside of it. And I knew, then, that this was more than I understood. Maybe this, whatever *this* was, was okay for someone like me.

At least when it came to Demi.

CHAPTER 14

Demi

The next morning, an hour outside of the motel, we stopped at a gas station. The world was flat around us. Short stubs of cacti peppered the plain with big brown rocks casting shadows against the ground. Feeling energetic, I jumped out of the passenger seat, sitting on the back of the van, watching Axe. He pumped the gas, his eyes lingering over me. I swear he smiled. Any time he let his lips form into that subtle curve, I melted. It was like he was giving me a personal gift, and I wanted to wrap it up carefully in tissue paper, tucking it into my pocket so I'd never forget the way it made me feel.

Things were different. Axe was in his thirties, but after last night, knowing that he actually saw me as more than a little girl, made me stand up straighter. Pride swelling inside of me.

The pump shuddered to a stop. Axe put it back into the rack, then tilted his head towards the driver's seat. His eyes reflected the dusty cement underneath us.

"You want to drive?" he asked.

My heart fluttered in my chest. "Really?"

He shrugged as if to say, Why not? And stupid me, who had never been behind the wheel of a car, was too excited to let the opportunity pass. I went to the driver's side and plopped into the car. A few seconds later, Axe sat in the passenger seat.

"You do realize I've never even been behind the wheel before," I said. A sharp breath came out of Axe's nose, his only acknowledgment. I hope it didn't bother him *too* much. "My dad didn't want me to have a license."

"Seems strict."

I gave a forced laugh. Strict didn't cover half of it.

"Was he like that with you?" I asked. Axe's eyes flicked to mine, then back to the road, so I continued talking: "He was controlling as hell. Kept saying driving was too dangerous." Axe handed me the keys, and I found the right one, then put it into the ignition. The van quivered to a start as the engine roared awake. Jittery butterflies filled me because Axe trusted me to do this. "I mean," I paused, sitting up in the seat, "There are plenty of things that are dangerous. Way more dangerous than driving."

"Fix your seat and mirrors," he said. I adjusted accordingly. Then he added, "Driving actually has a lot of fatalities."

I huffed. "I guess."

"All right." He gestured in front of us. "Press the gas pedal gently. Not too much. Get a feel for it." It barely moved, but once it did, I gave it slightly more pressure, letting the slow speed travel through my body. "Good. Now, let's go around the back of the store."

"The back of the store?" I asked. The convenience store was ahead. I angled the car around the side.

"Around it," Axe said. "We'll do that a couple of times before we go on the highway."

"You're going to let me drive on the highway?"

He grunted, and I knew the answer.

We came around the curve of the building. Dusty desert dirt surrounded the gas station. I steered off to the side, and the tiny rocks beneath us made the car vibrate. I quickly saved it, driving back onto the cement.

It was lucky that we were in a spot where hardly anyone was around, so I could use the time to figure out the basics. No matter how jolty my gas and brake movements were, Axe stayed calm, letting me figure it out. There were so many times that I was so sure that he was going to make me get out of the driver's seat, but he didn't. He trusted me, and because of that, I settled into it.

"Now, pull out onto the highway," he said. I did, feeling the smooth asphalt underneath the tires, different from the slight cracks and dips of the parking lot. I gripped the wheel a little tighter. "Don't be nervous."

"I'm not," I said, a little too quickly, and the corner of his mouth twitched up, another almost-smile, teasing me. And as stupid as it was, I grinned too.

"This highway isn't used much anymore. Only locals use it." He leaned back. "You can take your time if you want."

I raised my brow, smiling as I tested his words, teasing him right on back. I let the gas go, the car drifting slower, then slower still. A huff escaped his lips.

"Pick up speed," he said. "A little more gas."

One or two cars passed around to the side of me, but once I was up to the speed limit, I felt better about it. The road was fairly empty. I was technically *not* supposed to be driving. I didn't have a learner's permit, though I had been studying the DMV handbook since I had gone to college—but *still*. I didn't know the ins and outs of what was required for driving.

And for once, I realized that it didn't matter. We were fairly safe. And there were far too many things beyond what we were doing right then to be focused on what was right and wrong and what the rules were. Life was bigger than that.

Once I was comfortable, I turned on the radio, only finding country stations, but that was okay. I turned up the music, giving a sideways-glance to see how Axe reacted. I swear he was tipping his head to the music. Actually enjoying himself.

Maybe you could be accepted for who you were. If you gave yourself the chance.

After about ten minutes, Axe straightened, glancing at the side mirrors. I looked too; a black SUV was in the distance. I had noticed it before but didn't care about it until I saw his reaction. I tightened my grip on the wheel.

"Take this off-ramp," Axe said. My stomach churned. I did as I was told, coming to a stop sign at the end, and sure enough, the black SUV was behind us, taking the same ramp. "Back onto the ramp up ahead," Axe directed. I followed his words, unconsciously picking up speed.

"Who is that?" I asked.

Axe stared at the side mirror, then opened the dashboard and pulled out a gun. I kept my eyes on the road, but it was hard to ignore the fact that he was checking the ammo for the gun from his holster and the one from the dashboard. What was happening?

The SUV sped up behind us.

Axe stuck the guns out of the window, shooting at the car. They fought back. Bullets ricocheted into the van, the metal frame shuddering around us. I sucked in a scream and kept my eyes on the road. Axe shot again, and a bullet from the other side landed in my side-view mirror.

"Shit!" I yelled, swerving.

"Keep driving," he said. "Stay on the highway." He stuck out his guns, shooting more, and I hit the gas, but there was only so much faster we could go. Burning rubber smoked to the sides of us.

"Axe," I said, trying to warn him.

"Keep going."

There was an off-ramp to the side. I switched lanes closer to it.

"Keep going," Axe instructed. But my gut told me not to. Told me to get the hell out. I grit my teeth. We needed the SUV to stop following us. The off-ramp was about to pass us up.

Suddenly, I jerked the wheel to the side, and the force of the turn made the van screech to a halt, the two of us slamming to the barrier. My head hit the window and Axe braced himself. Then the SUV slammed forward, crashing into our van with momentum making the SUV rollover.

Axe stared at me, waiting for my response.

Blood throbbed in my ears. "I'm okay," I said, though I wasn't sure that I was.

He nodded, then got out of the car, carrying both guns. He glanced across the highway, then went to the car. A voice called out, asking him to stop, but Axe didn't listen. Three shots went off in the driver, and though a bullet came out from inside of the vehicle, he leaned down and shot the rest of them too, even the ones who weren't moving.

He leaned down, picking something up, then tucked it in his pocket. It was quiet then. The van was ticking with condensation dripping off of the undercarriage. I let out a long breath. My face was lit up with heat.

"Did you kill them?" I asked. It was obvious that he had. I don't know why that came out of my mouth.

"Some of them were already dead," he said.

Which meant that those extra bullets were to *make sure* that they were dead, but that my driving had killed them. I had only been on the road for less than an hour and I had already killed someone. Some people.

Some people who had tried to kill us.

I kept repeating that line to myself, trying to make it better.

"Miles Muro's men," Axe said. He pulled out the object from his pocket; a matchbox with two Ms smushed together at the top. *Midnight Miles Corporation* was written in small text underneath it.

"Is that supposed to make this okay?" I asked.

Axe ignored my comment. "You want to drive?" he asked. I blinked; my hands were still clutching the wheel.

"It can still drive?" I asked. I was afraid to look back and see how mangled the cargo section of the van was from where the SUV had hit it.

"Until we find another."

A heavy weight settled on my chest. I let go of the steering wheel, unbuckled my belt, then walked around the front of the car. Axe passed around the back of the van, taking the driver's seat in silence. I don't know if the accident had turned off the radio or if Axe had turned it off, but the van was quiet again, the car rumbling louder than before, mechanically asking for help.

When we came to a used car lot, Axe bought the first nondescript vehicle, paying with cash.

Suddenly, I realized why Dad never wanted me to drive. Why it was too dangerous. If anyone had a reason to take me out, it would be easy to do so in a car. Because it *was* dangerous. A hell of a lot more than I thought.

So why did I feel empty? We had left a car in the middle of the road full of dead people, some of which had died because of me, and yet I didn't feel anything. At least, I didn't feel as awful as I knew I should.

Maybe it hadn't hit me yet.

"Are you mad?" I asked.

Axe raised a brow at me.

"You said to keep going, and I—" Was I panicking? Was that it? I had reacted on instinct; that was all I knew. "I almost got us killed."

"We're alive," he said. I should have felt better about that, but I didn't. "You did what you thought was right."

A flush of warmth ran through me, but I wasn't sure what to say. I wanted to be mad. He should have been reprimanding me for the damage I had caused, that he could have killed those people himself, that I could've gotten us killed. But Axe didn't say a word like that, and I was relieved. So damn relieved. He was the first person to trust me to do what was right, to not question my decisions. I had to think about that, and not think about the people I had just killed.

People who had tried to kill us.

I let out a sigh. Axe reached over and squeezed my thigh.

"This is only the beginning," he said.

I didn't have to question it. I knew he was right.

CHAPTER 15

Demi

When we arrived in Sage City, we immediately went to Axe's parents' house. I recognized most of the people around the dining table: Wil, Ellie, Derek, and Maddie. The table was flat, covered in a rose table runner. We were the last two to join them; they looked up at us. Maddie smiled at me. Axe and I took seats next to her.

"Where's Gerard?" Wil asked.

"Taking care of Clara," Derek said. Wil let out a small hiss. I noticed things seemed normal between Wil and Axe. That was good; the fight about Ellie's safety must have been over by now. Axe's eyes flicked away, then back to Derek.

"Figures that he wouldn't be here," Wil said.

"Give it a break. Clara has food poisoning," Derek said. "He'll be here in a few minutes. Anyway..." Derek crossed his arms. "Wil and Ellie were attacked last night."

Ellie lifted her hand, her wrist bandaged. "I'm fine," she said. A small bright pink spot was still healing near her nose. The woman couldn't catch a break.

Wil blinked away the rage, then said, "She is *not* fine. I'm tired of dealing with Muro."

"You know it's Muro?" I asked. Everyone in the group turned towards me, and I realized that I was the one who always tagged along, but never spoke. Axe's perfect shadow, until now. I rolled my eyes. "What? Axe told me. I know what's going on."

"Yeah," Axe said, turning back to Wil. "Was it Muro?"

"What happened?" Maddie asked.

"We were supposed to be going to the island, but the ferries were broken, and I didn't feel like sailing," he said with such aristocracy that I realized he must not hold himself to the same minimalist standards that Axe did. Sailing? Axe didn't seem like he'd ever consider a past time like sailing. "Got a hotel room on the water to make up for it. Anyway, I don't know how the hell they got in."

"I disarmed," Ellie said.

"And I put the bullet in between his eyes," Wil said, looking at Ellie. They turned back to us.

"Did you find the logo?" Derek asked.

"On the neck," Wil said.

Axe lifted his chin. "We were attacked too," he said. He turned to me, which made the rest of them look at me too.

So Axe wanted me to talk *for* him? All right, then. I shrugged. "Yeah, they were chasing us."

"Where?" Derek asked.

"In the desert," I said. "By car."

"Shit," Derek muttered. "And we know for sure it was Muro?"

Axe lifted the matchbox from his pocket, showing the logo.

"They must have had a plan for when Cannon was taken out," Derek said. "Maybe he was a cover."

"Or there's a rat," Axe said.

The room fell silent, the accusation hovering in the air. Then Maddie cleared her throat, and Wil sat up straight.

"What do we do now?" Wil asked.

Gerard popped his head in, then tilted backward, motioning for the brothers to follow him. Derek and Wil stood up.

Axe put a hand on my shoulder as he stood up too, then said, "I'll be back." Ellie followed behind them, leaving Maddie and me alone.

"You're not allowed in the business talk either?" I asked.

"Oh," Maddie lifted her shoulders, "I don't mind taking a break." She rolled her wrists. "A few hours where I get to sit around and wait is fine by me."

Huh. What was she waiting for? "What's going on with you?" I asked.

"Derek's trying to convince his dad that it's fine if I clean their place regularly." She forced a smile. "I guess Clara prefers to do most of the work herself. And Gerard doesn't like extra women in the house." Extra women? She must have read the confusion, because she added, "He has a history of infidelity. Knows he needs to keep himself in check."

My jaw dropped slightly, but then I straightened. "But you'd never do that," I said.

"Of course not," she smiled. "But if that's what he needs to do to make his wife feel safe, then by all means," she knocked her shoulder into mine playfully, "I understand. But Derek hates letting his mom do that kind of stuff. She's getting older, you know?" She looked at the door as if she could see Derek through it, and her eyes softened. "He's so damn protective," she said, her voice wistful. Then she shook away the daydream and turned to me. "Anyway, I hear you went to Las Vegas. Did you get to do any gambling?"

I wrinkled my nose. The kitty machine in Sour Times must have counted.

"I guess," I said.

"Good," she chuckled.

"So what do you think they should do?" I asked. "Based on what you know."

Maddie breathed in deeply, staring at the wood-paneled walls. In here, with no windows, it made the room seem darker and closed in.

"Muro is unpredictable. It's hard to know the best option with him," she said quietly.

"How do you know Muro?" I asked.

Her jaw went rigid. "I used to live in Brackston. A long, long time ago." Her eyes narrowed, recalling the memories. "Luckily, the brothers have been taking care of his contacts one at a time. Muro is probably getting a little desperate by now."

"So where does that leave him?" I sat up, resting my elbows on the table. There were grooves and spots in the wood that created a pattern. It was an older table, but well cared for. "Who does he have left? Or better yet, who can the brothers turn to for help?"

"What about the police?" Maddie asked. "The odds are that they're in with Muro, but you never know. Maybe some of them want to put him in prison?"

"What do you mean?"

Her eyes fluttered to the side. "I mean, there's a possibility for it both ways. Either they're under Muro's grip, or they aren't. But maybe it's worth a shot." She shrugged. "You've got to believe in something around here."

And that filled me with hope. Stupid, foolish hope, knowing that we had been in the middle of this war on a regular basis, and yet, there was still a chance that law enforcement was on our side. Maybe we could have the upper hand.

We.

When had it become 'we'? I smiled to myself, and Maddie pushed my shoulder.

"Hey," she said in a sing-song voice. "What are you keeping from me?"

"It's just that," I shook my head, "I didn't realize that we can end this. If we work together. Use all of our resources."

Maddie gave a soft laugh. The sound made me anxious, not understanding why what I had said was so funny. But I told myself it was nothing: I was overreacting. So I focused on that word: *we*. There was a 'we' in all of this.

Maddie squeezed my shoulder. "I hope they can end this," she said. "Axe likes you, you know."

"He doesn't like me," I said. Axe liked having someone around that he could play with, torturing and pleasuring alike.

Or, maybe he liked having someone he could talk to. Maybe he felt more comfortable with me because of the situation. Because he could keep me in a cage.

But a hope lingered inside of me that Maddie was right. That he wanted me for more reasons than that.

"Oh, hush," Maddie said. "You're here, aren't you?"

Maddie's red hair dye had grown out slightly, exposing a thin line of brown hair. It was fake, but I liked the red; it went well with her deep emerald eyes. In a world where I was somewhere between Axe's ward and his captive, she was the only other friend I had. She was nice, even though she didn't have to be.

"Why are you so nice to everyone?" I asked.

She smiled, then sighed, leaning back in her seat. "You should be nice to everyone."

"But why?"

"You don't know what secrets they're hiding."

I stared at her for a moment; the smile had almost faded, but she was still hinting at it, looking up at the ceiling. What secrets was Maddie hiding? Or me? Or more importantly, what secrets was Axe keeping from me? I had a feeling I got to see him when he was most secretive, so what did it mean for Axe to have secrets? What side of himself was he hiding?

"Anyway," she shrugged her shoulders, "Make sure you don't do anything you regret," she said. "You're still young."

"I'm eighteen," I said.

"Exactly." She tossed her hair over her shoulder. "If this all blows over, you can go back to a normal life."

She said that like she couldn't. "Can't you?" I asked.

"We'll see," she said.

Axe opened the door to the dining room. When those narrowed eyes finally found me, they opened and lit up with warmth. I followed him out. I expected us to go through the woods to his workroom, but instead, he led me back to the newly-purchased sedan. We grabbed our bags from it, switching to another white work van waiting nearby. They had four others waiting in that clearing; I guessed the one we had left behind didn't matter much in the end.

At his apartment, he opened the door for me. I put my backpack on the ground, and Axe placed my duffel bags next to them, but I immediately noticed something: the mattress wasn't in the front room anymore.

"What happened to your bed?" I asked.

He pointed down the hallway. I leaned over, looking through the opening. A queen bed was elevated on a box spring, as well as a recliner sitting at the foot of it. There was even a comforter on the bed.

I raised a brow. "Not the floor?"

He shrugged.

"What's with the recliner?" I asked.

"For me. I don't sleep much anyway," Axe said.

"So you want to sleep sitting up?" He didn't answer, but before he went off to that faraway place to ruminate, I interjected: "Do you think the police are involved?"

Axe's eyes turned to me, staring coldly.

"We own the police station."

I stepped forward. I had figured that much for Sage City, but that didn't mean they owned law enforcement everywhere else too.

"But what about the police in Brackston?" His jaw went slack, and I realized that I didn't know half of what was going on, and when I said things like that, it made it feel all the more real. I felt stupid and flustered, but like the stubborn woman that I am, I kept going at it. "It's worth a shot, isn't it? I'm not the only one who thinks it's a good idea. Maddie does too."

He studied me for a moment, then shook his head. "I thought an idea like that would have come straight from you."

I could see why, but that wasn't the point.

"You know she used to live in Brackston, right?" I asked. "She knows what it's like there."

"Living in Brackston doesn't make her an expert."

"Come on," I said. I could feel the tension rising in my voice. I had finally decided to help his family, with whatever their crisis was, and he was being so resistant. All I wanted was for him to confirm that he knew I wanted to help, but even that was still hard for me. "I don't know exactly what's going on. But I know you need to give every option a chance."

Please, I thought. *Give me a chance.*

I came towards him, raising a hand to hold his face. That scar on his ear caught my eye. Did it still hurt? My fingers ran over the scruff, the weathered skin that held so much tension every day. His lips were soft, giving that dip an aching feel, reminding me of what it felt like when he rubbed his lips against my clit. He leaned in closer, his breath on my lips. What would it be like to kiss Axe? How could he kiss me *there*, but hadn't yet kissed me on the lips?

Axe lowered his eyes, then shifted away. He pulled out his phone and dialed Derek, going down to the bedroom. I stayed in the hallway, out of sight.

"Have we checked the Brackston PD?" he asked.

Those knots in my stomach turned to heat. Axe might not have kissed me, but he was giving my ideas, as stupid as they might have been, a chance. And that meant something.

CHAPTER 16

Axe

I adjusted the phone against my ear. "The PD?" Derek asked. "I doubt they'd be any help inside of Brackston."

I knew that. Just as our local municipalities were on our side, the law enforcement in Brackston would be on Muro's side as well. It was possible that even the neighboring territories would know to direct any of their calls about Midnight Miles Corporation over to Brackston.

But I also knew that Demi needed this more than I did.

"Have you verified?" I asked.

"I'll put Wil on it. And Axe?" I didn't say a word, which was Derek's cue to continue. "That woman, Demi?" He paused, waiting for a reaction, but I gave none. He couldn't see me straightening my curled fingers, one by one. "You realize you don't have to keep that promise to Shep, right? Gerard would understand." He sighed as if the arranged marriage would affect *him* more than me. "She doesn't need to be trapped in a world like this."

He must have known that it was her idea to call the police, then. It was a hopeful view of the world, but also ridiculous because despite everything that had happened, she still believed in the order of the world. That the police helped victims. As if we, the Adlers, were the victims, and that would make everything we did okay. But we were as culpable as Muro himself. I wanted to shake her until she realized that this, *our war*, was bigger than the police, bigger than the government, more powerful than anything she had ever encountered. There was no right or wrong. Only dead or alive.

"She's alive," I said into the phone. That was all that Shep truly wanted. Derek knew that. He cleared his throat.

"I've got a job for you," Derek said. He took a breath, adjusting the phone. "There's a banker. One of Muro's. I tried to reason with him, but…" A few buttons clicked on the other end, then he put his phone back to his ear. "Have him end the accounts with Muro. The rest of it is up to you."

"Send me the coordinates," I said. We hung up. I turned around. Demi had been waiting in the hallway, but she wasn't there anymore. I ran a hand over my face. A few seconds later, my phone pinged through an encrypted app. A set of coordinates and a name. When I checked the location, it looked like the banker was staying in a hotel, which meant that he wasn't from Brackston. Perhaps Muro's accounts were all offshore. Another ping; a message from Derek: *Wil is bringing the key card now.*

I turned off the screen and stowed my phone. When I returned to the main area, Demi was leaning on the counter as she read a light orange takeout pamphlet from one of the drawers. She wasn't reading; she was trying to appear distracted as if she *hadn't* been eavesdropping on my conversation. She looked up at me and gave me one of those smiles that made my breath catch in my chest. As if she was trying to communicate her wishes to me. As if I could fulfill them.

But I needed to see if she would run. Whether she could still face me after seeing what I was capable of first hand. My ugliness.

I didn't return the smile this time.

"Don't get comfortable," I said. "We're going."

***

The drives to Brackston were beginning to get on my nerves; I would have preferred to stay there indefinitely. But with Demi around, the risk wasn't worth it. Dressed in a button-up shirt and slacks, a suit jacket hiding my holsters, and Demi in a blazer, a hat hiding her hair, both of us in gloves—we walked through the empty hotel lobby to the elevator. Derek had already assigned one of our men to disable the security system from afar. The lights on the cameras shone red, but the images were full of static on the receiving end. Using the key card from Wil, the elevator cart flew up to the twentieth floor. It was late at night, and because there were few oversized suites on that floor, we had an easy time getting to the banker's room without being noticed.

I stood beside the door, taking Demi in. She removed the hat, her pale, cool-colored hair astray. She smoothed a few tendrils behind her ears. She looked at me, her gunmetal eyes lost, and she bit her lip. With a quick movement of my brows, I asked if she was ready. She nodded, holding her breath.

I swiped the key card. The pad beeped, then unlocked the door. A hallway, then a large open room, the ceiling fifteen feet high, a few doors off to the sides. The place was dark. A television chattered in one of the rooms, but other than that, there was no evidence of anyone staying there. I motioned behind me, and Demi fell in line, close to me. We inched toward the noise. The television could have been a distraction to keep potential intruders busy *if* the banker were smart. Or it could have been like I suspected: an oblivious man who didn't know the kind of devil he had made a deal with.

Peeking around the open doorway, a bed faced the opposite wall, a fifty-inch screen hanging above a dresser. A man, still fully clothed in his button-up shirt and tie, sat glued to the screen. His jacket rested on top of his laptop. The light from the television flickered on his face.

I put up a hand, telling Demi to stay.

"What?" she whispered. "I—"

I shot a look, narrowing my coal eyes at her, and she stiffened. She took in a breath, and before the man could turn to see what the noise was, I was behind him, putting him in a chokehold. He pulled at my arms frantically. I held him tighter.

"He-help!" the banker gasped. "Help me!"

He locked eyes with Demi, pleading to her. Using my free hand, I shoved the barrel of my gun into his temple. He whimpered, and I let him go, letting him cough himself into a fit. He was too easy. If I were anyone else, I would have felt the pang of guilt in my chest.

But I wasn't anyone else. I had seen this kind of death, induced it myself, since I was a child.

I swung my gun at his laptop. "Cut the accounts to Muro," I said.

"W-what?" the man asked, his voice shaking. "C-c-cut the accounts?"

"All of his accounts. Dump the funds. I don't care where." He didn't move, so I pulled the hammer back. "Cut his accounts."

Shivering, the man pulled the computer into his lap and started jabbing at the buttons, repeatedly stopping to erase, then type again.

"I don't understand," the man said, his voice wavering. "I just—" He shook his head, then pressed enter. "I just—"

"Close the accounts," I repeated.

The man stammered, but did as he was told, his breathing haggard. Demi was in the corner, hugging her blazer around her chest, reminding me of myself" standing in the corner, observing Shep. But I couldn't pay attention to her right then; I turned back to the man.

"It'll take a few days," the man said.

That didn't concern me. I had a job to do, and part one of that job was now completed.

"We gave you a chance," I said in a low voice.

"Who the hell are you?" the man begged, his voice turning to tears. I knew my brothers were proud to brag about our name. Annihilate. Conquer. Rule. That was our way of life, and while my only purpose was *annihilation*—I also knew that this stranger deserved to know. To know that if he had listened to his gut instinct, if had declined Muro, maybe he wouldn't be looking into the face of death.

"We're the Adlers," I said.

A sob escaped from his chest, telling me all I needed to know. Wanting to leave a statement for Muro, I pulled my cleaver from its sheath, holding down the man's hand as the blade sliced through the forearm. He flailed, and I grabbed the other hand, about to do the same.

"Can I help—"

I heard her voice, but I didn't stop. I sliced the man's other hand. He didn't fight. The man wailed in a piercing noise that made me grind my teeth. Blood bubbled from his stumps, oozing onto the white comforter. It must have been expensive. What would the housekeepers think?

I turned to Demi. Could she help *what?* We both knew she didn't mean it. She was trying hard to figure out where her moral lines actually landed, if she was anything like her father, testing that boundary. Could she help kill a man who had helped a criminal launder money?

No. I didn't think she could.

But she stared at me with passion in her eyes. She was trying to figure it out.

"Axe," she whispered. "Let me be a part of this."

I blinked, and the man whimpered.

"You want to be a part of this," I repeated.

"Yes," she said, so softly, I almost didn't hear it.

I dropped the man on the bed, then bounded over to her, seizing my grip around her waist. I pulled her into me. Her body went rigid with tension. I placed the cleaver in her hand, wrapping our fingers around the handle together. Her chest tightened; she wasn't breathing, too anxious to do even that. It was hard for me to remember that this wasn't normal. Death, like this, wasn't an everyday occurrence for someone like Demi. I shouldn't have exposed her to this.

But I needed her to know. I needed to see what happened when I made it her new life.

I moved my hand, holding her wrist, letting her feel the heavy blade in her hand. She was trembling, her eyes flicking over the man, his skin ghostly white, mouth opened, his lips dry and parched. She was second-guessing herself, but I thought of this as a gift. Something she could never undo. It would be part of her. Like her father had made it a part of me too.

I had to know what she would do.

"You asked for this," I whispered in her ear. "You asked to be a part of this."

"But I—"

I tightened my grip on her wrist. "If you don't do this, it will take minutes for him to die. Excruciating, painful minutes. It will be a long time before he has his final heartbeat." The truth was that I didn't know how long it would take. But after doing this for as long as I had, you had an instinct about these things. She could make it easy, or harder for him. It was her choice. "Or you can end it now," I said. "Give him peace."

Demi stared for a moment, and when the man's eyes opened widely, his lips quivering to form words, she turned her chin to me, keeping her eyes on him.

"He was bad to your family," she whispered.

I didn't answer.

She brought the cleaver down on his neck. The blade sliced through the first part, splitting the skin of his throat and the wall of his esophagus, cylindrical pieces of flesh torn open, but it wasn't enough. She started shaking, so I grabbed her hands, holding onto the cleaver with her palm, and I forced her hand down the rest of the way.

The spinal cord spotted pink, the head rolled on the bed, the eyes fluttered open. Demi took a deep breath, jumping back, her eyes full of tears. She flung her own body against the wall in shock. She shook her head, holding her face. Then her eyes were vacant, staring past the man's corpse, but then she hit her hands against her chest, her body swelling with air.

"I did it," she said, more to herself than to me. "I did it." Her face contorted, her eyebrows bunched, her mouth dropped open. "I actually did it." She shook her head. "He was a criminal?" she asked. "Right, Axe? He was a bad person?"

He laundered money. A white-collar crime. Would that be enough for Demi? I should have expected it, but it stunned me that she needed a reason. She cared about what was just. I admired that about her. But I wanted to teach her too.

The reason didn't matter anymore. He was already dead.

Her chin trembled. "I just killed someone," she said. She pleaded to me. "But he was a bad person," she stammered. "Wasn't he?"

Her gloves crunched in her hands. I touched her arm; she was ice cold. She needed comfort from me, the answer to her worries. A way to explain what she had done to that man. To tell herself that it wasn't for nothing. Because it wasn't simply a murder; it was a death so brutal that even I saved it for special occasions like this: the moment we told Muro that we were coming for his head next; the day that I showed Demi who I really was. When I stopped holding back. When I stopped trying to save her from me.

CHAPTER 17

Demi

I couldn't let myself look at that head. But I had to. It felt wrong not to face what I had done. Those half-drawn eyes. The open mouth.

"Tell me, Axe," I demanded, trying to find vigor in my voice. "Who was he?"

My entire body trembled, knowing that those answers would never erase what I had done. How had I let myself make an impulsive decision like that? Axe grabbed my shoulders, lightly at first, then firmly moved me until I was sitting on the bed. The mattress was taut, tension holding where the man's dismembered body laid. My legs were jelly. He parted my knees, standing between them. His body brushed against mine as he looked down at me. As I lifted my face, my eyes caught on his bulge.

Why the hell was he hard right now?

"What is wrong with you?" I asked. "You're turned on? Right now? By *this*?"

Axe didn't move. And if I was honest, I wasn't sure I wanted the answer right then. I pleaded that he was turned on by my reaction, by what I had done, and not that he was turned on by death. Axe's gloved fingers ran down the sides of my arms; even through the thick blazer, his touch was magnetic. I turned my chin to the side, not wanting to give in to the sensation, knowing that his touch meant more to me than I could logically explain. Then I saw the man's arm lying there. It didn't look real. More like a prop from a movie. Or maybe that's what I told myself to feel better.

The worst part was that I had asked. I had wanted to do it. To prove to myself that I understood Axe, that I could put myself in his shoes and did what he did.

Axe traced the curve of my breast through the blazer, then pulled on the button. There was blood on both of us. That man's blood. His *life* staining us.

Axe might not have cared who the man was, but that blood would mark me forever.

He undid those three large buttons on my blazer, and I let him. It was better to let him do that, to take my mind off of it, then to think about the headless, armless man next to me. I closed my eyes, holding back the tears. I didn't know if he had a family. If his friends would miss him. If I had done the right thing.

I tried so damn hard to understand. I wanted to know Axe better. I wanted to see what my dad was like. I wanted to see how it felt. I wanted—

Axe pulled up my shirt, exposing my bra and stomach. I inhaled, taking in the smell of blood, the tinny smell that was always lingering on Axe's skin. His murders had seemed so surreal from inside of that metal cage, like I would never be a part of it. Would never bathe in blood like he did. But now it was on my clothes, in my hair, staining my skin. And Axe wanted to touch me?

Why wouldn't I stop him?

"We first started making contact with Miles Muro a while ago," Axe said, his voice monotone. He pulled down the cup of my bra, exposing one breast. My nipple was hard before he even touched it, awakening to his presence. "We had a man, this thief who had stolen a diamond from Muro's wife. And we had the thief's daughter." He paused, his finger grazing over the tops of my breasts. I stared at the red-splattered shirt covering his stomach, the piece of flesh on his wrists, his hands manipulating me. Calling to me. My body responded, but it didn't feel like it wasn't me anymore.

"We were supposed to deliver them both," he said. "Use their lives as a tool to spread our empire with Muro's. But my half-brother, one you haven't met." He skimmed his fingers across my areola, making me shiver. "He fell for the daughter. Didn't care about what saving her life meant to the family."

I looked up at Axe, and those black eyes narrowed in on my soul, telling me that he didn't see anything there. Not the room. Not the corpse behind us. Not me. And I realized then, that I didn't want to feel or see any of it either. All I wanted was Axe. I could let myself go with him. Forget everything. Make it all disappear in a mindless, brainless orgasm. None of it felt real, anyway.

"He saved her," Axe said. "Saved her life. Threw away our one chance at having a partnership with Muro." Axe pinched my nipple, his fingernails biting into the skin as if to make me pay for his brother's mistake. I pressed my lips together, trying not to make a sound. I had to let Axe say everything. He had held it all in for so long.

"We knew that a relationship with Muro wouldn't have lasted," he said, "but we didn't get to try. Ethan took that one chance away from us. For a fucking woman."

For a woman? Why did that make Axe angry? Because *that* woman could have been me?

"Eventually, we delivered the thief to Muro." He let go of the pressure on my nipples, and a small gasp escaped my lips. "We tried to have a normal business relationship. Tried to put it all in the past. To do what Gerard wanted. But Muro trained soldiers to find us, trained them to have certain qualities that would attract the men in my family. Using our own desires against us."

Their own desires against them? "What do you mean?" I asked.

He turned his chin to the side, but never let his eyes stray from mine, always studying, always scrutinizing me. "Muro thought that if we were distracted, we'd slip up. Get ourselves killed." He leaned down, breathing onto my face in hot bursts. "The only mistake I made was gifting one of the soldiers to my brother. And Wil fell for her too. Another fucking woman." He clenched his fists, his grips around my breasts, one clothed and the other bare, and I grimaced, the pain shooting through me like tendrils of fire. "And when more soldiers came after us, I told my brothers we should have killed them. Each and every one of them. But they didn't listen. Didn't think it was fair."

Finally, he let go, then pulled my other breast out of the cup, twisting my nipples slowly. My breathing hitched.

"And you know how I feel about what's fair," he said in a low voice.

I searched his eyes. That might have been true, but he also held onto the promise to my dad. To me.

"You still wanted to kill them?" I asked.

He nodded, his eyes vacant. "Derek thought the soldiers could be recruited. And my father didn't want to start a war. Wil was a lost cause." He laughed darkly to himself, then beamed into me with ice in his eyes. "I don't care if you're a man or a woman. If you can be of use to our family, or if you're a scrap of meat. I'll kill anyone I have to. Every single person has a messed up past. I'm only doing what nature intends."

But nature wasn't a bullet or a cleaver. His fingers had stopped moving, as if waiting for me to speak, but my body stayed in his hands, both of us looking at each other, wondering what we should do next.

"If it were up to me," he pulled me up by the nipples, making me stand beside him, his cock hard against me, pulsing in frantic twitches as if it needed to be free to touch me, "None of them would have lived. I would have killed Teagen myself. I would have killed Ellie too." My heart clenched; he would have killed his own sister-in-law? "I don't care who you are. This is who I am. If I have to kill you, I will."

Was he trying to warn me that he didn't care about me? "Then why haven't you?"

I didn't need to finish the sentence. We both knew what I meant. He blinked, then curled his fingers into my spine, digging in between the plates, the pain kicking against me. Finally, I cried out.

"The only thing that's saving you from that end is my promise to your father. He saved my life. And I'll save yours. But once that debt is repaid," he put a hand around my throat, tightening his grip. "You're just like them."

I don't care who you are. If I have to kill you, I will.

But I knew in my heart that it was a lie. He was trying to convince himself of these words. He didn't believe it either.

"I'm not afraid of you," I said, gritting my teeth. I had just killed a man. Goody-two-shoes me, the daughter of an overly strict father, the child of an ex-mafia enforcer, had killed a man. And like Axe could threaten to kill me, I knew, given the opportunity, I could do the same thing to him.

His cock stretched against me. "What a stupid girl," he said.

He scooped me up, tossing me over his shoulder, knocking the breath out of my chest, then he slammed me back down, my body thudding into something hard. Fluid warmed my ear and I screamed in terror, getting off of the body as quickly as I could.

I yelled in fright, in sadness, in complete disgust. Axe unbuttoned his pants, taking out his cock, and by some strange will buried inside of me, I spread my legs for him and screamed.

I understood why he never spoke. He was full of hatred, of nothingness that swallowed him whole, and never let him feel anything. *I don't care who you are.* These were words he was forcing onto me, to punish me, to protect himself, to show me that I wasn't supposed to be there. That everything I thought was right. That there wasn't any good in anyone. And Axe's heart was pure darkness.

He stroked his cock and I pulled down my pants and underwear, then clung to his body, wrapping around him, begging him to do it already. But he pushed me down, making me lie on the bed, then flicked the head of his cock along my pussy lips, wet for him. Teasing me. *Just do it already. Make me pay.* But he pulled back, replacing his cock with two fingers, stabbing them inside of me like a knife. Like he could break me in two with those fingers alone, pounding into my cervix, making me cringe in pain, and shake in pleasure.

"You're turned on by death," I said, my voice full of accusation. Because I wanted, and desperately needed, for him to tell me I was wrong. "You're turned on by murder!"

"Yes," he growled, "It does turn me on."

There was power in death for him, the flood of adrenaline that rushed through his face each time he killed someone. Axe might have thought that meant it turned him on. But I didn't believe it. Wouldn't let myself.

He flicked a finger over my ass, then pressed inside, my insides tightening, and I squealed. He pressed his hand on my throat, cutting off my air, staring into my eyes as he pumped inside of me. Using my holes.

I don't care who you are.

Why was he trying to convince me that he only had darkness inside of him?

Why was he punishing me?

Then the air wasn't enough and my vision went blurry, my face filling with pressure, and I choked, thrashed, tried hard to get out from under his grasp, but he fucked me harder with his hand, harder, and harder, until finally, he let go. I coughed to the side, holding myself up by my hands. Once I was finished, he rubbed his cock against my pussy lips, never penetrating me. Like he couldn't resist it. Then with his free hand, he pressed a gun to my temple.

Adrenaline surged through me in a white hot rush, making sweat bead on my entire body. A tear slipped out of my eye. He could have killed me right then. He wouldn't have cared. My dad was the only thing keeping me alive. He wanted me to understand that completely.

I don't care who you are.

But he did care. I had seen it. Felt it.

Dad's words echoed in my mind: *You can't be afraid to see someone at their worst, Demi,* he had said. *Nothing can change the worst, because it's real.*

The hair on the back of my neck stood up as Axe pressed the cold barrel into my skin. Was this his worst?

"When are you going to learn?" he asked. "When? Tell me. When will you be afraid? All it takes is one pull." He pulled back the hammer, holding it to my head. "One pull, Demi. One flick of my finger. And you're gone. Do you really think I care about that promise to your father? Do you think I care about you?"

I stared at him, fighting him with all I had. "You must think I care too," I hissed through my teeth.

And for the slightest second, he stopped, staring down at me.

"Stupid girl," he said.

CHAPTER 18

Axe

With Muro's accounts out of the way, plans moved forward. We had one serious advantage: some of Wil's men had secured one of the warehouses. They were carrying on, as usual, pretending to be Muro's own complicit men. Using them as a decoy, we could lure Muro out, and then take down his men, for real, this time. We had a much larger group of our best, plus the help of Zaid's old team from Veil Security Services. In theory, it was perfect.

But it didn't sit right with me. I trusted Wil's men to be on our side, and Zaid had never let me down before. But I wondered about our attempt to gain access to the police. Wil's contact in the BPD confirmed that no one was willing to budge; Muro had a firm grip on their balls. And on top of that, we still had a rat among our ranks.

Something was off. I didn't trust it at all.

A knock sounded on the apartment door. I went past the kitchen, where Demi was eating a microwavable breakfast sandwich, and opened the door. Maddie lifted her pink flamingo cleaning bag at me, then went to Demi.

"You're eating without me?" Maddie asked. "I guess we can get lunch then."

"Huh?" Demi asked.

"I'm heading out," I explained. I nodded to the two of them, making eye contact with Maddie. She knew what I expected.

"What?" Demi asked. "You're leaving me here?"

I wasn't leaving her anywhere. I was keeping her away from danger. After decapitating her first victim, she didn't need any more of the war in her life. Demi protested, but I shut the door behind me.

It was for her own good. I could never decide if I wanted to break or protect her.

I met my brothers, Zaid and his men, as well as Ron and Billy (one of Ellie's friends) at the warehouses in Brackston. We picked through Muro's stock. There were the usual cocaine and heroin, but beyond that, there were guns and explosives, cases of them, hidden in the bellies of frozen fish and TV boxes. Our men were sporting the classic white Midnight Miles Corporation uniform, two Ms embroidered on their breast pockets. I knew that soon, Wil would take over the rest of the warehouses.

One of our men, pretending to be one of the Midnight Miles deliverers, called Muro on the burner phone he had acquired from the previous handler.

"Boss," he said. "Nan is out. I'm—" He paused again, listening. "Right. But we've got a little problem here. Could you come down to the—" He stopped, shaking his head. "But sir, can we move a product like this when—" He went silent again. "Understood, boss." Then he hung up.

He looked at me. "He wants me to drive to the headquarters."

The semi was still packed, to make it look like a shipment had arrived. Driving wasn't an issue; we could move our plans accordingly. It would give us a chance to confirm that his servers were out.

I turned to Zaid. "Can your men hide around the headquarters?" I asked. "The security will be armed."

"Not a problem," Zaid said.

The rest of us, including my men, Derek, Wil, Ron, and Billy, got into the back of the semi-truck.

I turned to Wil. He had convinced Ellie to stay home and heal while her friend, Billy, took her place. Knowing he was protecting his wife made me satisfied that Demi was safe too. But I ignored that relief. Demi would be safer once Muro was gone.

"And your connection hasn't notified the police?" I asked. Wil nodded, but the slight twitch of his lips told me what I needed to know. My gut instinct was right. "A new connection?" He nodded again. I clenched my fists, but I didn't blame him. Desperate times called for desperate measures, which meant potentially leaking our plans. It was too dangerous now. I turned to Derek. "We need to turn back," I said.

"Why?" he asked. "We've got a fucking militia on our side."

"Muro knows," I said.

"Who told you that?"

"Instinct," I said. "We're better off waiting for another chance."

"This might be our last shot," Derek said. "All we have to do is take down Muro. The rest can wait."

I didn't like it, but I shut the hell up and trusted him. Derek was a better leader than our father. If we failed, it would be on all of us, but especially Derek.

I turned to Ron. "Make sure that the servers are down," I said, handing him a set of deadly explosives with twice the power we had last time. Then I tapped my earpiece. "I'll be waiting for confirmation."

"You've got it, boss," Ron said.

We all listened as our driver stopped at the security checkpoint, which sounded quieter than usual, as if there weren't as many guards on duty. Then the truck was given clearance and the engine started again, driving to the unloading side of the headquarters. The truck reversed into the loading dock, shielding us from the parking lot.

Several feet shuffled to the side of the truck. As long as Muro thought this was routine, we would succeed, but we needed him to come down himself.

The back door opened, revealing a group of four men. None of them was Muro.

"Where's Muro?" Derek asked. The men's eyes widened.

"Who are you?"

I lifted my gun.

We took them out, then hopped out of the truck. Several more men exited from the lobby. I nodded to Wil. "You sure your BPD connection didn't notify Muro?"

"Don't know," he said, blasting a guard in the face. "But I'll kill him if he did."

Bullets flew and Zaid's men joined us. Ron made his way to the lobby while the rest of us stayed there, shooting down Muro's men. Billy gave a warrior's cry, but then a bullet hit her chest and she collapsed. Wil looked at her, then went back to fighting. He must have been thinking about Ellie. That at least it wasn't her.

Or Demi.

We all kept going, bullets zoomed around us. I went around the side of the building, driven by instinct. I gestured for Wil and Derek to follow me. In the back, there was a courtyard with a single man and a woman, the man holding a knife to the woman's throat.

A wide scar was on her cheek as if someone had scraped a layer of her skin off with their fingernail. The sides of her face were too tight to be natural. And black hair gleamed in the shadow of the building, her jade eyes pleading. The man holding her cracked his neck, his hair tied into a low ponytail, a lightning bolt tattoo to the side of his eye.

Miles Muro.

"I see you got started without me," he said with a smile. "Tsk, tsk. But thanks for the fair warning from the police, there, Little Adler," Muro winked, turning to Wil. "I always do like notice before being told my attendance is expected at a party."

"Fuck you, Muro," Wil said, lifting his gun, but Derek stopped him.

Muro looked at me. "You must be the missing Adler. And to think, all of this time, I thought you never left your torture cave." I readied my gun, aimed at his head, but Derek knocked the back of his hand into me too. The things I would do to him in my workroom.

"Don't shoot," Derek said, his eyes focused on the older woman.

"Thanks for always looking out for me, Derek," Muro said. "I always know I can count on you."

"It's over, Muro," Derek said, his voice loud. "Let her go."

Wil glanced at Derek, then back to Muro.

"Let her die," I muttered.

"Let her go, Muro," Derek said again, ignoring me.

Muro pressed the knife into the woman's neck, a sliver of blood collecting at the point. She gasped, holding back tears.

"This knife is the last of her worries," Muro said. "My wife here has seen much worse. Haven't you, Margot?"

She closed her eyes, her bottom lip trembling. "Yes, Master."

"Boss," Ron said on the earpiece. "We've got a problem."

"Go," I said. Muro, Derek, and Wil kept talking, everyone's barrels still trained on Muro. I turned to the sides, making sure that none of Muro's men were coming up behind us.

"There's a door here," Ron said. "It's not listed on the blueprints. And it's locked."

I didn't have time to worry about a door. For all we knew, it was a last-minute closet.

"Set the explosives," I ordered. "Then get out of there."

"Sir, I—"

"Now, Ron!"

"Yes, sir."

I adjusted my grip on the gun, listening to the bullets in the loading docks, trying to figure out which side was winning. Footsteps. I turned, then shot a man in a white uniform in the face, his body falling backward. Then an ear-splitting roar sounded from the front, knocking out the glass, brushing us in heat, so powerful it threw me on my face. After a moment, I lifted my head, waiting for the fog to subside. Derek stumbled to his feet and ran forward. Wil pushed himself up. Muro was gone, but Margot lay on her side, a knife wound on her cheek.

I glanced behind us; the window panes were empty. A quiet hum settled over the building, People yelled. Zaid came running around the side.

"Muro?" he asked.

I shook my head. "Not yet," I said. I tapped my earpiece. "Ron, what's your status?" No response. I clicked it again. "Ron, status." Again, I was met with silence, until Wil howled at Derek.

"Why the hell are you helping her?" Wil yelled. Derek held a hand to Margot's cheek to stop the bleeding, then dialed someone on his phone. Margot stared at me, then her eyes flinched back to Wil, then to Zaid, then to me again, as if she could never settle on who to trust. "Kill her. Or use her as bait. But don't help her."

"Let it go," Derek said in a warning voice.

"No," Wil said. "This is stupid. She's his wife. Don't help her."

I stood beside him. "There's no reason to keep her alive," I said.

Derek spoke to our family doctor, then hung up and turned to us: "No one is going to kill her."

Wil threw up his fists. "Why the fuck are you defending her? She's—"

"Because if Gerard doesn't defend her, then who the fuck will?" Derek demanded, his voice booming. Wil turned to me, then looked back at Derek.

"What?"

Margot stammered. "We—" she paused, "Your father and I, we—"

"They fucked and Gerard is too much of a chicken shit to own up to his mistakes," Derek said. "He might not be man enough, but I'm not going to let him ruin our family's name."

Derek's face was red, full of rage. He wanted her dead too, but it was different. He wanted Gerard to end Margot's life himself. To make Gerard face his mistakes head-on.

But something was holding Derek back.

"You mean to tell me this started because our father can't keep his dick in his pants?" Wil groaned. "You've got to be kidding me."

But it wasn't much of a surprise. Our half-brother, Ethan, was evidence of Gerard's earlier transgressions.

"This is the only way you fix loyalty and respect," Derek said. "Gerard has to own up to it," Derek stood, leaving Margot lying on the cement. "Our father claims he loves her." Derek clenched his fists, spit flying through his teeth. "Then I want him to prove it."

Wil and I fell silent, watching Derek. Anger boiled inside of him, eating him alive. The desire to kill the woman who had the power to ruin our family's name was at war with his belief that he had to respect his family, above all else. Even when his family was wrong.

"We don't even know her," Wil said.

Derek shook his head, then redialed the doctor again. "If she's meant to die, then Gerard will do it himself."

Derek spoke quietly, arranging Margot's treatment. Wil looked at me, and we stepped off to the side.

"What do we do?" Wil asked.

I stared at Derek. Out of the three of us, he was the most driven to lead and had strived to learn from the way our father had failed. Even if his leading title was part of a criminal organization, he wanted to be different. To earn respect himself.

"We stick by him," I said to Wil. "We need to trust that Derek knows what he's doing."

"But he doesn't know her," Wil said.

"Neither do we."

Derek had a strong urge to guard others, to make sure that transgressions were paid for, one that neither Wil nor I understood. But maybe we did. Wil was fiercely protective over Ellie, willing to fight his own brothers for it, and me? When it came to Demi, I—

Demi.

I wanted her to have the life that she believed in. A life where the police helped victims, when bad people were locked away for the things they did, and the good prospered. But I had forced her to become a part of our world, in hopes that it would make her stronger.

But it only reinforced that she didn't belong here. And she never would.

Demi wasn't like Margot. A girl like her shouldn't have had to endure any of this.

I clenched my fists, looking at Margot and Derek, then turned to Zaid. The rest of our combined men were moving the deceased to the vans. We had won, for now.

But anger flowed through me. How did my father have time to fuck our rival's wife, and yet growing up, he let me and my brothers wander? He never had time for any of us. Not even when I was almost beat to death. As if proving that being an enforcer was the only purpose for the second-born son.

Zaid came to my side, his eyes distant. "How many?" I asked.

"Three of mine. Yours, six."

"Ron?" I asked.

Zaid nodded. "That woman, too."

Billy. Ellie wasn't going to be happy about that. But her pain wasn't my problem. I was glad, so damn glad, that I had made Demi stay back.

My throat went dry. That was *my* problem. I cared about Demi. She should have been as disposable as Billy or Margot.

"Where do you think Muro is?" Zaid asked.

I looked up at the tall building, the cloudy sky reflected in what was left of the jagged gray windows.

"Not here," I said.

"Margot says she can put a tracking device on him," Derek said, interrupting us.

We turned to Margot. She started, "In exchange for—"

"Protection," Derek said.

I didn't trust her. How could she go from one side to the other without a fight? Derek read my mind, straightening up.

"She's fleeing for her life," he explained.

"Then how does she expect to put a tracking device on Muro?" I asked.

We both turned to Margot.

"I'll do it," she murmured, "Just please don't let him kill me or my—"

But she couldn't finish and fell into a sobbing fit.

I shook my head. That's what caring did to you.

CHAPTER 19

Demi

Maddie leaned on the counter as she took a bite, the crunch of her panini loud between the two of us in that empty apartment. Once she finished, she gestured at my bowl resting on the empty counter space.

"Are you going to eat?" she asked.

"I'm not hungry," I said.

My stomach grumbled in protest, but I stared out the windows. Axe's apartment was on the first floor, which meant we were underneath an awning, so I couldn't see much. But I could tell that the sky was dark and gray, the kind of sky that Dad would have called 'a storm from the other side.' The weather didn't help my stomach. Something was wrong. Axe wasn't okay.

What was Axe doing that was so bad, that he had left me home when he had taken me on other tasks? Why did I need a babysitter now?

Maddie cleared her throat and I turned back to the bowl. The steam hit my face. It smelled good, but I couldn't stomach it. Taking a bite seemed like too much.

"That's a lie," Maddie said, then she took another bite.

"Seriously. That breakfast sandwich was a lot," I said. She raised a brow at me, and I knew she wasn't going to let it go unless I had *at least* a bite or two. I raised the spoon to my mouth, sighing before I swallowed. The broth was addictive. It was one of those soups with spicy Italian sausage. I took a few more spoonfuls.

"See? Not so bad," she said.

I managed to finish half of the bowl. I pushed it back, then stared out the window again. At the storm from hell.

"What do you think they're doing out there?" I asked.

"Oh, Axe?" Maddie shrugged. "You know, the usual. Adler business."

She said it casually as if it wasn't a big deal to her. How could she be so flippant about the mob? Had she grown up with them?

"How long have you known them?" I asked.

"A year or two now, not sure. I don't keep track," she said. "But Wil hired me to clean his penthouse, and once his brothers saw how well I took care of his place, they hired me too. Between the three of them, and the occasional job at the Adler House, I'm pretty set. They don't pay too badly either."

I would hope not. I assumed they would be flush with cash, considering what they did for a living. But it was hard to tell in Axe's apartment. He didn't even have a dining table.

But that still didn't explain her blasé attitude.

"Doesn't it bother you?" I asked.

"What?"

"The—" I didn't know how to put it without sounding crass, but none of my words seemed to work. "I don't know. The mafia stuff."

She lifted her shoulders again, then started putting our disposable cutlery into a pile between us.

"You know, all families have their own skeletons," she said. "Sometimes, they're just secrets, and sometimes, they're actually skeletons." She snickered. "In their case, it's a backyard full of bones."

I could agree with that. Dad had kept his association with the Adlers a secret for all of my life. If I had known about it, how different would my life be? Who would I be now? Would I have killed as a kid, just like Axe?

Would I have turned out cold like him too?

"And what about yours?" I asked. Maddie blinked, holding her chin steady. "You know. What skeletons does your family hide away?"

"Ah," she sighed. "Don't know. I hardly ever talk to most of them." I nodded. That would be my future now too. "And yours?"

"Same," I said.

I didn't have any family now. Maybe that was part of why I was drawn to Axe. He knew my father in such an intimate way, a side of him that I knew nothing about. If I held onto Axe long enough, would everything start to make sense?

Would my life *ever* make sense?

After I helped Maddie clear our takeout from the counter, she started cleaning the apartment. There wasn't much to do, but she did it all anyway: vacuumed the carpet, mopped the tiles, wiped the counters, cleaned the sinks, the toilets. I offered to help, but she wouldn't let me, so I stayed in the living area, letting her do her thing, chatting whenever something came up.

Just as she was working in the kitchen, a shadow crossed the back window of the living room. I watched for a second, not sure if I had actually seen anything, but then it crossed again, this time going the opposite direction. With the cloud cover, it was hard to tell what it was.

"Did you see that?" I asked.

Maddie put down her rag and looked out the window. "What are you—"

Then it happened again. That same shadow. Round, like a hunched over person.

"That's weird," she said. "Maybe it's Axe's neighbor?"

"Not a neighbor. They're usually smoking or yelling."

We stood there for a while, watching the shadow walk back and forth. It was as if they were hunting. Dark hair. Beady eyes. A bubbled chin.

"Screw it," I said, going to the door. "I'm going to see what's going on."

"Demi," Maddie said. "Stay in here. I told Axe—"

I went around the building. The back alley stretched, full of concrete, bicycles, and tiny plots of white and gray rocks. But it was empty.

Where was he?

Then a hand covered my mouth, a mildew scent penetrating me. A thin film of dirt brushed from his clothes onto my skin. I tried to scream, but he held my chest tighter. I couldn't breathe. The rain came down, beating into us like pebbles, echoing in the alley. I swung my elbows, but his grip was firm. He breathed into my ear, hauling me back.

A gunshot sounded and the man let go of me. I fell to the ground. Maddie held a gun with a silencer, her elbows straight. The storm was so loud, you could barely hear her gun. Three more soft explosions, then nothing.

"Are you all right?" Maddie asked, racing to me. I looked back; the alley was empty. He was gone. My heart pounded.

"Did you get him?" I asked.

She shook her head. "But he's gone now. And you're safe."

Maddie helped me inside; I could barely walk with the adrenaline. What did that man want? After we dried off, we sat on the floor, facing the back window.

The rain pounded into the apartment. You could hear it pummeling the entire building, echoing in the walkways between the units. I crossed my arms in front of my chest, while Maddie told stories that I didn't listen to. The entire space darkened. A dark figure crept across the back again, but this time, it stopped in front of the window across from us. I couldn't tell if it was a person or a shadow.

Axe's van pulled up, the headlights visible from the front window. Maddie grabbed her bag.

"Don't forget to tell Axe," she said. "Good luck."

Axe nodded at Maddie, then came through the door.

"What happened?" I asked. He closed the front door shut behind him, storming to the bathroom. There was dust caked in his fingernails and hair, and though it looked like he had rinsed his face, he was still oily. There wasn't any blood on his clothes, but all that meant was that he had probably changed outfits. He ripped off his shirt, and I saw the flash of his hatchet tattoo, but no visible wounds. The tension released in my chest.

He closed the bathroom door in my face. I stood there, waiting. The shower started, and the splash of the water against the tub seemed abrupt, like he was scrubbing away his skin. I waited in the bedroom, sitting on the bed, and by the time he came out, wrapped in a towel, his skin was red, some patches darker than others. Scratched in places. Sweat beaded on his neck and face. Now that the dust was gone, I could see that his face was scraped up.

"What happened?" I asked. Axe said nothing. "You take me everywhere with you, and then suddenly, you leave me at home with a babysitter?"

"Are you a baby?" he asked. I shook my head. "Then she's not a babysitter."

"You made her come here to *watch* over me like I'm a child."

"She's supposed to clean," he said, running a hand through his damp hair.

"You know it's more than that."

"Fuck, Demi. What more do you want? There's a war going on and I'm not going to be able to think straight unless I know you're—"

He stopped suddenly, his words slamming into his chest, making him halt.

Say it, I thought. *Say it. Admit it. You do care. Just like I care.*

"You don't have to do this," I said, my voice quiet. "All of this for the war? You don't have to do it." I stood up, stepping closer to him. "You can choose to do the right thing, Axe."

"It wasn't my choice to be born into the mafia," he scowled, then leaned away from me. "I didn't choose to be scouted by your father. I didn't choose to live that day."

Heat boiled in my chest. My dad wasn't the enemy. Axe had to take responsibility for his own choices. He had made that call.

I would never win this argument, but I needed to understand. To know why he chose this life. Because I cared for him, so what did that say about me? I had killed someone for him. And deep down, I knew I would do it again. I wanted to help him, in whatever way I could. Even if it meant arguing his choice to death.

Because in the end, I had chosen Axe.

"You chose the knife," I said. "You told me yourself. Dad gave you the option." I put a hand on his arm. "You didn't have to."

He shook me away as if he couldn't stand to be beside me. "And so what if I choose this life? I've told you, Demi. You shouldn't stick around to see if I turn out to be a nice guy. Because I'm not, and I never will be." He grabbed my arms, holding me tight, forcing me to lock eyes with him. "There's nothing left inside of my soul. Absolutely nothing. I made sure of that."

His eyes were glossy with anger, ripping apart what little I had left. But I saw it there. He hated that he cared, but he did. He cared about his family. And he also cared about me. And not because of some stupid promise he made to my dad.

"Why was Maddie saying to tell me?" he asked, still beaming into my face.

My gut wrenched. He wasn't going to like this.

"There was a guy," I said.

"A guy?"

I shrugged. "Behind the building."

"Demi," he scowled. I swallowed a gulp.

"He may have attacked me."

He clenched his fists, then brought them to the wall, knocking a dent into the wall. "Get your shit," he growled. My heart leaped in my chest. I grabbed my bag and Axe took the other one and the backpack out of the closet. "Let's go."

"Where?"

"To the workroom."

This time, inside of the workroom, he got a blowup mattress from one of the cabinets, then filled it until it was a full size. He crossed his arms, then pointed to the bed.

"Sleep," he said. Was I a dog, now?

"That's it? That's what we're doing?" I crossed my arms. "You can still choose the right thing. Call the police—"

"I am choosing *this*," his voice boomed. He grabbed my face. "Don't you see, Demi? Being in this workroom? I am choosing to be here. It's one of the safest places I know." He pointed to the door. "I don't see you leaving."

I stared at the door. It was right there.

"I could," I said, "if I wanted to."

"But you're choosing to stay here."

We stared at each other for a moment, unsure of what to say. My eyes fell down, looking at the ground between our feet: the scuffed floor, the trails of dried brown blood, the scratches in the cement. Axe went to the side of the room and started sharpening one of his knives, the slick slide of the metal like a pendulum swinging back and forth. His chest breathed in deeply, then exhaled, resuming his calm rhythm.

I could have walked out. Could have left this hell hole and never looked back. He was right.

So why couldn't I make myself leave?

There was so much here that I wasn't willing to let go. Not until I understood.

CHAPTER 20

Axe

Once Demi was asleep, I left a note on the table: *Out. Back later.* I nodded at my men waiting on each corner of the workroom, then set the alarm for the place. There was no way anyone was getting anywhere near Demi.

On the way back to the apartment, I armed myself with more than necessary. I wanted to torture this man, but I knew I couldn't indulge; it needed to be quick. We had more pressing matters to figure out than some stupid henchman following Demi around. In the darkness of the apartment, I waited, watching the sky get darker as night settled in above the storm clouds. A man, dressed in black with a large hood over his head, hovered by the back window. Once he moved away, I moved underneath that window and waited. A few minutes later, his shadow crossed again. I leaped up and shot my hand through the glass, grabbing him by the throat.

He groaned. I pulled him down to the ground, kneeling on his chest. No one fucked with what was mine. And you sure as hell didn't fuck with my girl. It didn't matter if she wasn't and would never truly be mine. No one would ever be allowed to fuck with her.

I knocked him in the face, each blow harder than the last, my knuckles numb to the pain, until he laid still, his eyes swollen shut. I took my knife and brought it down over his stomach, splitting it open, and he coughed up blood, gurgling to the side, trying hard not to drown. I stuck my hand into his stomach, the warmth sucking me in. I knotted his intestines in my fingers, then pulled them out like a ball of yarn.

He opened his mouth, trying to say something, but couldn't. And I didn't say a word. Those bloodshot eyes barely opened, and

I held up his insides, making him look at them, then twisted them around, watching each convulsion of his body with glee until his eyes went blank.

It felt good. Better than it should have.

My hands were wet, covered with his blood, and cooled by the still air. I stood up and kicked him to the side. A double M was tattooed on his neck. This war needed to end.

I got the cleaver from the holster, then brought it down on his arms. That sense of serenity washed over me, though it was different this time. I wasn't used to this… Whatever it was. This insatiable need to make sure Demi was safe. Hating those who hurt her. I needed that space where nothing mattered. Where I could live or die and nothing would change. I hadn't had that since Shep died. Since Demi came into my life.

Right as I dismembered the other arm, my phone buzzed. I pulled it out, wiping a smear of red across the screen.

"Margot placed the tracking device," Derek said.

"That was—" I paused, wiping my hands on a cloth, "—fast."

"We'll keep an eye on his location, make sure it's accurate." I brought down the cleaver in a loud *thwack!* Chopping off one leg, then the other. *Thwack!* "We'll see what happens. Make a move soon."

"Soon," I said.

"The last time," he said, resignation in his voice.

I hoped so. I hadn't expected Muro to send more of his men into our territory after how it had gone down today. But Muro was a beast.

And so was I.

We hung up. I wanted to enjoy tearing the corpse to pieces, but I knew time was precious. I had to be economical. Once he was in transport size, I brought in a barrel from the work van, getting him ready for acid. I couldn't enjoy torturing him, but I could watch his body burn. That was one indulgence I would allow.

When I returned to the workroom, I disabled the alarm. My men stayed posted as I entered. Demi immediately sat up.

"Where were you?"

I didn't answer. I went to the sink to wash my hands again, better this time. Though I had gotten most of it off in the apartment, the water still ran pink. I would have to call the landlord to explain the broken window. Luckily, he knew who I was and didn't mind the protection that came along with a mafia tenant. Still, no one liked dealing with maintenance requests.

"Was it that man from the apartment?"

I stayed silent, which was an answer itself.

"You killed him, didn't you?" Demi asked. "You did. Did you know his name? Why he was there?"

I wiped my hands on a black towel, then threw it in the corner of the room.

"I am what I am, Demi," I said as calmly as I could. "This is in my blood." I pointed to the wall of cabinets. "Do you know how many tools are in there because *I* knew they would make people talk? Tools your father didn't dare to think of." I slammed my palm against the wall. "Unthinkable ways to hurt people so that all they do is try to stay alive, and every time, I kill them anyway. I chose this."

"Your brothers didn't," she said. I stared at her, those stormy gray eyes watching me, flickering back and forth. What the fuck did this have to do with my brothers? "Derek doesn't enforce. Neither does Wil. He runs the gambling hall," she laughed. "But you? You choose to enforce. To kill people. You—"

I punched the cabinet behind her, denting it in a large crash. Seeing red. Everything painted red.

For the first time, Demi's eyes widened at me. Her pupils were dilated, and that rancid scent of fear came into my nose. I breathed it in, taking a deep, slow breath. Finally.

I had almost hurt her. I couldn't let that happen ever again.

So I did the only thing that made sense.

I grabbed her hips, then forced her down to her knees. I fisted her hair, digging my fingers in tight, until she cried out and I yanked her head back. A primal noise erupted from her throat. I twisted her neck to make her look at me, sneering down at her. With one hand, I unbuttoned and unzipped my pants, pulling out my heavy cock, never taking my eyes off of hers. Then I leaned down, shoving my hands into her pants, her folds slick with heat. My cock twitched.

"This will shut you up," I growled.

"Screw you," she hissed.

I slapped her face, twice, three times, until she opened up her mouth, and I shoved my fingers into her throat, making her suck off her juices. I couldn't get used to this—couldn't let myself. But I plunged the head of my cock deep into her throat because it was the only thing I could do. Because I should have killed her. I should have known that silence beyond this earth would be better for her than suffocating inside of mine. Demi couldn't see that there was no morality when it came to me. There was only death. I had to teach her that she needed to live her life, go to college like she wanted, make the world a better place. Not drown down here with me.

I pressed her against the wall, forcing her to stay kneeling, then leaned on the wall above her. I fucked her mouth. Her big eyes stared up at me, holding back tears. My stomach dropped, my dick starting to go limp. I should have enjoyed it. Should have licked the tears off of her cheeks. So what was I doing?

You chose the knife.

You choose to enforce. To kill people.

You can still choose the right thing.

Her words hit me because she was right. I had chosen this. All of it. And I had done the one thing I had sworn would never happen: she mattered to me. The Demi from before all of this, and the Demi now. Every part of her mattered.

And I needed to let her go.

I pumped my dick in my hand, staring into those eyes. I had to come, had to force myself to enjoy her pain, but no matter how hard I fucked myself, I couldn't stay hard. Then she pummeled her fists against me—my shins, my stomach, my thighs—anything she could reach. And I kept fucking myself, watching her do it, the tiny bursts of pressure lighting my nervous system on fire, her violence finally pushing me closer.

Hurt me, I thought. *You know I deserve it. You're better than me. Better than anything I could ever know.*

She stood up hastily and pulled at my neck, her lips open, ready to force her tongue inside of my mouth, but I held back. Kissing would be an admission. And I was close, so damn close, to letting her go. She howled with rage in her eyes, and the rejection filled my blood with lightning and I came, shooting my seed on her stomach, her disheveled clothes, getting it on her hands. She growled and kneeled down, sticking out her tongue to lick it all up, but I held the back of her head, not letting her. I loved seeing her like that, desperate for my come. But suddenly she lurched forward and bit me, her teeth grazing the middle of my shaft. My cock still pulsed with come, filling her throat. Her teeth couldn't stop me.

Then I let go of my grip, letting her find her balance. She shuddered, her eyes focused on my cock, still partly erect, the bruise on the shaft a shade darker red than the rest. She closed her lips, stunned at what she had done.

Once she was on her feet, I fixed my pants. I turned away, going to the sink.

This was nothing. And it always would be.

"Tomorrow, I'll take you back to the college," I said over my shoulder. PGU was a few hours away, almost all the way to Brackston, but I would take the drive if it meant that she was safe. Safe from me.

"What?" she asked, her shoulders sinking. "Why?"

"I'll have a team watching you from afar." I turned toward the door. There was nothing more to discuss. "They'll make sure you're safe."

She grabbed my hand, whipping me around.

"No," she said. "That's not an answer. Why, Axe? Why *now*? If that was always an option, then I deserve to know why."

I stared at her, letting her breathe erratically. My jaw tight, my facial expression never changed. As if this didn't affect me. As if I didn't care who she was.

I wanted her to believe that.

"Is it because I'm not good enough for the mafia?" she asked, tilting her head. Good enough for the mafia? That should never have been a goal in her mind. She was too ethical, too righteous, and those words proved how I had ruined her. She needed her view of the world, back to where everything was wrong or right. "Is it because I make you question your morals?" She pushed my chest. "Listen to yourself, Axe. That means you do have moral logic inside of you. You know that what I'm saying bothers you."

She was panting, her cheeks flushed, her gray eyes pinning me down. There was beauty and rage and lust inside of her, and I wanted so badly to take a hold of it, to twist it until her body convulsed, to never let it go, to know that I would be by her side, guaranteeing her safety.

But these emotions weren't real. I couldn't allow myself to feel. And I would never let Demi come before my truth. I would never be the man she needed me to be.

"I'm not you, Demi," I said quietly. I gestured around the space. Death was always on my side, and one day, it would swallow me too. "This is who I am. Don't let me kill you too."

"If you wanted to kill me, you would have done it ages ago." She tossed her hands up around the room. "Don't you get it? I'm not the girl I was before Dad died. You changed me, and for once in your life, I want you to admit that you can change too." She bared her teeth. "My past was full of lies. This is me now."

"It's not you," I growled. "It can never be you." I wouldn't let it. "You need to go back. Live your life."

"I would rather die than go back to that life."

Those words hung in the air, filling the space. I closed my mouth. Immediately, she clenched her palms, knowing the gravity of what she had said.

I took her by the hair, throwing her back into that small cage. Locked the wooden slats. Turned out the lights, listening to her scream my name as I headed out.

"Axe!" she yelled. "Axe! Come back here! Don't you dare—"

I closed the door behind me, acknowledging each of my men. Then I grabbed my shovel.

If she would rather die than leave me behind, then I would show her what that meant.

CHAPTER 21

Demi

Eventually, I fell asleep, but I didn't feel rested. The haze of unconsciousness was groggy and confusing; every time I woke up, I was stuck in the timeless warp of that workroom. My back and knees ached from being cramped up. I wasn't sure what was going on. Was he going to leave me locked in the cage until the war was over? How long until we could go back to normal?

What was normal?

I didn't know anymore. But I knew I believed in Axe. There was a heart stuck inside of him somewhere, and that heart was willing to fight. At least for me.

The door opened. The light flicked on, the buzz of electricity filling the room. Axe kneeled down at the cage. He removed the locks, then stood, looking down his nose at me. His arms and pants were covered in dirt. I crawled out, standing, too nervous to stretch. Then he pointed at the door.

"What now?" I asked. He stared at me, his eyes full of darkness. "Do I need my bags?"

He didn't give me an answer. Chills went down my spine. I looked at my bags on the floor and went to get them.

"You won't be needing those," he said in a low, controlled voice. I tilted my head, but he pointed to the door again, waiting for me.

Outside, it was darker than I expected. The first thin sliver of morning light had poked over the horizon, the trees blocking some of it, casting the world in a soft blue. I turned toward the Adler House, but Axe motioned to the woods. I raised a brow, but Axe's expression never changed. I trusted him to know what we were doing.

The leaves on the ground swallowed my shoes, and it smelled like earth. Rich, gritty dirt, and damp leaves. The deeper we went, the eerier it felt. No matter which direction I looked, the woods never seemed to end. A lone bird sang a song as we passed. The air was heavy with moisture, but the temperature from the ground kept us cool.

We stepped over a tree trunk lying on its side. In the middle of the trees and vines, there was a clearing with a hole in the middle. I went around it, to avoid falling in.

"Stop," Axe said.

I turned around slowly. He had his arms crossed, and behind him, there was a shovel leaning against one of the trees, a set of pig bones piled to the side of it. I tried not to let the situation get to me. It was just a hole. In the middle of the woods. There was no reason to think anything bad.

Yet.

"Take off your clothes," Axe said.

A flush of heat prickled over my skin, but I pinched my teeth together. I couldn't let this get to me.

"Why?" I asked, but Axe didn't say a word. I stayed still, trying to wait it out. Then he clenched his fist.

"We can do this the hard way," he said. I shook my head.

Once I had my clothes tucked under my hands, he gestured at the fallen tree trunk, and I put the clothes down on top. He motioned at my shoes, so I took them off too.

Then Axe pointed to the hole.

I looked around—at the trees, at the deep blue sky above us, in the direction of the Adler House—but I couldn't see his parents' home. A tried desperately to find it, as if it would help save me somehow. But there was nothing that would give me any comfort. I held my arms around myself, a breeze rustling the leaves in a soft murmur. Axe's eyes were as hard as onyx.

"Get in, Demi," he said.

I didn't move.

"Or I will put you in myself."

I bit my lip. "Are you getting in too?"

He waited for me to obey, not answering my question. I clenched my fists, then undid my fingers, one by one. What kind of game was this? I sucked in a breath, then turned, crouching down, and lowered myself into the hole, then fell a few more feet to the bottom of the pit. The sides of the hole were steep. I couldn't see the sky between the trees.

"Axe?" I asked. "What's going on?"

The hole was wide enough that I could lay down and spread my arms, but not big enough for someone like Axe. A clump of dirt hit my cheek, rolling down my shoulder. I stared at it. Had it fallen from the walls? The hairs on the back of my neck stood up. I looked up again, trying to see over the edge. I didn't hear or see anything.

"Are you still there?" I asked. "Axe?"

Then the dirt rained down. A few specks got in my eyes and I shielded my face. Then another assault of the dirt. Spraying me with the earth. Axe leaned over the edge, then took another shovel full. I hid my face again, covering my eyes, but the dirt didn't stop coming.

"What the hell are you doing?" I yelled.

The dirt hit my cheeks. He moved around the hole, then sent another shovel full, this time hitting me directly on the back.

"Damn it, Axe. Why are you doing this?" I shouted. "Let me out of here."

"You said you would rather die than go back to that life," he said. Another shovel full, this time hitting my chest so hard that I stepped back to catch myself. My skin was covered in streaks of brown earth. "I'm giving you that option."

"This is not what I meant," I said.

He went back to shoveling. My feet were almost covered, so I had to get on top of the new layer of earth.

"Don't do this, Axe," I said. Still, he didn't stop. I covered my eyes, letting the dirt hit my shoulders and chest, then I went to the opposite edge of him, grabbing onto the walls, trying to climb out.

"If you try to climb out," he said, "or move on top of the dirt, I will knock you unconscious."

And I knew he would keep his word. The grooves on the sides of my tongue were still there, might be there forever. I took a step away from the wall. He went to the side and let the dirt fall on top of my head.

"This isn't fair, Axe," I muttered.

All of those times that I had thought that he wanted to protect me, that we had an actual connection, it was nothing more than waiting for this. He wanted to get rid of me. Losing me wouldn't hurt Axe. He would never love me.

"Why?" I yelled. "Why, Axe?"

"It was always going to end like this," he muttered, "We both knew it."

Tears formed in my eyes. As hard as I tried to blink them away, once I felt another shovel full of dirt hit my stomach and arms, they slipped down, streaking muddy paths down my cheeks.

I shivered. "You've got to stop this," I said.

Another shovel full, each clump of dirt like white noise filling my brain. This time, when I saw Axe, he had removed his shirt, his shoulders and arms bulging with veins, sweat covering his body, that hatchet tattoo streaked with dirt.

Another shovel full. And then another.

"You don't want to kill me," I whispered, but I didn't know if it was true. I thought about my words: *I would rather die than go back to that life.* I had said those words in anger, in frustration. Because I knew that life didn't exist anymore. I would never be the same Demi who wanted to bring justice to the world. Everything felt wrong. Like I couldn't tell what I wanted, because I didn't see the world like I once did. And still, I believed that even Axe, the enforcer for the mafia, a man whose only job was to kill for his family, had a heart in there, somewhere.

But maybe that was wrong too.

"Fuck you!" I cried. "Fuck everything, you monster. Why don't you kill me already?"

Still, that same pattern. The swift movements of his arms, the quick step forward. More dirt. He had done this before.

How many people had he buried alive?

I must have looked like a monster too, covered in dirt and muck, tears going down my face. Only little spots of my skin stood out. And still, another shovel full of dirt. It was past my ankles now.

"Don't do this, Axe," I screamed, my voice going hoarse. For the next shovel, he stared at me for a moment, then went back to what he was doing. Another. Then another. The beads of dirt hitting my skin like the darts of water from a pressure hose. It was up to my shins, and still, he threw another shovel. Another. This couldn't be it. This couldn't be the way I died.

"I want to live," I whispered. Then I looked up at the edges of the hole. Louder, this time: "I want to live."

He paused, his shovel suspended in the air, then he tossed down the dirt.

"Not good enough," he said.

"I want to live. Fuck!" I raked my fingers across my thighs. My breathing was close to hyperventilation. Another shovel full. "Please, Axe," I cried. But still. More dirt hit my face. "I want to live," I screamed. He glanced over the edge, but never stopped his task. "I would rather live," I cried, my voice hoarse, "I would rather live. I would rather live. I would rather—"

Axe jumped into the pit, his boots hitting the earth in a loud thud. I closed my eyes, readying myself for his blow, but he pulled me out of the dirt, scooping me up by the ass, holding me against him.

"I would rather live," I cried, shaking in his arms. "I would rather live. I would rather live. I want to live, Axe. I do. I want to—"

And he kissed me so hard that I thought I might pass out. His lips were angry and passionate and completely locked on mine, shutting me up in that embrace, hungry and possessive, as if he wanted to show me that this, all of this, was because of me. It didn't matter that I was covered in dirt, that he was as filthy as I was, because Axe needed me, and that was enough. It wasn't about a promise; *he* wanted to keep me alive.

When I opened my eyes, his gaze was locked on mine, as if he was fascinated, watching me as we kissed. Hastily, he unbuttoned and unzipped his pants, pressing me against the wall of dirt, some clumps crumbling between us, and he looked me in the eyes, watching my face as he stopped holding himself back from me. He thrust his cock inside of me. I grimaced, biting my lip. But I was glad for the pain. It was real. It was real, and it was mine, and it was what this world gave me. A chance at life. A chance at pain. A chance at something real.

Axe held me there, pinned with his body against the dirt wall, and he moved his hips, throwing himself against me.

"Never forget this," he grunted. "Never forget what a gift this life is."

And how could I? Everything had changed so rapidly that I couldn't tell what my old life was anymore, and I knew, even if I had to leave Axe behind, that I wanted more of this world. The one we were living in, inside of that moment. I didn't want to die. I wanted to live. Because dying would mean that there would never be this again: his touch against my skin, his breath on my neck as he panted, his body rapt with just as much desire as mine, our bodies caked with mud and grime as he fucked me like he needed me, like it gave him life, because maybe it did. Maybe he needed to understand too. He was showing me what it meant to live, to have a chance at life, but he wanted to feel it all, to know the gift for himself.

The shadow from the sides of the hole swallowed us up, but his black eyes shined with the light beginning to filter in through the trees. I pressed my lips to his, and he didn't pull away. He stared into me and I savored him: his velvet tongue, the groove in his bottom lip, his slick teeth, his tongue sliding against mine, wrestling with those scars he had given me. His cock pulsed inside of me, so big and unforgiving that tears welled in my eyes, and I couldn't tell if it was from the physical pain or the emotional release. But I wanted it all. I wanted him in all of the ways. Biting me. Hurting me. Caressing me. Fucking me. Hating me. Teaching me. I wanted his passion, his love, and I knew in my heart that it was mine. That Axe needed me too.

"I love you," I cried, staring into him. His hips kept moving, but his eyes blinked, still locked on mine. "I love you. I do. I love you so fucking much."

He closed his lips, his rhythm hurried. But his eyes studied me, searching for the truth. He was a monster who had done unspeakable things, but he wasn't *lost*. He was here. Here with me. Inside of a hole in the ground where together, we could climb out. He had shown me the darkness and given me light, given me hope, given me *choice*, when I thought I had nothing left.

"I love you, Axe," I repeated, knowing he wouldn't say it back. With those words, he twitched, his cock pulsing as he hammered into me. Then he gushed inside of me and I held him tight, squeezing my muscles, clamping my arms and legs around him. And his eyes never left me. He wanted to see me. To understand.

And I saw him too. I saw all of him, and I didn't run away.

CHAPTER 22

Axe

After we both took a long shower, we drove to Pebble Garden University. The only thing I could do right then, was to get Demi to Pebble Garden. Deep breaths in, then out, a steady pattern, so that she would never know what this did to me. Demi stared out the passenger window, her pale blue and purple hair faded almost to white, her dark roots growing in.

We pulled into the parking lot next to the tennis courts. I rolled down my window and the sound of the ball and the racquets filled the van. Bicycle bells. Students talking. A few young adults leaned against one of the buildings, a few of them smoking, the others gesturing around. And down the way, a slackline was spread between two trees, while a group of fit and thin men took turns balancing on it, each time checking to see if the women reading at the park bench were watching. An acoustic guitar strummed in the distance.

This was where she was meant to be. Where things were simple. Where the biggest problem she would face was whether or not she could fit some slackline in before her next class. Demi tossed her hair behind her back, her PGU sweatshirt in her lap. She unzipped her backpack, stuffing in the sweatshirt, then putting *Crime and Evidence* on top, then closed it back up. She held the bags in her hands but then froze in place. Didn't open the door. I made sure it was unlocked, and once I confirmed that, her shoulders slumped, leaning back against the seat.

"You don't want me, do you?" she asked. I refused to answer. She sighed deeply, then turned to me. "I already missed most of this semester." She looked down at her bags. "I've failed those classes by now. And because of that, I'm probably not enrolled anymore. So I—"

"Wil talked to the dean," I said. I kept a stoic face, watching as her expression shifted from disappointed to confused. "They worked it out." And I had paid for the rest of her tuition and board for the next four years. Made it so that her future bills would come to me. "You can stay on campus, audit the rest of the term. Start next semester."

Her eyes lowered and my gut twisted into knots. This would have been easier if she fought me. If she tried to stop me. I would have been able to dismiss her.

But this wasn't like that. Even if she didn't like it, she knew, as well as I did, that this was for her own good.

"What about the promise?" she asked.

I thought about marriage. The idea seemed like a fantasy now, a woman as young as Demi, with so much life in front of her, who believed in justice, marrying me. A criminal. I killed for a living, and no matter how hard she tried to change me, I still felt no remorse.

And at the same time, I clenched my fists, as if I could grab that fantasy out of thin air and make it mine. Demi had unlocked a part of me that I didn't understand. The part that may not have cared for others, but cared for her. Only her.

But I couldn't do that. I wouldn't let myself. Keeping her here was her best option for survival. She couldn't be with me.

"I will make sure you're safe," I said. I couldn't decide whether to put one of my best men on her security or to leave her well-being completely to myself. If I did it myself, I knew I would be too tempted to see her again. And this? Whatever this was? It made me weak. Made me forget about my purpose. Made me care about things that didn't matter.

And yet I knew I would never trust another soul to watch her like I could. As soon as the war was over, I would take full control of her care.

"If you see me or my men," I turned for a second, watching the tennis game through the fence, then turned back to her, "Stay away.

Don't speak to us. We'll watch over you. But it's not safe for you to get close to us again."

"Axe?" she asked.

I turned forward, concentrating on anything but her.

"When will I see you again?" she asked. Her voice was small, like a child's, as if she couldn't bear to hear the answer. And I couldn't look at her like that. There was too much that she needed, things that I wasn't capable of giving. Even once the war was over, I knew our truth. She would never be safe with me. And that's what I needed for her. Safety.

"You won't," I said.

"Why are you doing this?" she asked, her tone hurt. I turned to her then, her quivering lips, her eyes glossy and full of loss. "Why?"

She deserved an answer.

"Because it would be easier for both of us if I killed you," I said.

I leaned across and opened her car door, then sat back in my seat, my hands resting on the steering wheel, waiting for her to go. I knew I would never hurt her. I would never let myself.

Which was why she had to go.

She didn't move. I turned the key. The engine started.

"So this is it?" she said, her tone rising in anger and strength. "You're giving up, just like that?"

"I'm giving you a chance to live," I said. I waved a dismissive hand.

Still, Demi refused to leave.

"Get out of the car," I said.

She stared at me, but then she finally grabbed her bags, pulling toward the open door. With her feet on the ground, she looked up at me, tiny and full of rage.

"You know, yesterday," she said. "I meant every word."

I love you, Axe. I do. I love you so fucking much.

But it didn't matter what she said.

"If this is what's better for you, then I'll go, Axe. But only if it's better for you. Not for me."

I gripped the steering wheel so hard it crunched under my grip.

"Go, Demi," I said sternly. Go. Be yourself. Go *live*.

Demi sucked in a breath, then closed the door and turned to the school. I watched her go past the tennis courts, the buildings, those slackliners, until she was smaller than a speck of dust. She never once looked back.

I reversed out of the parking space, leaving the university. Once I was on the road back to Sage City, I called one of my men to watch over her, and he said he would head up as soon as he finished his drops. I told myself that this was supposed to happen; this was good for Demi. I may not have been marrying her like Shep wanted, but she would be alive. *Safe*. Able to grow and love and survive.

I went to the Adler House. Gerard, for once in his life, was supposed to meet with the three of us to discuss the final phase of the war. My ears pounded at the thought. If it weren't for the family legacy, he would have been thrown out of the business by now, but the lucky bastard survived on shared blood alone.

But when I got to the study, only Derek and Wil were waiting. What a surprise. The two of them straightened as I burst in. A fire roared to the side. I wanted to smother it until it was ash.

I took a seat on the couch. "We're just waiting on Gerard, then," Derek said.

"If he shows up," I muttered.

Wil turned to me. "Whoa, there," Wil said, shaking his head. "You actually spoke up about it. You all right?"

This was *why* I didn't talk. They made a big deal out of nothing. I grunted, crossing my arms. If I held onto the lack of response, they'd back off.

But not today.

"Michael said you went to PGU this morning," Derek said. "What's in PGU?"

Where the hell had Derek been? Demi had been wearing that damned PGU sweatshirt almost the entire time she was here.

Then again, I had kept her in a cage.

"I took Demi back," I said.

"That's Shep's daughter, right?" Wil asked. "She was at the wedding?"

It's not like he went full-mafia-style-wedding on his big day. He kept it small on purpose. And he still didn't know her name? I wanted to shake him until he remembered her damned name. *Demi Walcott, you fucking idiot.* Adrenaline rushed through my body.

"Her name," I said through my teeth, "is Demi Walcott."

Wil stared at me. I guess I wasn't being as subtle as I hoped.

"What's the deal with you and her?" he asked.

There was no me and her. *That* was what the deal was.

"She's a liability," I said.

The two of them nodded. The fire cracked in the corner, filling the silence hanging in the air. Which pissed me off even more, knowing that they were holding back, trying to respect my silence. I clenched the sides of the couch.

"Out with it," I barked. "Say it. Get it out now."

Derek took a deep breath. "It's been a while since you've been like this," he said. "You haven't been as..." He turned to Wil. "What's the best way to put it?"

"Angry," Wil said, that stupid grin on his face.

Derek gave him a look. "I was looking for the euphemism."

"Axe doesn't need us to sugarcoat it," Wil shrugged. "He isn't stupid. He knows what we're talking about."

"You were the one who told me she doesn't need to be in our world," I muttered, glaring at Derek.

"Until I realized how she changed you," Derek said.

I was getting angrier the longer this conversation went on. As if the rage had been suppressed ever since I met Demi, and now was coming back in full force, ready to boil over and burn everything to the ground.

But this was good. This was why she needed to go. I couldn't be around her like this.

"She must have been good for you," Derek said.

What the hell was his problem? "She's a good person," I said. "She'd be good for anyone."

"But she took the edge off," Wil said. "It's good to have a connection, especially with a woman."

He said that as if a monster like me wasn't supposed to connect with anyone. I clenched my fists.

The two of them glanced at each other, then looked at me. I knew that look. I wanted to punch it right off of their faces. But I knew they were right. Demi loved me, but that didn't mean I was capable of returning that love. If I killed her, this would all be over. There would be no chance to debate the effect Demi had on me, because she would be gone.

But my stupid brain wouldn't let me kill her. Couldn't do it. There wasn't supposed to be anyone to protect beyond my family. I was supposed to be able to kill anyone and everyone. So why couldn't I look her in her steel-gray eyes and put a bullet in her head?

Fuck.

"She's a liability," he shrugged. "You're right about that. But once this war is over—" he turned to me, "—will she still be a liability?"

"Just fuck her already," Wil said.

I railed a fist at the table, instead Wil's head. The wood cracked in a loud snap.

"All right," Wil whistled. "Point taken."

Right then, Gerard entered, running a hand through his peppered hair. I clenched my fists all over again, the blood pounding hot in my ears. If it wasn't for his stupid ass, we wouldn't be in this war. And then, maybe then, I could...

But what could I do? What would protect Demi?

I needed to focus. My family's legacy was at stake, and until we took down Muro, nothing would last. Gerard may have aggravated the situation by fucking Muro's wife, but Muro always had it out for expansion. It was simply more personal now, for all of us.

Including me. Our family was on the line. And if a person wasn't family, they were no one. Like Shep had taught me.

What was Shep teaching me now?

"All right," Derek said. "The politicians aren't on his side," Derek made eye contact with Wil and me. "But the police are still an issue."

"Is that only in Brackston or surrounding areas too?" Gerard asked.

"We have Brackston confirmed," Wil said.

"And his source of funds are locked out," Derek nodded at Wil and me again, referring to the man Demi had decapitated in the hotel, "Now, we've taken over the warehouses," Derek said. Wil nodded. "All that's left are the headquarters and Muro himself."

"Do we still have enough people?" Wil asked. "I thought they were all killed the last time we tried to take them down."

"Not all of them," Derek said.

"I told you three I didn't want a blood bath," Gerard said.

I turned to him, my eyes bulging from their sockets.

"It's too late now," I said.

He stared at me. "Watch your tone, son," he said.

"You fucked Muro's wife," I said. "Watch your dick."

Gerard raised the back of his hand to backhand me and I blocked it, about to punch him in the face. Derek jumped in between us and Wil pulled me back.

"Damn it, you two!" Derek said. "Enough! We've got too much shit to deal with to add family problems on top of it."

"You're a piece of shit leader," I shouted. "You're a joke. Derek runs this place better than—"

"And I can end you as easily as I created you," Gerard said.

"And I will kick the shit out of both of you if you don't get it together," Derek said. "You," he pointed to Gerard, leering into his face, "Own up to what you did like a man. And you," Derek turned to me. "You know better. We've got a war to win. Get your shit together."

Gerard and I stared at each other. I knew he wouldn't kill me; he was too much of a coward. And when it came to blood, I knew to respect our family's name, even if it came down to a stupid dispute. But I would be lying if I said I wouldn't love to show *him* how to respect *our* family, one agonizing torture at a time.

Derek looked at both of us individually. "You good?" he asked. We both nodded. "All right. As I was saying," he paused, "not all of them were killed. Zaid agreed to find more and meet us back here in time. And thanks to Ethan, the neighboring states are sending reinforcements now. But we've got to work together. All of us."

"Zaid?" Gerard asked. "I haven't seen him in ages."

I wanted to point out that he hadn't seen Zaid because he was hardly involved in the family business, but I held my tongue. For Derek's sake.

"We have intel that says most of his men are down, save for a handful still left in the main building," Derek said. "If we take down the building while Muro is there, that will effectively wipe him and the men out. And we'll still have the full operation of his warehouses."

"And the GPS?" Wil asked.

"I've been watching it," Derek said. "He goes to the headquarters, goes back home. That's all he does now."

"And we're sure it's not a plant?" I asked.

Derek turned to Gerard, who said nothing. "You want to tell him?" Derek asked.

"Margot confirmed it," Gerard said, gritting his teeth. So he was still talking to her then. The man would never learn.

But Derek was right. We had to move on.

"So when does it all go down?" I asked.

"As soon as Zaid's men get here," Derek said. "The day after tomorrow."

I nodded to myself, then stood. After that, I would focus on figuring out a plan for Demi's protection. I looked at Derek.

"I'll put Randy on explosives," I said. Derek bowed his head in acknowledgement. At the door, I stopped and turned to Gerard. "You didn't want a bloodbath? You could have done more to prevent," I said. "But you didn't."

"Son," he said. But he had no other words.

I headed to the backyard, making my way toward the workroom, where it was dark and empty.

CHAPTER 23

Demi

At the edge of the dining commons, I lifted the burger to my mouth, my eyes more interested in the rest of the room. The endless lines: the salad bar, the pizza trays, the fried tofu, the ice cream station. Everything orderly and in its place. The burger was cold, but that was my fault. I had wanted a burger because I couldn't stop thinking about the motel in the desert with Axe. But the burger was bland, worse than the fast food we had eaten, which made me feel worse. I stared at everyone and fumed. What were we all doing?

I ate about half of it, then dumped the rest in the appropriate bins for recycling, compost, and waste.

"Wait, wait. It's you!" a squeaky female voice said. "We all thought you got kicked out. Where have you been?"

I flipped around and blinked at her. Strawberry blond hair and blue eyes, only slightly taller than me. "Who are you again?" I asked.

"It's Dolly," she said, patting her chest. "Dolly Kate. You don't remember me?" She tilted her head. "We were supposed to go to that party together, down on Frat Row?"

Oh, right. She was from the second floor of the dorm rooms and had somehow managed to smuggle in a handle of cheap vodka during our first week. I had gone to college wanting so desperately to break the rules, to drink like my peers did, like Dad never allowed. But I was always too nervous to be 'rebellious,' and that made me feel out of place now. Underage drinking seemed so angelic.

"Are you still rooming with Olivia?" Dolly asked. I nodded, holding back a cringe. "Ugh. She's the worst. You know, I filed a report on her to Judicial Affairs last week. Still waiting to hear back."

How long would something like that take? It seemed like a struggle with no reward, but part of me hoped, even wished, that maybe it would work.

"So where've you been, girl?" Dolly asked. "There was another rumor that you went abroad on a scholarship. So go on," she nudged my shoulder, "Spill."

If I said a small part of the truth, it would be easier to keep up with the lies. *I butcher meat*, Dad had said. That must have been how he felt when I was growing up.

"My dad passed away," I said. I immediately heard Axe's voice in my head: *Don't be afraid of death.* He was always careful with that, knowing how our words showed our true emotions. And I couldn't be afraid of death. Not anymore. I shook my head, then corrected myself: "He died."

"Oh," Dolly said. She gave me a quick hug. "I'm so sorry. You must be so strong to go through something like that. Seriously, you're a fighter," she smiled, "Anyway, we're going to a house party later. You should come. Get your mind off of it."

The idea of suffering through a party seemed absolutely unnecessary now.

"Thanks," I said. "I've got to catch up on my classes."

"I get it. You know where to find me."

She curtseyed and walked off, and I let out a sigh of relief. Was that how Axe felt when he was around people? He always seemed like he was waiting for that moment when they left, when they died, when he wouldn't have to engage anymore.

Except when it came to me.

There I was again, holding onto something that didn't exist. Axe had chosen his path. Why couldn't I choose mine?

I had always been a walking contradiction, full of the need to rebel against my dad, and to respect what he had taught me: how important it was to go to school, to find a good job, to always trust in justice, to believe in right and wrong. But criminal justice classes seemed pointless now, and yet I went to the lectures anyway. The professor had a slideshow, which switched from words and bullet points to generic pictures of models dressed as criminals. A burglar in a ski mask. A violent criminal with a chain resting on his shoulders. A serial killer in a hockey mask. Part of me wondered if the professor was ever a professional, or if he was a grad student scraping by on a temporary position.

"Nature versus nurture is always the argument. Sometimes, it's about the environment, but sometimes, it's in their blood," the lecturer said. I perked up. In their blood? "It's a part of human nature. Violence and peace must have an equilibrium. So—"

"Isn't that a little outdated?" a student said. "That's the antiquated and oppressive thinking that puts criminals in jail for miscellaneous—"

"All I'm saying is that some people are *born* sadistic," the lecturer said. "That's what I meant. Sadism is a part of human nature."

The lecturer's way of thinking seemed too simple, too... defined. Criminals, like Axe—like *every person alive,* really—had messy lives. You couldn't narrow it down to nature versus nurture. That implied clear cut definitions and an easy view of the world. Like everything could be fixed.

And maybe that was what my problem was. I was trying to fix a man who wasn't broken. Why couldn't I accept him for who he was? What was holding me back?

I stayed outside of the lecture hall, leaning against the old building. It was painted a pale pink and white, and reminded me of Sour Times Casino, except it was bigger, cleaner, and I could actually breathe inside of it. And still, my mind went to Axe.

But maybe that lecturer did have a point. Maybe Axe was born with a sadistic streak, one that screamed until he quenched its thirst, drowning it in the quiet. Maybe Dad had a sadistic streak too.

Maybe I did.

I thought about the second time I was grounded. At my private grade school, an upperclassman had picked on one of my friends, and instead of telling the headmaster, I punched the girl, square in the jaw, giving her a bruise that lasted a week. Right before I did it, this strange memory kept repeating in my head. Dad talking to Mom: *I'm going to teach them a lesson with my fists. With my bare hands, baby.* Dad had been so adamant about it and hadn't known I was listening from my bedroom.

And so, it seemed like a logical step to hit her in the face. To teach her a lesson. She never messed with my friend again, but I was suspended and on the verge of expulsion. Now that I thought of it, I should have been expelled. Maybe Dad's association with the Adlers was why I was able to stay.

With my bare hands, he had said, with blood in his eyes. How had I missed it?

After that, Dad made me sit in the corner for a month. Ate my dinners there. Did my homework. Slept. Everything in that corner. And then he put me in kickboxing lessons. He wanted me to release my aggression and stressed that I had to learn to respect authority. *If something is wrong, you don't use your fists,* he had said, *You go to the headmaster.*

But what happened when authority wasn't around anymore? What if the sadistic streak ran in my blood too?

I got up, heading back to the dorm room. Maybe I wasn't a sadist, but I did have an impulse to fight. And if that's what was in Dad's blood, and Axe's too, then how could I judge them, when Dad had raised Axe and me? Maybe I was only trying to change Axe because I was ashamed of myself. Of what it meant to be an enforcer's daughter. To be in love with a murderer.

I wouldn't always understand Axe's reasons, but I knew he always had them. Always.

Like he had his reason for leaving me.

Maybe he wanted to protect me.

As I made my way across campus, I felt lighter. It didn't matter if Axe loved me back. What mattered was that I did what was right for myself, and that meant learning not to judge him, or anyone else, on what I didn't know or understand. Everyone had their reasons. Including Axe. And me.

And I wanted to help Axe.

In the dorm, my roommate, Olivia, snickered. "Still got your V-card, huh?" she said laughing to herself, pointing at my hair. "You know, Tommy said he'd take it from you. But when he heard you dye your hair to get attention, he thought you might be a little too clingy."

She tossed her hair behind her shoulders, fixing her lip gloss. I balled my fists.

Maybe it was okay to break the rules. At least sometimes. Because sometimes, you had your reasons. Violence wasn't *always* the answer, but sometimes, it just felt good.

But that didn't mean I had to fight like that. I could fight like *me*. And that was okay.

"I'm on my way to report you to the Office of Judicial Affairs for bullying," I said. "Get enough of those, and something's gotta give." I grabbed my duffel bag, leaving my backup on the bed. "Good luck. You're going to need it."

Her jaw gaped. "What's the matter with you?" she stumbled over her words. "You're going to report *me*? But I did nothing."

"I'm not the only one who thinks you did."

"Now you're bullying *me*, Demi."

She kept yelling, but I tuned her out and left.

The whole mess with the Adlers and Miles Muro was more than a report to the Office of Judicial Affairs could handle, but I had faith that I could help the Adlers, in my own way. Maybe if I brought in help from outside of Brackston, I could make a difference. The Brackston police were part of Muro's territory, but Pebble Garden was a sleepy college town. There was no reason for Muro to take an interest here.

After I filed the report on Olivia, I got a ride from one of my classmates to the police station. I leaned on the counter. In my mind, I could do both; I could respect authority, like Dad taught me, and still help the vigilantes—if you could call the Adlers that. But that discussion was neither here, nor there. I was going to help them, no matter what.

"I'd like to file a report," I said. The clerk raised her brow at me. "It's about Miles Muro."

A few people stopped, turning to stare at me.

"You said Muro?" she asked. I nodded, my eyes darting around. Why were they looking at me like that? He couldn't have possibly been known here. "I think we've got Shines on that case. Let me get him for you."

She wandered into the back, while I waited in the front, dragging my finger across the counter, wiping the stray pen marks with my thumb. A man with a clean-cut face nodded at me, his thumbs in his pockets.

"I'm Officer Shines," he said, holding out his hand. I shook it. His hand was sweaty.

"Demi," I said.

"You say you got something on Muro?"

"I know what's going on with him. His warehouses. The drugs. The weapons." I shrugged my shoulders. "Tell me where to sign and I'll write it all down."

"I like your attitude," he said. "We've got a friend from the next city over who just came back from apprehending one of his men. I'd like to introduce you two."

"Anything I can do to help," I said.

He gestured toward the front door, and I followed him out of the entrance. We went around to the line of police cars all parked together. Seeing the vehicles like that, my stomach clenched, another thing I had gotten from Dad; he never liked police officers. But Shines seemed nice, and he was listening to me.

But my stomach lurched. Could I actually do this?

"You know," I said slowly, "I don't think I can do this today. Maybe tomorrow."

"Demi," he said, his jaw pinched tight, his shoulders tensed. "Crime doesn't wait for when we're ready. And after what Muro's done, we've got to make moves *now*. Before it's too late."

That made sense. But it didn't help the feeling in my stomach.

He opened the back seat for me. "Rules, I'm afraid," he said.

I tapped my fingers on my legs. He was an officer. This was normal. A simple regulation.

"It's fine," I said, sliding into the backseat.

Once we were driving, Shines immediately merged onto the highway. My gut twisted in knots.

"Where are we meeting him?" I asked.

"Just a little way farther now."

He kept talking about his glory days, the police radio chattering every so often, Shines ignoring it. He asked me what I was majoring in at PGU and was pleased to hear that I was studying criminal justice. I shuffled my feet, trying to listen and have a real conversation, but I couldn't keep still. Something wasn't right. Then I saw that thin, red double M logo on a skyscraper that stretched up high, like an all-seeing eye looking down on everything around it.

"What are we doing here?" I asked. "I thought we were meeting your friend? Another officer?"

"Look at it this way: I figure that with your help, we have enough on Muro," he flashed his white teeth, "You've got the info. Now we can arrest him." He put a hand on my shoulder. I shook my head. I hated when people did that. He laughed.

"You're just one man," I said.

"What is he going to do?" Shines asked. "Kill me?"

"Kill *us.*"

He tapped his handheld radio. "That's what backup is for," he said. But I wasn't stupid; I knew this wasn't the way things worked. "Trust me, kiddo." He slid out of the car, then opened the back door. "Think of this as your first assignment," he beamed, gesturing at the building. Most of the windows on the bottom floor had been taped up with sheets of plastic, some of which were loose and fluttering in the wind. The bottom floor was empty, with a withered brown flower near the exit. He clicked the button for the elevator.

"Does it work?" I asked. The elevator dinged, and he tilted his head, gesturing inside.

"Let's see."

He punched the button for the top floor. I held my breath, watching the numbers increase on the digital pad. My gut twisted even more.

"How do you know what floor he's on?" I asked quietly.

"I've been here plenty of times," Shines sighed. "But we can't arrest him. Can't figure it out."

This wasn't right.

I needed to run.

The elevator stopped, the soft ding sounded overhead. The doors opened. At the end of the lobby were two black double doors. Officer Shines opened one and ushered me inside. I tucked my hands behind my back, wishing I had a knife or a gun with me right now. Anything. Absolutely anything at all. I'd even take a cleaver if it meant defending myself against Muro.

Even if logic seemed backward, I had to trust myself.

"Come on," Shines said, pointing inside.

I shook my head and walked back to the elevator. "I'm going to go," I said.

"Not without me."

"I'll take a cab."

I pushed the button, but the elevator was already a few floors down, picking up someone else. Shines stomped toward me and I panicked, hitting the button again and again. Where were the stairs?

Shines grabbed my shoulders and I kneed him in the groin as hard as I could, using my height to my advantage. He crumpled to his knees. The door to the stairs came into my vision and I ran toward it. A sharp object busted me in the back of the head. I fell down.

Another man, dressed in white, picked me up by the hair, my scalp tight with tension as if it would tear off if I wasn't careful. Shines stood up, nursing his crotch.

"Don't make this harder on yourself than it already is," the man holding me said.

Inside the office, the man dropped me to the floor.

A swivel chair turned around slowly. A jagged black bolt tattooed on the side of his face, his skin burned and marred, the like peel of a damaged beet. His hair was tucked into a bun, his clothes impeccable.

If it weren't for the wounds on his face, he would have seemed well put together.

He smiled. I swallowed hard.

"Muro," Shines said, limping in behind us. A chill ran through me. "I brought something for you." I looked up at Shines, but he was still focused on Muro. "She says she's got enough on you to put you away."

"And what might that be, Demi?" Muro asked.

My gut dropped. "How do you know my name?" I asked.

"Funny. I never would have thought the daughter of a notorious enforcer would grow up to be so oblivious," Muro laughed, an eerie grin on his face. "You thought you could waltz in here and destroy me? That the police would be on your side?" He leaned forward on the desk, peering down at me, then flicked a hand toward Shines. "Cuff her. Send in James on your way out. Tell him to disable the elevator."

"You got it, Boss," Shines said. I shot a glare at him, scooting back as he came toward me.

"You can't do this," I said.

"I can," Shines said. Then he kicked me in the ribs, the pain ricocheting through me as if he could split the bones apart. Then he kicked my face. My stomach. The pain searing me alive. I lifted a fist, but Shines stepped on my hand, crushing my fingers. I ran my tongue over my teeth with each blow, trying to feel the scars. I had survived so much with Axe. I could survive this too.

But every time I tried, he kicked me, and I couldn't find the scars.

Then a man picked me up. Exotic cologne filled my nostrils, and an arm went around my neck, sucking the wind from my chest.

"It's over, Demi," Muro whispered in my ear. "The Adlers won't be able to save you this time."

Then an object struck me in the back of the head again, and everything went black.

CHAPTER 24

Axe

On the final drive to Brackston, I kept expecting problems. Another car chasing us. An explosion. An unexplained traffic stop. But the drive was smooth. Too smooth. Even the guard station at Midnight Miles Headquarters was empty, the bar for entry permanently lifted. Though we could have gone in, we circled the neighboring streets, waiting for Derek's confirmation. Finally, my phone buzzed.

"He's there," Derek said, referencing Muro's location.

I turned the SUV back toward the building and went through the empty station, parking as far away as I could get. The rest of the group followed. Immediately, Randy went inside, setting up his explosives. The rest of us, including Zaid's men, our men, as well as my brothers and myself, surrounded the building. If Muro left the premises, we would know.

My phone vibrated; one of my men texted: *Which dorm in PGU?*

I scowled, then texted quickly, *North Tower Terrace.* That question shouldn't have been an option, but I would happily deal with Demi's security as soon as this was over. *Notify when you have eyes on her,* I sent.

Immediately, he responded: *Yes, sir.*

My phone buzzed again; this time, it was Gerard. *M's home is secure,* he sent. What that meant was that Margot was there, but no Muro. Once Muro was a corpse, Margot would be free, and Gerard had sworn to protect her. Me? I would *never* choose to protect her. But if Gerard didn't want me to kill her, then that was his choice.

But none of that mattered right then.

The flaps of tarps covering the missing windows beat like wings in the wind. Through the gaps in the exterior, I scouted the place. The door had been replaced, but everything else was still broken. It was empty. Too empty. I expected, at minimum, a guard or two on the bottom floor. Where were they?

"He's in there?" I said, asking for confirmation. Derek pulled out his phone and showed me the GPS tracking app, a red dot signaling Muro's location inside of the building. I turned back to the headquarters. Randy rushed back out, coming to my side, handing me a tablet.

"Sir?" Randy said. "Should I go ahead with it?"

I stared at those top windows, the ones from Muro's office. I had never been in there myself; those business interactions, before we declared war, were always left to my brothers. But something held me back. It was too easy. Why wasn't Muro fighting back? We had him surrounded. He would know we were here by now.

"Wait," I said.

"Come on," Wil said. "Let's kill this bastard already."

"Give it a few minutes," Derek said to Wil. His expression said, *Trust Axe on this*. I nodded my thanks to the two of them.

Still, nothing happened. I motioned to Derek.

"Call him," I said. He dialed, and we waited, but it kept ringing. "Do we trust Margot?" I asked. "What if she placed the tracking device on someone else?"

"All we have is her word," Derek said.

And I didn't have time to trust her word. A gut instinct inside of me pressed forward, needing to see Muro for myself. I checked the ammunition on my guns, then stowed them in their holsters. Patted my cleaver's sheath. Everything was in place.

"I'll give the signal," I said.

Once at the building, I lifted one of the tarps, stepping over the shattered remains of the windows. A flower, crumpled and decaying, lay near the wall. The elevator's light was dim. I hit the button, but it made no movement. After searching the lobby, I found a door that led to another door and a staircase. I tried the other door's handle, but it was locked. Then I remembered: one of my men had mentioned this;

this door wasn't on the blueprints. There was no time to deal with that now. I had to move up.

At the second floor, I went inside, pulling out office materials and filing cabinets, chairs, trash bins, anything to make going to the ground floor more difficult for Muro. Then I continued up. Six flights up, the door opened and I shot at the target. A man, dressed in white, hung over the railing, my bullet in his head. I held my breath, continuing up the stairs, checking each floor with caution. As I neared the top, another two men burst through the doors, their automatic weapons echoing in the stairway, but I nailed each of them quickly, stepping over their bodies as I made my way up.

Then it was quiet. There were no noises to fill in the blanks.

And for the first time in my life, that silence made me uneasy.

On the top floor, I opened the final door to a long lobby. I crossed the threshold slowly, my footsteps inaudible, ready to shoot. Double doors were propped open, and on the floor, there was a lifeless heap of clothes. A college sweatshirt. A splash of blue and purple hair, muddied with blood.

Demi.

I ran to her. Letting my gun fall beside me, I pulled her soft body into my arms. Her face was bloody, one of her eyes swollen shut, her arms bruised, matching the color of her hair, tattered with bloodied cuts.

How had this happened?

I had a man watching her. Was he one of Muro's informants?

Shit!

"What happened?" I asked. But Demi gave no answer. "Demi?" She stirred, her eyelids fluttering with movement. A soft moan escaped her lips and her eyes closed again. *Fuck!*

"What's it going to be?" a raspy male voice asked. I tightened my grip on Demi. Muro stood in the doorway, his gun pointed at us. I reached for my weapon too, but then he moved, his weapon aimed at Demi. I stilled. My gun was just out of reach.

"She doesn't have much time left, you know," Muro said.

"She's innocent," I said.

"I would hardly call her innocent," Muro said, narrowing his eyes. "Though I admire her tenacity. She came in here with the best of intentions. Thought she was going to save the world. Save you Adlers." He tilted his head. "She would still be conscious if it weren't for the way she attacked my best officer."

She was cuffed to a metal ring protruding from the floor. I pulled on the links.

"Now, now, I thought you would have killed me by now," Muro said, tsking through his teeth. "You should be ashamed of yourself. Never living up to the name."

I growled, finally grabbing my gun and aiming at his chest, but he pulled back his hammer, his gun still directed at Demi.

"If you kill me, you'll kill her too."

I howled in rage, then looked around. The key had to be somewhere. It had to be.

"Where is the key?" I asked. Muro didn't answer. I looked around frantically. It had to be close. It had to be somewhere. "Tell me *now*, Muro. Where the fuck is the key?"

But when I looked up, he was gone.

"Muro!" I howled. I gently placed Demi on the ground, then ran to the entrance lobby. The door to the staircase was closed, but when I opened it, I heard nothing. No footsteps. No doors swinging shut. *Nothing.* The elevator to the top floor was jammed too. The bathroom in the entrance lobby was dark. The lights flicked on, but it was empty. There was no sign of Muro. I raced down the stairs, throwing open the door to the next floor.

An overhead speaker crackled on. "Demi doesn't have much time," Muro's voice echoed through the floor. "Now, what will it be, champ?" He laughed. "Will you save the girl, or search for me? Take your pick, but get moving. Time is winding down for sweet little Demi."

I looked around. The key. I needed the key. I bolted back to Muro's office.

"Good luck," Muro's sing-song voice rang out over the speakers.

I clenched my fists as I ran through his office. My heart raced. I stumbled over the desk, tearing out all of the drawers, looking for a key. Any key. A black disc in the shape of a button, our tracking device, crunched under my feet. Papers flew. A filing cabinet. An empty suitcase. Objects clattered to the ground. But not one of them was what I needed. I checked the floor of the bathroom, then the toilets and urinals themselves. Where was it?

I ran back to the next floor, racing through rooms. As I went through a desk, I realized I could cut off her arm. Only one of them was cuffed, leaving her other hand free. She might hate me for that, but at least she would have a chance at staying alive. But I knew that any further loss of blood would cut her time shorter. It wasn't an option right then.

I couldn't think about anything. All I could do was keep going, trying to save her. Demi. My Demi. Not my Demi. Just Demi. I needed her to be safe. I needed her to be alive.

Muro laughed over the speakers. "This is exciting, isn't it?" he said. "Run along now, Adler. The clock is ticking."

Finally, in the next room, a hacksaw lay flat on a drop cloth next to a bloody chair. I didn't know if the cuffs would be soft enough to cut through, but I had to try. I ran back up, leaping toward her. I moved her to the side but then used the hacksaw. It gave way, cutting through the metal, then I switched to my cleaver, to see if anything moved faster. But it didn't, so I went back to the hacksaw. Back and forth. Trying to work it with the little patience I usually had, the calmness escaping me. *Come on,* I thought. *Stay alive.*

Finally, the metal chain clattered to the floor. I scooped her into my arms. We raced to the stairs.

"Axe?" she asked, her voice hoarse. She started coughing, and the sound made my heart pound.

"Don't speak," I said in a soft voice. "Concentrate on breathing."

She moved around, wiggling in my grasp, and I glanced down, but I had to keep my eyes open, on our surroundings, to make sure

Muro wasn't there. I had to get her to the ground floor. I had to keep her safe. Suddenly, her limp hand lifted my gun. She hoisted herself up, angling it over my shoulder.

"Where is he?" she asked.

"Stay still," I said. "Focus on you."

The only thing I knew was that there were just as many reasons to die as there were to live. *And I need you, Demi,* I thought. *I need you to stay alive.*

I went as fast as we could manage, skipping steps when I could.

"I'm fine," she said, trying to be louder. But her hands were weak. She was barely holding onto the gun.

"That's adrenaline," I said. "You need to be careful."

The gun went off. A crash echoed in the stairwell. I glanced back, but we had already turned the corner; I couldn't see what had happened.

"I got him," Demi said, but then she cringed, and I held her tighter.

"Concentrate on you," I said. "Just you, Demi."

She closed her eyes. By the second floor, the barricade looked more spread out than before, but I didn't question it. I would have heard if someone had moved it out of the way. I went through the second floor, finding the window. I ripped down the tarp with one hand, holding Demi with the other. Immediately, a few of my men came running toward me. I jumped out, holding her in my arms, landing on my feet, the shock of the ground heavy in my knees. I ran as fast I could, holding Demi close to my heart. Halfway across the parking lot. Almost there. I locked eyes with Randy.

"Go!" I shouted.

The world was silent for a second. There were no birds chirping. No cars. Not even my breath or hers. Only Demi in my arms. Then the explosion ignited, bursting through the building in loud pulses, shocking through me, making me fall to my knees. I covered her with my body. The blast of heat washed over us. Her eyes stay closed.

Come on, I thought. *Stay alive, Demi. Stay alive.*

CHAPTER 25

Demi

In the darkness, I saw my dad. Instead of the skinny, shriveled arms I had gotten used to seeing, he was full, standing upright, a strong smile on his face, the kind he used to have when Mom was alive. His white hair was cut short, his shoulders straight. An apron sprinkled with blood was strewn across his chest. This time, I knew it wasn't animal's blood, but I wasn't ashamed. He was the same dad I had always had. He had raised me to respect authority, to believe in the order of the world. Even with his past, those teachings didn't change. Only my understanding did.

Axe, his bottom lip with that deep, pitted scar, his dark eyes somehow narrowed and warm at the same time, stood beside Dad, towering over him. Dad put a hand on Axe's arm and nodded at him.

That's my boy, Dad said. *Take care of my girl.*

Dad vanished into dust and Axe came forward, scooping me into his arms, his brows furrowed with desperation. His eyes darkened and he mouthed the same words over and over again. *I need you, Demi. I need you. Stay alive. Stay alive.*

Stay.

***

I blinked my eyes, letting the light flood in. I closed them again, then squeezed my fingers, feeling a warm presence inside of my palm. I turned toward it. Axe was beside me, holding my hand. He was whispering to himself, words I had to concentrate to hear: "Stay alive, Demi," he said to himself, almost like a prayer. "Stay alive."

"I am alive," I croaked.

Axe startled. "Demi," he said. He ran a hand over his face, dust and dirt and blood in the creases of his forehead and in his hairline. I cleared my throat, but it hurt like hell. Axe found me a cup of water.

"What happened?" I asked. Fluorescent lights hummed above us and the table-cloth curtains hung in neat lines. "Where are we?"

"A hospital," he said.

"Where?"

"Brackston."

Miles Muro. I sat up, and the pain coursed through me, charging through my spine, knocking me back down.

"Lay down," he said. "You need rest."

Rest? How was I supposed to rest when we were still in Brackston?!

"Why are we still in Brackston?" I asked, my voice panicked.

"Muro is gone," Axe said. "Went down with the building."

"With the building?" I pictured it, peering over the other structures like a monster with its head in the clouds. Had they actually taken it all down? "It's gone?" I asked.

"Most of it is a pile of rubble."

"Where's everyone else?"

"Wil went home to Ellie. Derek went back to make sure Gerard, Margot, and Clara are all safe."

"Who's Margot?"

Axe cringed. "Muro's wife."

I gave him a look, but by the expression on his face, I could tell he didn't want to talk about it.

"But everyone's okay?" I asked.

"For the most part," he said. His eyes were heavy, full of sorrow and longing, an expression I had never seen before.

Then I realized he was talking about me.

"Axe," I said. I sat up slowly, trying not to let the searing pain affect my facial expression. I put a hand on his arm. "I'm fine."

"It's my fault you were hurt," he said.

"How?" I rasped.

"If I hadn't promised to marry you, Shep would never have trusted you with me."

"It's not your fault that my dad trusted *you* to take care of me," I said. I squeezed his arm. "And trust me, if it wasn't you, it would have been someone else." I shook my head. "Who knows how *that* would have ended up."

He bared his teeth. "One of my men was supposed to be watching you." He looked out of the crisscrossed window. "I should have been doing it myself."

I wanted to know why he hadn't been doing it himself, but I knew why. He didn't want to be near me, because he was afraid that he wouldn't be able to stay away. Because he needed to keep me safe, and the only way he could do that was by keeping himself away.

"What happened to that man?" I asked. "The one who was supposed to be watching me."

He closed his fist and lowered his voice, "I killed him."

Axe was never one for softening the blow. I felt guilty, but I knew now nothing I could say would bring him back.

A nurse entered the room in a flutter of energy. Axe backed away, letting her get close to me, and I kept my eyes on him, too distracted to answer the nurse's questions coherently. Axe inched toward the door, and I mouthed, *Stay.*

"Excuse me, ma'am?" the nurse asked.

"I'm telling him to stay," I said, motioning to Axe.

"That's right," she said, turning toward him too. "You don't have to leave for this. Not if the patient wants you here." She smiled. "Come on. It'll be good for her healing. The body is mental just as much as it is physical."

He slunk back in but stayed against the edge of the wall as if he needed to be as far away as possible. I turned back to the nurse and started answering her questions. She told me that although I had a few broken ribs, I was lucky that none of my organs had been damaged. I had been beaten to hell and back, but somehow, I had managed to survive. I could even heal at home.

Once she left, Axe turned toward the door again.

"Where are you going?" I asked.

"I'll watch you from afar," he said. "But you need your own life."

"Stop it," I said. My tone must have been harsher than I intended it, because he flinched, then turned, scrutinizing me under that glare.

"Could you please come here?" I asked. "I would love to chase you right now, but I can't," I said, lifting my hand pincushioned with an IV.

He stepped forward slowly. I waited until he took the chair again, then I took a few seconds to sit up, wincing at the pain.

"Demi," Axe said.

"You keep telling me," I said, squeezing my eyes shut, then opening them again once the pain subsided, "that it's not safe for me to be around you. And obviously," I pointed to my swollen face, "That's true." He looked away and I grabbed his hand, clenching it tightly. "But I need to do this for myself." He faced me. "You are who you are. And I am who I am. We can't force ourselves into boxes that make sense. And right now, all I want is *you*, Axe. If you'll have me."

He shook his head solemnly. "You don't know what you're getting into."

I lifted a hand toward my bruised face again. "I think I do."

The corners of his mouth twitched, and then a smile formed—a real, heartfelt smile, that was made for me. He leaned forward, putting a thick hand behind my head, cupping my skull and making me feel safe. The warmth in my stomach coursed up, making it easier to forget the pain because Axe was holding me, and that's all I wanted. His ear had mostly healed, but part of it was missing. Impulsively, I rubbed my tongue along my teeth, along those bumpy scars, where I was missing flesh too. I rubbed some of the dust on his face away with my thumb, marveling at how intimate each moment was with him. There had been so much that I had felt on his skin—blood from the murders, dirt from the hole, and now debris from a ruined building. It seemed fitting, in a way.

"I love you," I said.

I waited for the returned gesture of those words, but Axe was silent. He stared at me, at the shape of my lips, probably looking at the bruises on my face. It was hard for him, wasn't it? To admit something like love. He must have thought it put us both at risk. Or he was afraid of what that meant.

But I realized that I was okay with that. That's who he was. I wasn't going to force him to be anyone anymore. Just like he let me be myself, I had to do the same for him. Because I loved him, the real him.

Instead of words, our lips met, but this time, Axe let himself go, closing his eyes, breathing life and fury into that kiss, and I closed my eyes too, relishing in the way his scarred bottom lip felt against mine, wondering if he could feel his scars on my tongue. Our tongues twisted with each other, not fighting one another for once, but working together, figuring this out. One step at a time.

He pulled back, peering deep into my eyes.

"You're not afraid of me," he said, almost like a question, as if he was stunned.

"Nope. Never have been." I smiled weakly. "You're just a misunderstood ogre."

"An ogre?" he asked.

I beamed, and he shrugged, letting it drop. One day I would remind him of the first time we met, but for now, I just wanted to enjoy the smiles crossing his face.

Once the doctor discharged me, we headed to the parking garage, Axe pushing me in the wheelchair.

"So Miles Muro is really gone, huh?" I asked. "What was that like?"

"I think you shot him," he said.

"Really?" I asked, surprised.

"When we were coming out of the building, you shot someone." He shrugged. "I didn't see who."

"Huh." I thought about it. A flash of a memory came to the surface, but I couldn't quite place it. Everything had been so blurry, but I did remember shooting at someone, or something. But it seemed fitting, in a way. "I'll take credit for that."

He opened the passenger door for me, then carefully helped me stand up. Once I was settled and comfortable to both of our liking, he got into the driver's seat. He looked in the side-view mirror, then leaned down to adjust it.

"I love you too," he said, focusing on the mirror, avoiding my gaze. "You know that, right?"

He turned the key and the engine rumbled on. I smiled. I knew that may be one of the only times he would ever admit it, and so I held onto that moment, savoring the petroleum smell of the engine, the patched seats underneath me, the way the moonlight washed over his face as we backed out of the parking space, and made our way out of the hospital's garage.

"I do," I said.

He smiled, then put an arm around the back of my seat. For a few seconds, I was afraid to move, to break the moment, to somehow cut it short. As if one small gesture could break the spell and remind him of where we really were. But then I leaned in closer, over the gear shift, and laid my head against his shoulder. Because this wasn't a spell that would magically break. We didn't have to worry about that anymore. With a bond like we had, a moment like this wouldn't be the last time.

When we made it to the Adler House, well into the night, a party was roaring inside, the whole house lit up like a firework. Cars were parked out front in a maze. It almost reminded me of the funeral, but this time, I recognized almost everyone there. Zaid held a glass of amber-colored liquid. Heather had the same drink too, her collar wound tightly around her neck. She smiled and waved at me. Then Maddie grabbed my arm.

"You are *insane,* woman!" Maddie laughed. "You stormed the Midnight Miles Headquarters all by yourself?"

"Actually, I was escorted by a corrupt policeman," I said. "Not as cool as you make it out to be." I turned to Axe. "What happened to the police anyway?"

"Wil's getting their info," he said, gesturing at his brother. "We'll get rid of them one by one."

"Let's focus on having fun tonight," Maddie said, rolling her eyes at us. She went to smack my back but then froze in mid-air, realizing that it might hurt. "You need a new ice pack?" she asked. She headed to the freezer in the kitchen before I could answer. Derek leaned against the wall, letting his eyes follow Maddie as she made her way into the kitchen, hypnotized by her hips.

"Demi," Wil said. He nodded at Axe, then winked at me, then pulled Ellie into his arms. "Good to see you again."

"What an introduction, huh?" Ellie laughed. She lifted her bandaged wrist. "I would say it's not always like this, but," she shrugged, "it is pretty much always like this. Maybe it'll be better now though."

"Maybe," I said, warmth running through me. After all, I had helped get rid of Muro.

No. I had killed him. *Killed* was the word I was looking for. And that was okay.

Axe put an arm around me and I flushed from head to toe. He grabbed a beer and got me some water. Maddie was holding an ice pack in the air, distracted by Derek, who had hooked her into a conversation. Axe grabbed the ice pack from her hands without her noticing, then headed back to me.

I knew that a party like this was different for Axe. If it was up to him, he would have been patrolling the perimeter, watching for intruders. Killing the enemy was his safe space. But for now, he seemed content. He could relax for once, even in a group of people. Maybe I was his safe space too.

Axe held the ice pack to my ribs. I was cold, but Axe held me close, his body like a personal heater, soothing me. There might have been a lot of bad in the world, but that didn't matter right then. Right or wrong, good or evil, all of it was shades and variations, and I knew most people had their reasons. If you could stand behind those reasons, that's what mattered.

And I could live with Axe's reasons.

EPILOGUE

Axe

There were promises you made out of respect. But sometimes, you made those promises because of a stupid emotion, like love.

Like rearranging an office a thousand times, because you promised your future wife the perfect space where she could take her online classes in peace.

Demi gave a haughty glare at the white-washed wooden desk, then pointed to the other side of the room.

"No," she said. "I think it'll look better over there."

"There?" I asked. This would be the fifth time we had moved it.

"Yeah," she said. "I can totally sit through an online lecture right there."

I moved the desk to the other corner. The light from the window crossed the desk's surface.

"See? Natural lighting," she said. The light she craved would probably mess with her computer's screen. And then we would move it again until she found the perfect spot for it. And I would do it happily.

After selling Shep's house, we had searched for our own place. We had only been in the new house for a month, and with all of the new furniture we had bought and the items we had taken from Shep's house, it would take a long while to figure out where everything fit. Unlike my old apartment, this place was spacious, with plenty of windows to bring in those gloomy, but reflective, Sage City clouds. We even had a backyard.

Once we were settled in, I'd broach the idea of a pet. If she wanted one.

"All right," she said. "That should do it for now."

Later on, I adjusted the maroon tie in the full-length mirror in the master bedroom. I had taken the day off from enforcing, telling Derek and Gerard that I had an appointment to keep, when what we were doing was *more* than an appointment. But business had been slow lately. Things were quiet with Miles Muro gone, which was the way I liked it, so I could focus on other things. Important things. Like creative ways to torture prisoners.

Important things, like Demi.

When I had tried to buy a new suit for the occasion, Demi had told me not to. She liked my only suit, and convinced me that if I bought a new one, my family would find out. So I smoothed the red tie, making sure it was neat. In the reflection, I saw Demi. I stopped in my tracks, then spun around.

The dress went down to her feet, with thin straps and a low-cut V in the front. Her white sandals and rainbow-painted toenails poked out of the hem. The dress was mild but elegant, and with her bright hair splashed against it, my mouth watered, thinking about how she would look later when I fucked her, still wearing that dress.

"Is it too much?" she asked.

I shook my head, not sure of how to say it. Her hair was freshly dyed, this time in shades of a deep pink mixed with the blues and purples, like the sunset over the ocean. Her eyes always seemed to change with those colors, as if they could be more outstanding, even when her hair tried to take the show. But it was that smile that danced on her lips that took my breath away. But luckily, she spoke before I had to answer.

"So this promise to my dad," she said. "It is a very practical matter."

"A practical matter," I repeated. "Should I ask for your dad's approval?"

"If I remember correctly, he *begged* you to marry me," she smirked. I couldn't help it. I kissed her, pressing her against the wall, her body tensing with passion, then relaxing, dropping against me.

She broke from the kiss. "We're going to be late!" she cackled with laughter.

We took the van to the courthouse. It was a quiet affair, without anyone, like I wanted. I had purposefully picked a day that Clara was out at a spa treatment facility and wouldn't be back until late that evening. Luckily, Demi didn't mind the small event at all.

Afterward, we took a bottle of champagne and three glasses to the cemetery, where Shep had been buried. We clinked our glasses together, Shep's flute nudged against his tombstone. I would tell my family about the wedding later. But for now? This was Demi's night. And she wanted to see Shep.

We took our sips, and Demi cringed. I chuckled at her puckered face.

"*This* is champagne?" she asked. "I've been waiting to drink *this* since I turned sixteen?"

I shrugged. "Some people like it with orange juice."

"My dad would be *pissed* if he knew I was drinking," she said, staring at the tombstone. I disagreed—I figured Shep wouldn't mind a night of celebration—but it didn't matter what I thought.

Demi's face softened, her hand stroking the top of the stone. "You think he's smiling down on us right now?" she asked.

I put an arm around her. Wherever he was, I knew he'd be happy for us.

***

And like good newly-weds, I fucked my wife until she fell asleep. It left me satisfied to see her that way. We had a cage in our bedroom that I sometimes locked her inside of, but most nights, I wanted her beside me. And both of us couldn't fit in that cage.

But at one a.m., my phone rattled on the nightstand. I sat up quickly. Demi stirred in the bed, but never woke up. *Derek* flashed on the screen. I went to the hallway to answer his call, closing the door behind me.

I waited for him to speak.

"You need to come here," he said.

"Where are you?" I asked.

"The Adler House."

"What is it?"

He sighed, and in the background, I heard Clara howling, the sobs raking from inside of her. That was all I needed to hear.

I hung up. I gently woke Demi, helping her into some jeans and her old PGU sweatshirt. She mumbled about a headache as we went to the van, and I strapped her into the seat. My chest tightened. Every nerve ending in my body sat on the end, but I breathed deeply, in a practiced pattern. As long as Demi was safe, there was nothing that would disturb me.

Once we were inside of the Adler House, I put Demi in my old room, tucking her in bed. Then I followed the sounds of Clara up to my parents' bedroom. Wil, Derek, and Ellie were standing outside the room. Clara's sobs vibrated through the walls, louder than I knew was possible coming from her.

Derek tilted his head toward the door. "Go in," he said.

Clara was on her knees, covering her face with her hands. The bed laid disheveled, the comforter halfway on the ground, and two lifeless bodies laid on top. Blood splattered the sheets. A brownish-peach chunk of flesh was stuck to the headboard. Margot's black hair laid across my father's face, like the tendrils of a loose scarf. Gerard's blank eyes stared up at the ceiling. Both of their necks were split from end to end, broken like a branch snapped in half. From right below their shoulders to the bottom of their stomachs, two curved hills were carved into each of their abdomens. A symbol. An M. Miles Muro's mark. I grit my teeth, my vision going red.

I was glad, so damn glad, that I had Demi with me. I would never let her out of my sight until I stood over Muro's dead body.

Because this war was far from over.

ALSO BY AUDREY RUSH

Dark Romance

The Adler Brothers Series
Dangerous Deviance
Dangerous Command (April 2021)

The Dahlia District Series
Ruined
Shattered
Crushed
Ravaged
Devoured

The Afterglow Series
His Toy
His Pet
His Pain

The Dreams of Glass Trilogy
Yield to Me
Surrender to Me
Love Me

—

Romantic Comedy

Standalone
The Last One Standing

ACKNOWLEDGMENTS

Thank you to my husband, Kai, for doing *all* of the graphic design, reading *all* of the action scenes, and for helping with *all* of the brainstorming; you are *all* of the things, a.k.a. the very best. Thank you to my alpha reader and brainstorming extraordinaire, Michelle; I hope you know how explosively amazing your feedback is. Thank you to my dad for your critical feedback on the blurb; I always know I can count on you for honesty and on-point suggestions. Thank you to my ARC readers for your honest reviews; you give these books an amazing start. And thank you to my daughter, Emma, for taking long, productive naps and tolerating my writing sprints.

But most of all, thank you to my readers. You are the reason I love to turn my daydreams into stories. I would love to hear from you. Feel free to leave a review online or to email me directly at audreyrushbooks@gmail.com with your feedback, or join my Facebook group at bit.ly/rushreaders.

ABOUT THE AUTHOR

Audrey Rush writes dark romance featuring redeemable antiheroes and the badass heroines who love to challenge them. She grew up on the West Coast, but currently lives in the South, where she raises her daughter and snuggles her husband. She writes during naptime.

Website: audreyrush.com
Amazon: amazon.com/author/audreyrush
Newsletter: bit.ly/audreysletters
Facebook: fb.me/audreyrushbooks
Reader Group: bit.ly/rushreaders
Email: audreyrushbooks@gmail.com
Twitter: @audreyrushbooks
Instagram: audreyrushbooks

Made in the USA
Columbia, SC
21 April 2021

36570400R00117